TABLE OF CONTENTS

Title Page
Copyright
Dedication
Haima
Prologue - page 6
Chapter 1 - page 26
Chapter 2 - page 33
Chapter 3 - page 41
Chapter 4 - page 51
Chapter 5 - page 62
Chapter 6 - page 74
Chapter 7 - page 86
Chapter 8 - page 98
Chapter 9 - page 112
Chapter 10 - page 131
Chapter 11 - page 152
Chapter 12 - page 175
Chapter 13 - page 192
Chapter 14 - page 209
Chapter 15 - page 234
keep in touch
About The Author

BLOOD WITCH

Kelly Coulter

Copyright © 2021 Kelly Coulter

All rights reserved.

The characters and events portrayed in this book are fictitious. Any similarity to real persons, living or dead, is coincidental and not intended by the author.

No part of this book may be reproduced, or stored in a retrieval system, or transmitted in any form or by any means, electronic, mechanical, photocopying, recording, or otherwise, without express written permission of the author.

Cover design by: Vanessa Mendozzi
kellycoulterauthor@gmail.com

I could not have done any of this without the unwavering support of my husband, and my very own BeeBee - you know who you are!

I hope you love this book as much I loved writing it.

HAIMA

From Greek meaning 'blood'.

The Goddess of Blood and Witchcraft, daughter of the Goddess Asteria and a mortal man, and half-sister to
Hecate, Goddess of Witchcraft and Magic.

Her only blooded daughter was Tisiphone, the first Blood Witch.

PROLOGUE

Leanachan Forest, Scotland 1558

Caitlyn

The wind howled as I ran through the forest. The branches and leaves whipped at my face and body as I hurtled through the trees; my once beautiful dress - now caked in mud and the detritus from a savage woodland - was lashing at my legs trying to slow me down, creating another obstacle to our escape. I could not slow down to remove it, so I gathered as much of the material into my free hand as I could whilst still moving, bunching it into my fist to keep it still and away from my legs as I fled. Holding the abrasive wool with my left hand bunched at my side, I picked up the pace, whilst also trying to make sure the roots and brambles did not trip me up. I couldn't afford to lose time. I looked from the floor and up again, placing my feet in places that I had stepped before countless times; on the crushed leaves, then leaping over the fallen log that had been there since before I was born and now covered in lichen, and a leap over the hidden puddle that was deeper than it looked. The forest used to be my haven, my safe place. But now it was the enemy, trying to stop me from reaching the river, from reaching safety. I couldn't stop. I wouldn't. I risked a quick glance at the precious bundle swaddled tightly against my chest, her tiny breaths feeling warm and sweet against the opening of my blouse, and wrapped my right arm tighter around the only thing that mattered any more - the only thing I had left.
As I ran, I could feel the cuts and abrasions from the branches opening up on my arms, my face, my legs. There was not a bit of skin left untouched by the ravages of the Highlands. A forest that

was as familiar to me as my own face, was now a hindrance. I couldn't get through the trees quick enough, it was like they were adamant I would not get past them. Would not get to safety. I suppose it was right that nature had turned its back on me, especially after what I had done. But regrets would not save me now, regrets would not keep my daughter safe from the beasts that pursued us. As if my daughter could hear my screaming thoughts, she began to wriggle against the wrappings of the linen that I had used to hold her tight to me.

My whispered words were meant to soothe, but my voice was raspy from the exertions; all of the running, jumping, climbing had my breaths coming out heavy with each spoken word and footfall. "Hush now wee one, everything will be alright". Damn it. I sounded like the Bean-Nighe, raspy and hag-like. I probably looked like one too after all of this. But thinking about the words I had just used to comfort my baby, I didn't think it would ever be alright again.

      The baying of the beasts was not far behind, it sounded like they were gaining on me, or maybe I was slowing down? Goddess, I fucking hoped not, I needed to quicken my pace; I muttered a prayer to the Goddess Haima, hoping that - for one last time - She would hear my plea and grant me the swiftness to carry my babe away from this mess and devastation that I had wrought. My daughter was sinless, pure and untouched by the corruption of this world, and she was a descendant of the line of Haima, a blood witch (eventually) and a sister of the coven; surely she would not be abandoned in her time of need? But I had no time to think on what would happen if the Great Mother did not listen to my prayer because within the darkness, a light burned amongst the trees, a beacon of hope when I had thought all was lost, it was the only light that I had seen for hours, since the sun had set. Maybe this was Haima sending me a sign? Telling me to go towards it? Perhaps my plea had been heard and she forgives me for my transgression? All of these thoughts ran through my mind as I raced towards the only spark of light for miles; not even the moon provided a source of light, because it was a new moon, a night when the moon was hidden and darkness reigned, a time for anarchy, carnage and magic. But could I really lead those monsters to what are probably innocent people sleeping under the stars, hoping for a restful sleep? Well, I had no choice, my daughter *had* to be saved. She was innocent too dammit!

  I veered off the well-worn track that I had been racing down, and sharply turned towards the spark of light that was behind all of the Hazel trees, they were more like giant bushes, but they were great for hiding in - not that I could hide behind a bush to escape *them,* they could smell me from miles away. The weather, and everything else, was not on my side either; it blew towards me, carrying my scent downwind where the hunters would be able to follow. They would always be able to track me, not only for the fact that it had been days since I had been able to bathe properly, but my blood ran freely from my cuts; that smell alone was enough to fragrance the air with my location, and I knew how well they could hunt things, I'd made the fucking things after all.
As I rushed towards the light, and off of the man-made path that I had traipsed so many times, I dropped my skirts and wrapped both arms around Lauren in the hopes that the great trees and foliage would not harm her. Protecting my child was the only thing that mattered; from the trees, from the beasts…from me.

  I sprinted. My precious cargo was bouncing up and down, and despite the grip I had on her, Lauren let out a high-pitched wail, telling me that she was not happy with the current situation, but all I could think was 'shite, they definitely would have heard that'. And like my daughter's cries had manifested the beasts from miles behind me, I looked over my shoulder and glimpsed the burning eyes of the Lycan in front of the pack. It's gigantic paws eating up the ground beneath it…and gaining on me. I knew he was hoping to be the victor: my killer, murderer. He probably would be. But like fuck would I make it easy on him. The pounding of dozens of feet made the earth tremble beneath me, my heart was hammering in my chest at how close they were, the thudding of their many feet overshadowed the drumming of my heartbeat in my ears. I broke through the trees and as I did, I saw a lone male figure sitting beside a campfire, a musket leaning against his cocked leg. As soon as I saw him, it was like my legs had decided that it was time to rest. I didn't need help, no normal man could help me - but Lauren, aye, he could help her.

He had a kind face, soulful brown eyes surrounded by heavy lines, like he laughed a lot - or frowned a lot. I would find out soon enough, and yet when I looked deeper, I could see a great sadness; the grey of his aura swirled around him, intertwined with a rich blue that denoted his caring and loyal personality. I knew he was the right one. Haima had not forsaken me.

The soles of my feet were burning from the mad dash through the forest; my leather shoes were coming apart at the seams. The shoes, beautifully hand-crafted with the finest of leather, and laces that wrapped around my ankle, were not made for this type of adventure. Noooo, I thought bitterly, they had been made for my wedding. They were made for dancing and showing off to my husband. That would never happen again. Before I could rest, I had to make sure we were safe - or as safe as we could be with a pack of Lycans chasing our tails. As a blood witch, my magic was always with me, I could feel it in every finger and toe, in every organ, it was everywhere. But the events of the past few months had drained me, I was running on empty, and it was the only reason I had not been able to get out of this goddess-damned crisis.

The scratches on my face and arms were seeping dots of blood; my life-blood. That life giving liquid that them damned demons were after. They were like the old tales of the Vampires that granny used to tell me about. Those nightmarish stories of the Nosferatu, the undead, the evil ones who drank your blood so that they could survive and live off of other's suffering, and gain power from their slaughtering ways. It was said that the Nosferatu would track down any wayward blood sisters, the girls who refused to pay homage to the Great Mother. But they were just old stories told to young blood witches to make sure they stayed in line and made sure that they protected themselves

from those who would abuse their magic, made sure they protected every bit of that essence within them and did not let it be taken from them.
But this was reality, and the reality was, I was not getting out of this in one piece.

      I wiped my hands up and down my arms and brushed them over my face trying to gather as much of the blood as I could. It was not much but it would have to do; besides, I had lost my athame in the flight for survival so I could not even prick my finger at the moment.
I looked down at the hands that were held out in front of me, palms up. They were coated in colours of red, brown and green. They showed the story of the past hours of my life: red for the life-blood that *they* wanted, green for the stains of the grasses from home that had rubbed on my hands as I'd raced through the trees and brown for the mud of the earth that had stuck to me as I had fallen over and over in an attempt to get myself and my daughter away safely from the massacre that had befallen our people. Eyes raised to the night sky, I could see the stars shining from my spot in the clearing, but no moon. Never mind, I could do this part without the new moon's slight outline taunting me from its place of safety above me. I did not need another reminder of what I had done on the last new moon and the spell I had cast. A night exactly four months ago from tonight.

      Hunched over my spot in the grass, I started wiping my stained hands on the blades closest to me, then rising onto my knees, I imagined my blood worming its way through the thin stalks creating a circle around us, the strange man and the campfire, blocking everything out. As I pictured the circle being completed, a dome of pure white brilliance formed around us, veins of crimson spread throughout the hemisphere, culminating into a pentacle directly above our heads. I felt the familiar rush of magic spread through my body, it was like when you had pins and needles and the relief when you got the feeling back into your hands or feet, arms or legs, that tingly sensation, knowing you would be able to use your limbs again, it was comforting, but at the moment I was exhausted, that last spell - despite being an easy one - had wiped me out, My eyes felt heavy, and the thick weight of my raven hair hanging loose behind me caused a trail of sweat to trickle down my neck. Gathering the mass into both hands, I tied it into a knot at the base of my neck, hopefully taking some of the weight off my pounding head. Appearances didn't matter right now, and if I'd had my knife, I would have just lopped the whole thing off, saving myself the hassle of having to deal with it. The once shiny locks that were the envy of all of the other girls, was now matted and riddled with twigs and bits of goddess knows what.

Looking up at the dome, I knew it would only protect us temporarily, it shut out all sounds from either side so the beasts could not hear me, unfortunately, I could not hear them either, but more importantly, it created a barrier between me and my enemies; they could not break through until I lowered the shield, or died. Hopefully not the latter anytime soon. It was the most basic of protection spells, the spell taught to every novice when they started practicing the craft at the age of seven - and now at the age of nineteen, I was a master at it.

  Slowly sinking down to sit on my haunches, resting my bum on my aching feet behind me, I let out a breath, it felt like I had been holding it for months. For just a little while, I could relax while planning our next move and where they would go from here. A wriggling, squeaking baby at my chest pulled my thoughts away from the future and, taking my tiny bundle of energy out from the cloth, I brought Lauren towards my face and buried my nose in her shock of chestnut hair, smelling the sweet scent of the lavender lotion that I had rubbed on my wee bairn this afternoon, a smile crept on my face, because seeing that she was none the worse for wear from our escape made everything that had happened worthwhile. She gazed up at me with her striking azure eyes, eyes that she had inherited from her father, the man who started this whole fiasco. Lauren trusted me to keep her safe, and so far I had made a mess of things, but I would do everything in my power to make sure she survived and lived a long, happy life. Even if that life was a human one.

I looked towards the unfamiliar man, whose mouth hung agape, like a carp that was not expecting that hook and smiled. "A fine night for a stroll, doona ya think" my voice was still scratchy and my words came out with each pant of breath, but it was slowly returning to its normal silvery sound, along with my heart rate. He looked at me, then up at the dome and back to me, his mouth moving but no sound was made. Obviously, I had made him speechless.

Daniel

I had made camp as I knew I wouldn't make it home by dark, and I daren't travel this unfamiliar place in the gloom, where men could be turned around and lost, bad things happened when men didn't know where they were goin'. Lighting a fire to keep the chill away, I had every intention of spending my night thinking about my failed journey, and that I would be returning home to my wife with no answers. Again.

A rustling in the trees brought my attention to the darkness, crashing footsteps and howls from further away had me leaning my gun where I could easily reach it if I needed to. I was hopin' whatever it was that was being hunted, would go straight past my sleeping place, leaving me to my melancholy thoughts.

A woman, a young one at that, broke through the tree line and collapsed to her knees before my fire, it was obvious she was a great beauty with eyes like emeralds, her skin - beneath the blood and dirt - looked clear and unblemished, no easy feat out 'ere. She must be wealthy, her dress certainly looked of the finest quality. No sooner had I finished my perusal of her, did she start rubbing her hands on the grass at her feet.

"Lassie, what are ye doin' oot 'ere at this time o' night? What happened to ye?" My words went unheard, because she was too busy doing witchy shite. A barrier of some kind trapped me in with her, a cage meant to keep us in, or keep something out? I was'na sure yet?

I had spent years travelling around Scotland, spent money we did'na have to speak to different healers, doctors, even witches. I had tracked them all down in the hopes of giving my beloved wife her greatest desire - a child. But no matter what remedy or tincture or potion or lotion they gave us, nothing worked.

But I had never seen magic of this magnitude before. I had never seen anything like it, and I'm no' gonna lie, I was man enough to admit that if I had been a lesser man, I would have shit my pants. I wanted to hide too, but there was nowhere to go, so I stood there and watched, shocked that I was actually witnessing something so momentous - and terrifying - that I had lost all my words. My wife would be crackin' a joke about now, about how I was finally without somethin' to say. She'd probably think that I had drunk too much o' the moonshine and passed out, she'd been warning me o' that for years. The thought of the "I told ye so" that was coming was enough to snap me out of my surprise.

"A fine night for a stroll, doona ya think?"

"A stroll? It's a bit late for that, you should be at home in bed, tucked up safely". Her shoulder's drooped and a lone tear made it's trek down her cheek, leaving a trail through the grime that coated her skin; sadness enveloped her whole frame, she looked like someone who had suffered much loss. But what could a wee young thing like her have to be sad about? The babe she carried looked hale and hearty, and a pang of longing swept through my chest, aye, she knew nothing about loss.

Caitlyn

His words reverberated around in my head, aye I should be at home, snuggled up in my sheepskin throw in the house my husband had built for us. He would be stroking my hair, softly speaking to me about his day in his baritone voice, but there is nothing left now; no husband, no home, no family, no friends. "My home is gone, it's just me and Lauren now", his face fell at my reply, then he looked around at the protection that I had put in place.

"What's with the cage?"

"You'll find out about…..now" I had timed my comment perfectly, because at that moment a monster crashed against the outside of my dome, the impact caused vibrations all around us, I could see those ruby veins that surrounded us quake at the force of it's collision. Six feet tall on all fours, the beast shook it's furry hide and got right back up. Those resilient bastards. It looked right at me through the crystalline ward, it's eyes burning with hunger, it raised it's front right paw and placed it on the barrier. A promise that he would have me once it fell. Goddess, that paw was the size of my head. As it dragged it's clawed forepaw down the side of the dome, it left a streak of blood - my sister's blood - and as it stepped away from the dome, I glimpsed the rest of the pack rush forward, fighting to taste the remnants of my family from the outside. They were all fighting each other for the right to have the last of us, they were tearing each other apart, biting and ripping, I could see bits of fur and flesh fly off as they raced to be the victor. Finally, a lycan with murderous black eyes stepped forward, it's bright pink tongue licked the ichor clean away. It's body shuddered in ecstasy, it's eyes closing as it savoured the morsel his packmate had left for him. Yes, it was a 'him', I knew those eyes. As I watched him regain his composure, he glared at me, his tongue hanging out leaving those sharp, glistening fangs on display. What I had known as Jacob, was now a monster. But then, he had been a cunt as a human man too, the only difference now was, he had the power to kill me.

"Holy Mary, mother of Jesus, what the feck are they?" The poor man sounded horrified, I didn't blame him. I was the same when I first saw them.

I turned to him, giving him my full attention, he was after all the one who would be saving my daughter, he just didn't know it yet. "My name is Caitlyn, and this is Lauren" nodding my head towards the now sleeping babe. "Might I have the pleasure of your name?"

"Daniel, my lady, Daniel Fraser. And now maybe you could explain to me what is happenin'?"

I couldn't tell him everything, I couldn't tell him that this was all my fault, he may never agree to help me if he knew the truth. "Well Daniel, it's a really long story, and I don't have much time to explain everything, because the wards will no' hold all night, and I'm exhausted. The minute my body gives in, this comes crashing down and we are all dog food". I could no' afford to spare his feelings too much, this had to be quick, and he had to help me.

What little colour that was left in his cheeks from the cold, washed away with my speech, his face devoid of everything except fear. Fear was good, fear I could work with. "They're chasing us Daniel, they have killed my entire family. I watched my mother and my sisters be torn apart, their bodies picked clean; I can still hear their cries for mercy in my mind. Now they want to do the same to us...to my baby".

Anger replaced his terror, "I'll protect ya, you and the bairn, I have my weapon, and I'll no' let them get to ya". Relief washed through me, relief that he would help. Some people wouldn't, especially knowing that I was a witch. These were perilous times, and not many trusted us anymore.

"Come and sit with me" I took his arm and led him towards the fire, we could be warm while I explained. I picked up some branches that he had obviously put there to feed the fire, and chucked some onto the dimming flames, watching as they gradually ate away at the fresh wood and rose to new heights, providing more light and warmth. "Do you have children Daniel?" I turned to him, my legs crossed in front of me and my arms cuddling a sleeping Lauren. I watched as that ever-present sadness became his most prominent emotion, overtaking the anger he had felt for us. "Nay, we were never blessed with young, God saw fit to give us a different purpose in life". He tried to smile and cover up his sorrow, make excuses that it was ok and they had accepted their childless existence. I had seen it before in the human women who came to the coven for help in their quest for a baby, but unfortunately some things we are incapable of fixing. They never fully accepted that it was not meant to be. Some of them got on with things, trying to make the best of their life and took on maternal roles in other ways. The rest of the women didn't accept it at all, and they kept coming back to us, adamant that we had not done the spell properly. Those were the worst ones.

"Would you like to hold her? She's asleep right now so she's not wiggling around, she's quite the mover when she's awake". I untied the linen that was knotted behind me and started to unwrap her, Lauren's eyelashes fluttered against her cheeks, that was the only movement she made; all of the excitement must have tuckered her out. Cradling her in both arms, I reached towards Daniel, and with one hand shifting to hold her head, I slowly moved her away from me, and into the arms of a stranger. Daniel held out both arms, his gun being put to the side but still within easy reach should he need it, and he took her in his arms; her head cushioned by the crook of his elbow and his other arm coming up under her bottom to hold her body to him. Daniel was not a big man, slightly taller than me and with a shock of ginger hair, but his face and arms were tanned, his hands roughened and calloused from hard work. "You know how to hold a baby, she's still sleeping soundly, and she looks comfortable there". He looked up at me, hearing the strange inflection in my voice.

"Aye, I have lots of nieces and nephews".
"I need you to do me a favour Daniel Fraser, and I will forever be in your debt". I paused at what I was about to say, I knew it was the best - and only possible - option, but it still broke my heart. I was about to put all of my trust, my entire life into the hands of a stranger, insane, I know. But what choice did I have right now? There was no-one left. "I need you to take Lauren away from here, take her home, keep her safe." My voice broke on that last part, and grief that I had not allowed myself to feel for my murdered family now welled up inside me at the thought that she would no longer be mine, that I would never see my family or my daughter again after this wretched night.
His head whipped around sharply towards me, taking his attention away from the child. "What are ye saying woman! I canna just take your bairn". His Scottish brogue got heavier with

the shock of my request, but I'm sure I could hear a faint yearning in his words too.

"I need her to be safe, and I may not know you Daniel Fraser, but I can see your heart, I can see that you are a just and loyal man, despite your fear, you were willing to protect a woman you had just met from monstrous beasts. You are a good man. Please, I beg you". I shuffled towards him on my knees, my skirts dragging across the floor, I placed my hand on his arm that cradled my child and looked at him, beseeching him with my eyes and my words. "Please take her away from this horror and death. I'll distract the lycans so you will have enough time to get her far away".

He returned to staring at Lauren, looking down at her with a mixture of hope and pain, "I canna take her with me, because I canna risk loving her - my wife loving her and cherishing her above all others - only for ye to come back and take her from us. I would risk death at the maws of those beasts out there to protect ye and the child, but I could never endure the heartbreak my wife would feel if she were given the one thing she has so desperately hoped for for years, for it to be robbed from us, please, doona ask this o' me." He looked at me with tears shining in his eyes, the love for his wife evident in his expression; knowing that he would rather face death than cause her any agony confirmed that I was making the right choice.

"No Daniel, you don't understand." I braced myself for the declaration I would make. I took a deep breath, steeled myself for the unending loss I would feel at Lauren's departure and told him. "Take her, raise her as your own. You must never ever tell her about me, she can never know that she is a witch, the minute *they* figure out who - what - she is, her life is over." I looked behind me and watched as six of the wolves paced outside, waiting for me to break, watching me with death in their eyes. I turned back to Daniel. "Look at them, do you honestly think I'm getting out of this alive?"

"What, wait, nay!" He grabbed my arm, thinking to stop me, that it may change the future. But it was inevitable. I could not escape them. "Yer a witch, you created this thing around us, you could get away."

"There is no point in trying to find another way. Every blood witch is dead. If I'm gone too, then maybe they will die with me. I created them..." I felt him grab me, the pads of his fingers digging into my upper arm, gripping me tightly.

"What do ya mean you created them", he growled angrily, his hand shook me, but even still, he was gentle, a tug on my arm meant to get my attention, not to harm me.

"You were willing to give up the chance to have a baby, wasn't you?", he looked at me confused. "When I asked you to take Lauren, you said no because you didn't want to upset your wife, because you love her, because you would do anything for her, right?" I needed him to understand why I had done the things I had done, and I think he, of all people, would know why I did it.

"I met Robert when I was fourteen years old, and he was the son of an English merchant who had travelled to Scotland to visit the coven. His father was hoping to procure a tonic for his ailing wife. As soon as I saw him, I loved him; my heart knew him and I knew he felt the same way. They stayed for a sennight. We didn't even get to speak a word to each other during that time, my mother kept an eye on them - on us - always, she didn't trust them. She always warned me about men you see, told me that they took too much and never gave enough, that they corrupted everything they touched. But whenever we saw each other, it was like I knew what he was thinking. The twinkle in his blue eyes, Lauren's eyes, would find me, and they looked only at me." Daniel listened with rapt attention to my story, and he nodded at me like he understood the feeling and what I was talking about, so I continued. "He left after that week, but he returned the following summer. A little bit taller, a little bit more handsome." I smiled to myself as I reminisced. "I remember he gave me a yellow rose. It had been slightly wilted, but he had brought it all the way from England with him, just for me. He had said that a yellow rose signified friendship, and he hoped that's what we could be, and that next time he saw me I would be sixteen, and he would give me a red rose. When I asked him what a red rose meant, he just looked at me and smiled, and said that he would tell me next year". I laughed out loud remembering how cheeky he had been and how happy we were. "We married when I turned eighteen, he had business to arrange in England once his father had passed, but then he moved here, gave it all up to be with me. So you see Daniel, I would have done anything for Robert; he was my other half, my soulmate and without him I couldn't breathe - I didn't *want* to breathe." My fingers trembled as I remembered the last time I had seen Robert, his pain and anguish. "My people...we are immortal, tied to the goddess Haima, so long as we practise blood magic, we will live forever."

"What if you stop practising blood magic?" he asked me.

"We become human, we live as humans, we die as humans but living just a little bit longer than a normal person. I couldn't live knowing that Robert would grow old without me, I couldn't bare the thought of watching the life fade from his eyes as I stayed like this. I was selfish, I wanted everything."

Daniel leaned away from me, suddenly realising that he still had a grip on my arm, he let go and looked at me with the knowledge that I had done something so terrible, so heinous, that monsters now roamed the earth, but that's not what was supposed to happen.

"What did you do?" He whispered.

"Every blood witch upon her inception, is gifted a familiar, a dog; a loyal and worthy companion that she will bind her life to, share her soul with and live out eternity with by her side. She shares everything with her familiar, and in return, the dog is devoted only to her. A constant presence in an ever-changing world. My familiar was named Atlas, named after the god who was condemned to spend eternity holding up the earth. That's who he was from the moment he approached me as a pup. He held me up, and never let me fall." I knew what he would ask before he even said it.

"Where is Atlas now?"

I looked straight into his eyes, "dead, I killed him," I muttered. This part was so hard to talk about, I had not allowed myself to think about Atlas, I had been too busy dealing with the fall-out of that spell and my selfishness. "In order for Robert to live forever, I sacrificed my familiar, transferring Atlas' immortality to my husband, but I did not know what would happen afterwards, I promise you that. If I had known..." My sentence trailed off unfinished, because if I *had* known, I would have given up my magic in a heartbeat, and lived out my life with Robert and Lauren - and goddess willing any other children we would have had together - to be with him for the thirty, fourty or fifty years that we would have been blessed with. But it's too late, my Robert was gone, and in his place was a monster of my own creation. My mother always said that men corrupted everything they touched...but what about us? We destroyed everything from the inside, watching the decency of good men decay before our eyes, because why? Because we were blood witches descended from the gods, so that automatically meant that we could do anything we wanted to? No! That could not be allowed to continue, I had to make my mistakes right. It would not bring back my sisters, but it would stop any other of my kind from making the same mistakes as me, we are descended from a goddess. We are *not* gods ourselves.

"This very night four months ago, I cast the spell that destroyed my Robert, he transformed before my very eyes, his body contorting in ways that the human body was not made to. His suffering lasted all night as did Atlas', and as Robert's body and soul took on another form, Atlas' soul left this realm, and I will never forgive myself for my betrayal. Robert disappeared that night, before the sun rose on the following day, and I haven't seen him since; but his eyes looked crazed, they were not the eyes of the man I had given my life to. Then, as the days passed, the local villagers started to disappear and these things were sighted in the area. I didn't connect them at first, thinking it a coincidence, but these hounds, I recognise them, recognise their auras; and I know that they are connected to Robert, I know that he made them somehow. I have to fix my mistake, the consequences are too high for me not to."

      Daniel sat there, silently watching me, I couldn't tell what he was thinking, my tale was a lot to swallow, and I had put his life in danger. He blinked, took a breath and didn't say anything, he just pulled me into his side, a one-armed hug. It was not something I would normally allow, but it was something I did not know that I needed. He sat there with his arm around my shoulders, not moving. "I'll take Lauren to safety, but promise me tha' once this is over, them beasts will be gone, they canna be allowed to roam free. I doona want them coming after my family." He looked at Lauren still nestled within his arm, and I knew he counted her as part of his family now. I would make sure they were safe, all of them.

"Get your stuff, leave what you don't need, I will distract them. You need to make your way east towards the river Arkaig, there you will find a boat which will carry you to Loch Lochy, from there you will be able to make your way to the town of Laggan, look for Aggie at the Inn and tell her Caitlyn sent you. Speak to no-one else but Aggie. Do you understand?" I looked to him for confirmation that he had understood my instructions. It was important that he made it to Aggie, she would help provide food for the bairn until the coast was clear, and Daniel could make his journey back to his wife.

He looked at me with determination. "I ken what I have to do lass, and she'll be safe with me, never you worry." He squeezed my arm affectionately, then he handed my baby back to me so that he could pack his belongings and put the fire out. I knew what he was really doing though, he was giving me privacy to say goodbye.

  I cuddled my darling against my breast, smelled her clean scent, stroked my fingers through her baby soft curls and lovingly caressed her silky cheeks. I touched her button nose softly and ran my finger over her smooth brow. She was flawless in every way, her features a mix of myself and her father, created with love from our union. She was everything that was perfect taken from our relationship, combined to create this one tiny being that I would die for. I saw Daniel standing across from me, the extinguished fire between us; smoke from it's remains drifted upwards and swirled around the top of the dome, it's escape impossible - a bit like me.

His satchel was strapped over his shoulder and his musket was across his back, the handle easy to grab from over his left shoulder. That left space in front for Lauren. I kissed her face over and over, whispering to her how much I loved her, I would always love her and that I would be watching over her. At that moment, she opened her eyes and looked straight at me, her little hand grasping at my hair, pulling me towards her open mouth and making growling noises. My little minx woke up starving. Daniel turned around, showing me his back and giving me a modicum of privacy while I fed her for the last time. Opening my blouse, I pulled apart the two halves of my shirt, pulled down my camisole and arranged Lauren at my breast, she latched on easily and immediately started feeding; she was an easy baby, and she would be satisfied for a little while, hopefully until they can make it to Aggie's.

Once Lauren had had her fill, I fixed my blouse and called out to Lauren's saviour, her new father. "We're ready Daniel." I wound the linen around Daniel and fitted my daughter to his chest, tying the cloth behind him underneath his gun, making sure it would not be in the way if he needed to grab the weapon. Then, I looked at them both, this man sent from the goddess Haima to save Lauren - because I knew he was not here by coincidence. It was fate that he was here, at this very moment to see to her safety, and also fulfilling his own wife's dream. Yes, this was meant to be. I stroked Lauren's head one last time, and braced myself for the events to come.

"I will create an opening over there," and I pointed to the area furthest away from where the beasts had congregated, "I'll make sure they don't follow you."

"How will you do that?" he questioned.

"That's not your problem, just make sure you get to the river, alright."

"Aye." He turned towards the dome where I would make an opening and waited, his body ready for the rapid departure. I closed my eyes and imagined a tear in the transparent barrier, the scarlet markings that covered the dome separated to reveal a doorway and the dark forest beyond. As Daniel stopped at the opening, he turned his head towards me so his face was in profile, the dim light from the hemisphere creating subtle shadows over his appearance. "Thank ye for this precious gift, I'll no' forget ye." And then he was gone, like the wind had picked them up and blown them away, taking my heart with them.

I sealed the dome shut and ran towards the firepit, I had to be quick now, the wolves would notice something was amiss, and my presence still inside the dome would not keep them occupied for long. I found a piece of wood that had been placed just outside of the fire, the heat had hardened its grains, creating a spear about the length of my forearm; I felt the tip with my finger, it was sharp enough to do what I needed it to.

I turned towards the lycans that had gathered for me, *what have you done Robert?* I thought to myself. I held the sharpest point of my make-shift knife to my wrist and pushed down sharply, my blood bubbled out of the wound and pooled in the palm of my hand. The pain was tolerable so far, I was used to making myself bleed for my spells. As quick as I could, I dragged the point up my wrist towards my elbow, opening a large gash and the blood streamed out. It covered my clothes and poured towards the ground, creating a puddle of viscous liquid beneath my feet. They could see it, their ambrosia, and they became frenzied. Clawing at the barrier, trying to break through, their jaws opened wide with their silent howling. Saliva dripped from their mouths in their lust for a taste. They could taste me over my dead body...literally.

I sank to the floor feeling light headed. I would have tried to make this go quicker by cutting my other wrist, but I couldn't make my ravaged arm move to take the stake, and my grip was slippery with blood. The tendons were severed, and I had lost all feeling in that hand; the stake had dropped somewhere, but I had no more need of it.

There was no pain; I thought death would hurt, but the pain in my heart far outweighed the pain in my arm. As my lifeblood continued to flow from my wound I grew weaker, I could feel the wards starting to fall, but at least they were disintegrating from the top first, it meant I had a bit more time to die. I could hear them now, their excited barking and the scratches from their claws. The bigger ones were using the smaller beasts as stepping stones to clear the top, that couldn't happen, I wasn't dead yet.

The wards were falling too fast and the crimson pattern was almost invisible, the shimmering barrier was fading, with patches of forest peaking through clearly. This is not the way it was supposed to happen dammit! My uninjured hand quickly grasped about the forest floor for my spear, running my hand through the soft brush frantically searching for my only way out. Where was my fucking stake? My fingers caught on the scratchy surface of my weapon, and I pulled it towards me. With only one hand, my only option was to brace myself on my knees and place the stake beneath me, the bluntest end braced against the ground and the sharpest point pointing towards my heart, I was going to throw myself on to it. But before I could figure out how to create enough momentum that would force the point through my chest bone, a heavy weight crashed into the side of me, throwing me away from my last chance of taking my own way out.

Holding my damaged arm to my side, I tried to pull myself up, but my body was tired, and I collapsed to the ground, landing on my damaged limb. They surrounded me now, sniffing at me and licking their jaws. What were they waiting for? And then I saw him. Jacob. That sleazy bastard who had worked for Robert. Changed into this vile beast. I would recognise his soulless eyes anywhere. He was the largest lycan there, and he shouldered his way through the growling ranks, pushing the smaller ones out of the way. It was like they had forgotten to be human, their animalistic sides taking over and controlling them. If this was the way I was going to go out of this world, I was going to do it the way I had lived. Speaking my mind.

"You always stank like a wet dog Jake, and now you look like one too. Fuck you." He roared and lunged at me, the dozens of needle-like fangs bit into my shoulder and I screamed, I felt my shoulder bone give way between the strength of his jaws, being crushed between his teeth. And then he reared his head back, pulling my arm with him until I felt a tear and the most unimaginable pain, like lightning bolts being stabbed into my body over and over, torturing me and burning me; and through it all I screamed, I felt liquid spill out of my mouth, my throat ripped up from the inside from my constant shrieking, I was choking on my own blood. My eyes cracked open, and through the fog of my pain, I glimpsed Jacob standing there, his four giant paws stationary, his lupine face half hidden by the contents of his mouth. An arm hung lifelessly from his great maw, torn flesh and tendons hung from the mutilated appendage, and blood splatter covered the area between us. It dripped from his face, and pooled around the clearing. I could hear the squelch of my blood as the other wolves pawed at the ground, lapping at the viscous liquid that had once been so precious to me. Now, it was a lycan delicacy. I was food for the dogs. Jacob laid down where I could still see him through my slitted eyes, his huge body stretched out to cover almost half the length of the clearing, and he placed my mangled arm between his forepaws and began to tear my flesh from the bone, gulping down the pieces in one swallow. I was panting now, dizzy from blood loss and the pain was unbearable, but I still had not lost consciousness. This was my punishment then, She was keeping me awake to watch and feel my death, this was Her retribution for what I did to Atlas. I would get no relief from Her.

Jacob's pause in my mutilation to eat was the impetus for the other wolves to take their turns, and as I closed my eyes, envisioning my family and my sweet Lauren being held in my beloved's arms, I felt teeth and claws ripping into me. My back arched off the ground as I screamed my pain and rage to the night sky, leaving my throat exposed, which was all the incentive one lycan needed to clasp his jaws around my windpipe and then, I knew no more.

CHAPTER 1

London, England. Present day

Zoe

      I was pissed. I stamped my feet with each step towards home, hoping that the 1, 2, 1, 2 of my tread would help ease my anger with the rhythmic beating of my Reebok Classics against the pavement. It was still warm for mid-September so I had left the flat this morning with only my cardy, and it would stay light out for a while yet; which meant that 'Mum' would probably be in the pub garden, drinking her benefits away…as usual. But that was ok, I didn't need her around right now, listening to her moan about her life - especially when mine was going down the shitter!

      I turned from the tree-lined road through the black waist-high metal gate and walked up the familiar gravel path towards home. The block of flats that I had grown up in stretched 7 maisonettes across, with a further storey above. Each home consisted of 3 beds, a bath and a tiny 80's style kitchen, they were uniform, and well kept by the tenants, but the council didn't let us do any work to the properties, hell, *they* didn't do any work on the properties. The only difference was the doors. Each family had rebelled against the strict 'council-code' and painted their doors in any colour they wanted. So along my row, there was a literal rainbow. I didn't even bother to get to know most of the tenants' names anymore, they were just "that's the blue-door family, and that's the green-door family." It worked for me. I stopped at my door, which I had painted a Hooker Red colour, (yea, that was the actual name on the tin) and before I could open my door, I heard the familiar strains of Wiley's 'Too Many Men' blast out from my neighbours window - yellow-door lady - or Marie for short. Everyone knew when she had a guy round because she turned the volume way up, this was because Marie was a screamer; and the irony of the song title wasn't lost on me either, because 'yellow-door lady' had too many fucking men.

I rolled my eyes, feeling myself getting even angrier, because where she had a revolving door of dick, I had only had one boyfriend, and that motherfucker just upped and left me - knocked up. "I can't have a baby Zo, I'm too young," I mimicked his stupid excuse in a high-pitched voice under my breath. Yea, well, what about me dickhead? His reply: get an abortion, but he "couldn't come with me because he was squeamish." What. the. Hell? You weren't bloody squeamish when you wanted to *go in raw because it felt better.* How had I put up with this dude for three whole years!

What's done is done though, I was having a baby and I would never get rid of it, ever. I knew what it was like to grow up unwanted, unloved, an orphan. My child would never feel the same way I did, I would love this little baby unconditionally, and they will never go a day without knowing how much I love them. Did I want kids in my current living situation? No way. I wanted off of this council estate, I wanted my own home, a car, a decent man to share it with (not necessarily in that order) But still living with your foster mum at the age of 25 and taking care of your foster brother because your lazy-ars foster uses all of her 'earnings' on fags and booze, didn't generally create a warm and stable environment for my future prince or princess. But, no use crying over spilled milk - or spilled semen in my case.

      Walking through the entryway, I toe'd my trainers off and pushed them to one side, and walked in my socked feet to the living room, where I saw my little brother sitting on the sofa still in his school uniform, head-phones on and fully engrossed in his Fortnite game. I looked at the clock on the wall, and noticed that school had been finished for almost two hours."Hey poo-head, did mum make you dinner?"

"Nah, she left me two pounds for a McDonalds Happy Meal. TWO POUNDS" he stressed. "They haven't been that cheap in years, not that a kid's meal would fill me up!" I don't even know why I was so shocked at her lack of care for him, it's not like it's a new thing for her, she was always going out when I was growing up, leaving us to fend for ourselves. As long as the place was clean and tidy, and she was here when the Social did their check-up, she let us do what we wanted. She got paid for being a foster mum, and as far as she was concerned, we had a roof over our heads and a bed. But come on, he was 15 years old, he needed nutrition and protein. Thinking about it, I suppose I was already technically a mum and had been for the past decade. "Go and have a shower and put your uniform away, you know the rules. Shower first, then games. I'll order food over Uber while you sort yourself out," Chucking his school blazer at him to hang up, I pulled my phone from my front pocket and went to the app.

      Hearing my front door open and slam closed, I looked around the door frame to see my bestie Lissa, walking towards me. She lived in the flat directly above us, and so I'd given her the spare key when we were 13, after we realised that her mum worked the night shift at the hospital and Jackie-the-shitty-foster-mum went to the pub, so rather than be by ourselves, we would stay together. At first I would go up to hers, but when I was 15, Nathan came to live with us and he was only 5, so she started staying down here. I would babysit Nathan, then we would sit up all night chatting shit and watching Friends re-runs. It played havoc on our attendance record at school. Not only that, but it had been 12 years, and Jackie still hadn't noticed that the spare key was gone. She wasn't winning any Mum Of The Year Awards any time soon.
She threw herself on the sofa, crashing lengthwise against the chocolate coloured cushions and flinging her right leg over the back of it, her multi-coloured braids cascading over the arm of the sofa and almost brushing the floor. I envied her plaits, not only because they looked awesome, but also because her mum spent hours weaving the rainbow extensions into her natural black hair, until she had these striking, psychedelic locks that immediately drew your eye wherever she went. I was envious of the love and care that Sarah, her mum, took to maintain them. She had offered to tame my own unruly curls so many times, but I didn't want to inconvenience her, she worked enough hours as it is; and I definitely couldn't afford to have it done at the salon.

So I kept my own hair cut short, shaved back and sides and curly on top, it was called a pixie style apparently, and way easier to maintain - bonus, the dude at the Barbers kept it lined up and sharp for only 20 quid - a bargain and it looked damn good.

"I'm ordering McDonalds, d'ya want anything?"
"Nah I'm good thanks, I already ate, mum bought food back from Brown Eagle earlier." I salivated at the thought of food from the Jamaican restaurant down the road, but I knew Nathan had his heart set on the greasy Big Mac meal. After ordering for us, I collapsed on the arm-chair across from her and released a sigh of relief.
"Soooo...." Lissa leaned forward on the sofa that she had commandeered, "do you wanna tell me why you were marching up the street like your ars was on fire?"
I listened intently for the shower running upstairs, knowing that he was occupied, I turned to face her; I wasn't ready for Nathan to know yet, but I knew that Liss could keep a secret. "I'm pregnant." Her eyes widened a fraction, but she didn't say anything.
"Aren't you gonna say anything?"
"What is there to say, I knew it would happen eventually after you told me that you weren't using protection, but nooooo, don't listen to me, what do I know"
Her sarcasm wasn't welcome at the moment, I just wasn't in the mood for it. "Look, I know what you're gonna say, that 'pulling out' wasn't the safest option bla bla, but I trusted Sean to have to have my back"
"Baby, if he'd had your back, you wouldn't be in this predicament in the first place."
"Haha very funny," I said drolly. The smirk on her face showed that she was pleased she was back in my good books, after her less than impressive comment on my recent initiation to 'the club'. "I just meant that we both did this, we both created this baby and he basically said he's not interested. I thought he would be there for me, ya know." That familiar tickling sensation at the back of my nose signified an incoming of tears, but I swallowed it down, I wouldn't cry over that dickhead again.

"Fuck that prick babe, I got you. And mum too, you know she will love havin' a baby around. I'll be that cool auntie that gives them sweets just before bedtime then send them back to your yard." She came over and perched on the arm of my chair, and wrapped her arm around my neck; I leaned towards her, resting my head against her shoulder. This right here, this was what family was. Not those people who only needed you when they wanted something. Not those people who only came around when you had something. They were the ones who were always there, regardless of what you did, or said. Through your mistakes, and highs, and lows family was what you made it, not blood, definitely not that. If blood made you family, then my birth mother never would have given me up, no matter what.
She kissed my forehead, "It's me and you yea."
"And me!" All of the air was forced out of my lungs as a giant man-child crashed on top of me, wrapping his spider-like arms around me.
"Umph, shit Nate, give a girl some warning will ya," I tried to push the big lug off of me, but he weighed a ton.
"Idiot boy, you can't jump on her like that in her condition." Lissa scolded.
He looked at Lissa sharply, concern marring his youthful face, "What condition Zoe? huh, what condition?"
"It's fine, I just have a headache," I rubbed my hand over his bicep, then turned towards Lissa, cutting my eyes and glaring. I *really* didn't want anyone else to know yet.
"You're lying Zo, I can always tell when you're lying. You get this little twitch at the corner of your eye."
"No I don't, and I'm not lying, I told you." His finger came right at my face, pointing straight at my left eye.
"There you see, you're twitchy." His finger stabbed repeatedly at my face, I shoved his hand out of the way.
"Ok, alright, fine. I'll tell you if you get the hell off me." He sat on the floor at my feet, and at this height, I could now look down at him from my seat. I put my hand on his head and stroked through his spiky hair. "I have to tell you something really important..." I looked to Liss, still sitting next to me with a stern look, a look that said 'don't say a word' then I gave Nate all of my

attention. "I have a really bad period, and the cramps are killing me." We cracked up laughing, but clearly he didn't find it funny. "Ugh, you two are gross, I don't need to hear that." I laughed so hard at his obvious disgust, my belly ached, this was just what I needed right now. My two favourite people in the world. He got up to go into the kitchen, and I shouted out to him around my laughter, "Well that's what you get for calling me twitchy." Our chuckles soon slowed down, then died a death at Lissa's "you know you have to tell him soon right." Yea, I would tell him soon...but not yet.

Later that evening, after we had eaten, Lissa broke the news that there was a party tomorrow night, and she expected me to go with her. I did *not* wanna go to a house party, where it would be full of drunken fools, all crammed into a small space, with guys grabbing my ars and saying "oh sorry sweetheart, accident," such bullshit, and I was getting too old for that party scene anyway, besides, I was pregnant and I had to start thinking about our future, not spending money on parties.

"But it'll be fun, you won't be drinking, so bring a Coke Zero with you, have a dance and we can leave early-ish to grab a kebab, whatd'ya think? It's a good plan right!" She begged. It did sound quite convincing, the thought of letting my hair down for a few hours and relaxing with some good tunes was swaying me, plus, a dirty doner kebab was sounding really good right now.

"You promise we will only stay for a couple hours." She immediately held her crossed fingers over her heart, and swore to me that we would leave no later than 11pm.

"Besides babe, you need to enjoy the time you have left as a single woman, the minute you have a kid in tow, you ain't going nowhere!" That idea didn't frighten me as much as I thought it might have, I was used to Nathan being around and I was so used to putting his needs first, making sure he had everything that would keep him happy and healthy, that having a baby in the house didn't intimidate me in the slightest.

"What d'ya think Jackie will say?"

"Honestly, she will probably be happy for the extra child benefit." Lissa kissed her teeth, I knew thinking about that money-grabbing bitch always upset her. "Don't worry, you know I've been saving and that won't change. Nate ages out in 3 years, and when he's free of her, we'll rent our own place together. Me, Nathan and baby Peanut. We'll save space for auntie Lissy too" Out of the corner of my eye, I noticed her discreetly wipe at her eyes. I didn't say anything to her about it, she hated being all emotional and shit. "Now turn the TV up, it's the one with Joey's hand twin."

CHAPTER 2

I finished getting ready in front of my full length mirror. Dark blue skinny jeans, fashionably ripped at the knees (that I wouldn't be fitting in for much longer) a white short sleeve crop-top that showed off a serious amount of abs and cleavage, and my black suede, chunky heeled combat boots finished off my outfit. I had never been much for lots of make-up, some girls could work that contouring shit, I always ended up looking like Pennywise when I tried it. So I kept my look simple: winged eye-liner, some bronzer to add some colour to my cheekbones and my favourite matte lipstick, Kourt K by Kylie, a deep purple that always makes my full lips look even plumper. I had styled my hair with my Blue Magic leave-in coconut conditioner, so that my curls were defined on the crown of my head. Giving my coils a ruffle, I pulled one of the front corkscrews to hang over my forehead, and *now* I was ready. Chucking my purse, keys and lippy into my small brown shoulder bag, I grabbed my black leather jacket - a splurge from TK Maxx - and hightailed it downstairs.

Nathan was on the sofa watching the new episode of Loki, "don't tell me what happens, I haven't seen this episode yet. I won't be too late, but call me if you need me, ok?"
"Is that what you're wearing?" he questioned, looking at my outfit.
"Yea, why? Is there something wrong with it?"
"Don't girls normally dress a bit.....sluttier when they go to parties?"
"Are you joking? Firstly, when the hell have I ever dressed slutty and why would I start doing it now?" This kid needed a slap.
"Well....Josh heard it from Jess who heard it from Tyler who heard it from Sean that you weren't together anymore, so I thought..."

"You thought that now I was single, I was gonna go out and get a new boyfriend?" rolling my eyes at his teenage-boy logic, I calmly stated, "I do not need to dress up slutty to get a boyfriend, and I for sure don't want another one right now, I'm gonna enjoy my single life for a while thank you very much."

Throwing his arm up into the air in a mock Rocky pose, he whooped "Yeesss, I knew you had more brains than that, Tyler said…."

I interrupted that one very quickly, because nothing good ever came out of Tyler's mouth, and he was always in trouble with someone for doing something he shouldn't have. "What have I told you about listening to Tyler." A sharp rap sounded at the door, that was Liss letting me know she was outside and ready to go. "I'm leaving now, remember no-one comes in, don't go out and call me if it's an emergency, I'll be back around midnight, love you."

As I walked to the front door, a "love ya sis" was called back at me.

We jumped in the cab and made our way to the party, which was being held only 10 minutes drive away in Tottenham. The house wasn't in the nicest of areas, but it was free to get in, and for Lissa's benefit, the drinks were free too. After paying the cabbie, we made our way inside, the heavy sounds of CliQ's 'Wavey' was being pumped out to the whole neighbourhood - I'm surprised the neighbours hadn't complained yet. The walls and floors vibrated with the bass of the tune, and the strobe lights that had been dotted around the ground floor flashed against the walls. Lissa grabbed my hand so we didn't get separated in the crowd, and we pushed our way through the grinding bodies to find a gap where we could dance.

The couch and coffee table had been pushed against the far wall, and the latter was being used as a chair for a couple to suck face; bodies swayed and bounced to the music while everyone else lined up against the walls. The floor was already littered with plastic cups and other rubbish - I did *not* want to be around for clean up duty.

Lissa pulled me towards the couple on the couch, a woman I recognised was talking animatedly to her partner, drink sloshing out of her cup to land on the floor. "There's Psycho Sally, let's go stand over there." I remembered her now, she was labelled Psycho Sally because she had set her ex-boyfriend's car on fire when she caught him shagging someone else, coppers didn't have any evidence for the arson, so she got off scot free. Then she went round and battered the shit out of the woman, left her drinkin' out of a straw for months and got sent down for that one - so yea, thats Psycho Sally for ya, not someone I wanted to hang around with, but she had a decent seat with a space right in front for dancin'.

"Hey Sal, how long you been out? Haven't seen you for ages." So of course Lissa addresses the elephant-in-the-room straight away, asking about Sally's jail time, because she has zero filter.
"Lissaaaa babe. You're looking fine as usual, how's your mum, still working at The Whit?"
My friend casually squeezed her way in between Sally and no-name dude, Sally didn't seem to mind, but he looked insulted that he'd been pushed aside, so he got up and stormed off. Aaaaand that was my cue to sit down, thank you no-name dude! While those two shouted at each other to be heard over the music, I looked around at the mass of shapes writhing with hands waving in the air to Banx and Ranx's 'Answerphone', and in the midst of the 'orgy' was a familiar body, with his hands up some skank's skirt - already.
This motherfucker dumped me because he didn't want a kid, and a day later he's all up in some random bird with his tongue shoved down her throat. Oh hell no! Fixing my jacket and pushing my curls back from my forehead - I didn't need anything in the way right now - I stalked towards the groping duo, sliding in between the mass of people crammed between us. Tapping him on the shoulder, hard (I used my finger nail for that extra little bit of hurt) he pulled himself away from his 'friend' and turned sharply towards me, glaring angrily and ready for a fight...until he saw me standing there, then his face went all kinds of pale. I could see his panic in the darkness of the house, the

lighting even made him look a little green. And although I had to shout the words at him because it was so fuckin loud, he knew exactly how angry I was, he could see that rage in my face…and he looked worried. "Aren't you gonna introduce me to your friend, who you clearly only just met right. Because there ain't no way you've known her for more than 24 hours." He looked towards Barbie, who clearly had no clue who I was, and I could see him gearing up to make some bullshit excuse - I knew him so well - and whatd'ya know, clearly he thought I was born yesterday because he actually tried to play the part of the confused ex with his "Hey, I didn't know you would be here" crap.

"I didn't know you would be here either, and with your side piece." Barbie 2.0 actually looked hurt at my comment, and for a moment I felt a bit bad for her; I didn't know her, and she most definitely didn't know Sean very well - but then, clearly I hadn't known him very well either, because I never thought he would turn out this way - he actually had the audacity to look annoyed at my outburst.

"Look Zoe, what we had was fun, but I've told you that we're over, please stop following me around."

"WHAT THE FUCK DID YOU JUST SAY! I have never followed you around, ever! You broke up with me because you found out I was pregnant and you're too much of a pussy to take responsibility." I was conscious that we were drawing a bit of attention, that despite how loud the music was, they could hear my words clearly. I could make myself be heard when I needed to. Plus, I was so far gone now, I didn't care. Let every Tom, Dick and Harry find out what a prick he was. Blondie was fixing her clothes and trying to make herself presentable during my tirade, but everyone could see her smudged lipstick and rumpled clothing, she made to leave, but Sean stepped in front of her to halt her.

"Wait babe, wait a second, she's clearly lying, look, she doesn't even look pregnant."

Laughter surrounded me as Lissa and Sally backed me up, standing either side of me, my wing-women. "D'ya want me to fuck him up for ya Zo?."

"Um, no thanks Sal"

"Are ya sure? I can make it look like an accident. I learnt some new stuff when I was inside."
As much as I really hated him right now, I really didn't want him maimed or dead, so I declined her really kind offer to murder the father of my unborn child - for now. Although I wasn't ruling it out.

And as if this night couldn't get any worse, our little love-triangle became a love-square when Ripped Randy (not his real name but I wasn't gonna ask him for it) turned up for Barbie; then the real drama began, because it looked like Sean was *her* side piece; and of course Sean being the little bitch that he was, took one look at RR - who was built like a brick shit house that flushed steroids - and decided to try and blag his way out of the frying pan. Meanwhile Sindy (because I've now decided Barbie is too high-class a name for her, so I renamed her after the poor-man's version) is trying to move RR away and take him outside, pulling on his tree-trunk arm, which didn't budge even a little bit, all whilst RR is squaring up to Sean and shouting in his face about 'touching his girl'.

Tion Wayne's 'Body' played over the trio's argument, but I could hear everything, until crunching sounded right in my ear. I looked behind me to see Lissa snacking on a bag of Butterkist popcorn, watching like it was a fucking movie. "Where did you get that?"
"Kitchen" she mumbled around a full mouth of sweet and salty. She held the bag out for me, "want some?"
I took a handful and shoved them in my mouth, I was ready to watch this show, I just needed a can of fizzy to wash the kernels out of my teeth, and I was set for the foreseeable.
Sean must have opened his big mouth and said something that RR didn't like, because he shoved Dickhead backwards, where he fell on another guy, toppling them both to the floor and spilling beer everywhere. I could see the guy flat on his back, his can of Bud laying empty next to him - because its contents were all down his white shirt; he pushed Sean off of him and rose quickly, shoving Sean into someone else. At this point, Dickhead just looked like a marble in a pinball machine, being pinged back and

forward between different people. I felt sorry for him a little bit, the poor guy looked like he was gonna cry....nah, he kinda deserved it. Until someone went a bit OTT and shoved him towards the DJ booth that had been set up in a corner of the living room, where he went flying into the set up, smashing one of the free-standing speakers and effectively killing the music - this did not look good.

The DJ went postal, laying a Hayemaker on Sean, knocking him out cold, but in the process causing pandemonium as his unconscious body knocked over several people. They were like bowling pins - people knocking over people. Shouts of anger and pain could be heard in the now silent house. Crashes of glass and moans as people littered the floor, chaos ensued as dozens of bodies all tried to get out at once. Lissa and I had moved back to stand by the sofa, but there were more people from the kitchen trying to push through and get out. As an opening appeared, we tried to squeeze through and get out of the melee, but a body flew towards us crashing into Lissa, separating us. "Liss!" I screamed, trying to fight my way through to her, but there were fists and elbows flying around freely now. Men and women who thought it was a WWE Smackdown episode. And as I reached down to grab at her, an elbow flew at my face, crashing into my nose. I felt the blood trickle past my lip, and tasted the metallic taste with the tip of my tongue. I left it to drip as I went back to get my friend. But I couldn't see her in the spot she had been a minute ago. I panicked. I couldn't see her. What if she was crushed underneath the mass of fighting forms? She needed me and I couldn't do anything.

A feeling of hopelessness swept over me, and tears spilled down my cheeks as I thought of how shit this night had gotten. That the one person I could count on was hurt - maybe worse - and I couldn't do anything to stop it. I imagined all of these people getting the fuck out of my way, I just wanted them gone more than anything else!

A strange sensation swept through me, a buzzing under my skin that made all of the hairs on my arms stand on end;

static electricity made my entire frame shudder, my bloody nose oozed down my chin and stained my top. And as I had the brief thought that I would never be able to wear this again because of these fucking crazy people, an explosion rent the air.
I ducked down and pulled the sofa cushions towards me, trying to create some form of protection from 'something'. Every single person was thrown with considerable force towards the walls. Thuds and crunches reverberated around me. 'Random dude' from earlier crashed face first into the wall-mounted TV, a woman in a red mini dress hurtled horizontally towards the kitchen doorway, her spine bending unnaturally so that her head was in the kitchen and her legs were still in the living room. Not an inch of wall space was left untouched. Blood, cracks and holes disfigured the cream paint, and in the hallway people were screaming and running out of the front door. The glass windows had blown outwards, a deafening shattering sound drowning out my scream.

  As the screams died down and only the moans of pain from the surrounding bodies were left, I slowly stood and surveyed the carnage, and right in the centre of it all, was a woman curled up into a ball, her arms wrapped around her rainbow coloured braids. She looked up, her hands over her face, but her brown eyes peered through the gaps in her fingers. Her eyes found mine "has it finished?"
I wanted to sink to the floor and cry in relief that she was ok, and untouched, not a scratch, not even a broken nail. But before I could spend even a second being thankful for our good luck, sirens sounded in the distance and they were getting closer. We couldn't be found here in this mess. We ran to each other at the same time, our arms folding around each other and quickly reassuring ourselves that we were alive...then we ran to the exit, the front door hanging loosely on a hinge.
On the high street we stopped to catch a breath, at least here, people (police) would think we were just out for a walk to the 24 hour corner shop.

  "What the fuck Zo. What did you do!"

"Me? I didn't do anythin', you was in the middle of it, what did *you* do?" I stated back to her, there was no need to say anything about that dodgy feeling I'd had right before the 'big bang.'
"You screamed, and then everything went nuclear, babe, it was you." Her tone had gentled, like she was babying me, and didn't want me to freak out. But it must have been an electrical issue right?
"No babe, it literally looked like you pushed everything and everyone out of your way - except me. That's why I was just left in the middle of the room, it was like something out of X-Men, some Jean Grey shit."
"That's crazy. there was a power outage, a...a...short circuit or something. People don't just do things like that Liss." We were both shaken, our night having taken a ridiculously unexpected turn, but in true Liss fashion, she steered me towards the kebab shop, sat me down at one of the formica tables and got my doner.
"How can you act so...so normal after watching that?"
"Because, we are safe and nothing happened to either of us. I know that sounds selfish, and that I'm pretty sure people died, but you are the only person - outside of mum and Nate - that I care about. Their problems are not my problems, *you* are my concern, and you're ok...which means I'm ok too. So, eat your food." The kebab was placed before me, covered in red cabbage, onions and chili sauce and my stomach let out a loud gurgle. Like seeing people get hammered by an unseen force made it hungry. And whatd'ya know" she said smugly, looking at the clock on the wall, "Its 11pm, didn't I promise to have you out before 11pm AND a kebab." Sticking a piece of the lamb into my mouth, I nodded, because yea, that's exactly what she'd promised.

CHAPTER 3

     I wiped the crust from my eyes. I could feel the burn in my eyeballs from lack of sleep, and I wanted to pull the cover over my head and go back to bed, but it was a sunday, and I had to work today. I had gotten hardly any rest last night; we got back home at midnight, where we each went back to our own places. Once I had washed and climbed into bed, it was almost 1am, and my mind was whirling with all of the events from the party. Scenarios spun in my mind, until I had pulled up Google on my phone and searched 'all the ways a house can implode around you.' and surprise, hardly anything came up except 'Can Crusher experiments' and 'How To Detonate a Building', not something I was interested in knowing.
I heard Jackie stumble in around 5. She must have met some chavvy guy in the bar and went back to his house. She didn't even bother to check if Nathan was home; I could hear her snores from the next room, she sounded like a freight train with a bum engine - all those years of smoking. I've been telling her for years that they would kill her.

     I dragged myself from bed, hearing my phone chime with a Whatsapp message. One of the girls I worked with had sent me a link to the newspaper, asking me if I had heard about what happened last night, the headline read 'Tragedy at House Party, multiple injuries'. "Fuck,"
I was ignoring that message. I had no idea what happened last night, and if anyone asks, that's exactly what I'd say.

     Completing my morning routine of a wee, shower, and donning my Ladbrokes uniform, I quickly poked my head into Nathan's room and saw him spread-eagle, and fast asleep, on his little single bed that was way too small for his growing frame. I headed downstairs to have some toast and coffee before remembering that I couldn't have normal coffee, and I had failed to pick up any decaf. Fuck my life right now. If there was ever a morning where I *needed* coffee, it was today! It's fine, I told myself, no big deal. I can stop at Costa on my way to work. Simple.

I didn't work far from home, less than 10 minutes walk, and when the weather was nice, I would take my time, but I wanted coffee. Now. After ordering my 'ughh' decaf , I turned to leave, and the cliche of all cliches, a big hairy bastard walked in to me, spilling my hot drink down *his* top - thankfully not mine, that stuff was scalding - but for fuck's sake, I just wanted a coffee.

"Watch where you're going, you could have burned me," I angrily told him, holding the disposable cup away from my body and closer to him. His red shirt was soaked with the brown stuff, but the heat didn't seem to bother him because he hadn't even flinched. "Isn't that hot?"

"What? Yes, actually, it's quite hot," looking down at his shirt, I could see his torso clearly defined beneath the wet cotton. It was like a wet T.Shirt contest for guys. I was actually enjoying this. His voice, when he spoke, was with a rough, gravelly cadence enriched with a posh accent; too posh for me, a pregnant single-mum with a dead-end job. With that negative thought in my head, I moved around his massive body and headed towards the door, pulling it open to leave, he called out. "Wait - I can buy you another coffee?"

"Nah, it's fine, I'm not in the mood for coffee anymore."

Ladbrokes was a gamblers haven. We had our newbies who rarely put a bet on, maybe once a year on the Grand National, then we had our regulars who popped in on weekends to make a cheeky bet when the other half was out, and finally, we had our regular regulars who came in every day to spend their winnings, only to lose them and come in again the next day to try and win them back; it was a vicious cycle that they couldn't break. Today would be extra busy, as a big football match was on this afternoon, so every man and his dog would be betting on who would win, who would score and how many goals. It became repetitive after a while.

Setting up my till, the bell on the front door alerted me to my first customer of the day, and in walked 'wet t.shirt man' holding a Costa cup of steamy goodness and placing it on the counter in front of the plexi-glass I was behind. "The lady at the coffee shop mentioned that you had decaf, so an apology cup for you, for spilling your drink."

I stared at him in amazement, because I wasn't expecting this to happen at all, I had relegated myself to a coffee-free morning, not to be gifted it by a tall, sexy specimen. And let's face it, I wasn't watching where I was going, too lost in thought about last night, that his first meeting with me turned into a coffee-bath that was most likely my fault. "Um, thanks. That's....sweet of you."

He stared intently, his lips turning up slightly at the corners, acknowledging my gratitude. "Are you putting a bet on?" I asked, looking at him, and dragging my eyes over him, taking in as much as I could.

He was beautiful, in a manly way of course, although he probably wouldn't appreciate being called 'beautiful.' He looked like someone who spent a limited time on his appearance; his dark hair was cropped short to his head - an all over job that he could do himself with the right clippers, and a beard that he didn't cut at all. It grew in a thick and wild mass - magnificent and coal-black; a beard that most men would be envious of, I wanted to grab it and stroke my fingers through it. His eyes were a golden amber that looked down at me from his (at least) towering 6ft 6 height. He was what I would expect a mountain man to look like, but dressed better, I most definitely wanted to climb him like a mountain - just call me Hazel Findlay.

If life wasn't so crazy right now, with a baby on the way, I would have been the first to ask for his number, but that wasn't in the cards for me any time soon, I had way more important things to worry about than sexy men bringing me coffee - even though it was super nice of him. He was still staring at me, so to break the spell his golden eyes had on me, I asked him again (but also I wanted to hear that sexy voice again) "will you be placing a bet today?"

"I have never been much for gambling to be honest, I'm not a risk taker - unless I know I'm going to win."

"Well, I can't give you any tips, you'll just have to check the odds to see who has the best chances of winning." I told him.
"Do you think I have a chance of winning?" he said pointedly, his eyes twinkling knowingly.
"That all depends on who you choose." ok, were we still talking about gambling here? I'm pretty sure we were flirting at this point. And after I had told myself I wouldn't do this, damn it.
"If I were to choose to ask you to have dinner with me, would I be successful?"
"Hmmm, you just said you weren't a risk taker, isn't asking me for dinner a risk?" I said cheekily.
"I do not see this as a risk, more like taking a chance that a beautiful woman would allow me the pleasure of her company - ladies choice of locations of course."

I decided then, why the hell not. The worst case scenario was he turned out to be a weirdo with a toe fetish, the best case scenario - I get a free meal at my choice of restaurants. I wasn't gonna think about where this was going, I was gonna accept because it was good food, some eye-candy to look at for the evening, and it helped take my mind off things. And yea, I was feeling a bit vindictive too, maybe Dickhead would see us out, or it would get back to him, that I was out with another guy, and I wasn't pining away over him.
"I don't even know your name, and you want me to have dinner with you, you could be a serial killer for all I know!" I joked.
He laughed loudly, a deep raspy sound that gave me the impression he didn't laugh very often, "I assure you Zoe, I am far from a serial killer"
I hesitated at his comment, looking at him warily and then checking over my shoulder to see if my colleague, Tina, had arrived yet, because I sure as shit had not told him my name.
"What's wrong?" clearly noticing my unease.
"I never told you my name."
For a split second, his face twisted to show his own unease before he covered it with a smile, revealing perfectly straight, white teeth, the points of his canines showing clearly behind his grin. "It's on your shirt." his eyes lowered to my burgundy polo,

and the name badge pinned above my left breast that clearly stated 'ZOE.'

      To cover up my idiocy, I used the old "good, I was just making sure you were paying attention." and although he obviously found my attempts at covering up my stupidity to be funny, he didn't mention it. Which - I think - was quite gentlemanly of him. I took a sticky pad from under the shelf, and wrote my digits on it, passing it to him through the slot between the counter and the plexi-glass, and as I slid it towards him, his hand came up to take it from me; his fingers - long with neatly trimmed nails - glided his fingers over mine, sliding the slip of paper from under my hand, stroking my fingers with his own. Just that touch alone, felt like a livewire had coursed through my system, sending my libido into overdrive - and all of this from a touch of his hand? I wasn't sure I could handle a touch from his 'anything else'. My breath came out in pants, his hand had been hot and rough, his eyes searched mine from behind the perspex, asking silently *'did I feel that too.'*

"My name is Lucian."

Lucian. I finally had a name for my handsome stranger. "Lucian, do you like Wagamama? There's a place in Islington, it's not far; we can eat there."

I cannot say I have ever tried it actually, I'm partial to steak, but I'm willing to try anything you suggest."

"Mmm yes. Their steak Bulgogi is to die for. You'll love it." I heard a rustling behind me, Tina was finally here - late as usual - and I had to get back to work, not ogle my mountain man all day. "I finish at 4, I need to shower and change, I can meet you there?" He was sexy, but I wasn't stupid enough to give a random guy my address, I needed to get back to work, the morning rush was starting, and he was a nice distraction that I couldn't afford at the moment.

      He took the hint, telling me that he would text me so I had his number, and that he would meet me there at 6pm. Walking backwards, still facing me, he blocked the doorway of the shop and smiled; and damn he actually looked excited at the prospect of a date...with me. It did wonders for a girl's ego. The bell above the door signified his exit, and I released the breath that I had been holding (not literally) since he asked me to dinner. Doing a jiggle on the spot, my arse shaking side to side and squealing, I revelled in the fact that I still had 'it', that someone as fine as Lucian would want to have dinner with me. Mentally digging through my wardrobe and considering what I was going to wear tonight, I was interrupted by a tap on my shoulder.

"What are you so excited about?" Tina asked.

I told her that it was nothing, because I didn't want her sticking her nose in my life. She was nice and all that, but she liked to talk about everybody's business. And on that note, my 'business' would have to be explained to Lucian later. I would see if he was interested in another date once he found out I would have a plus one in about 7 months; and no hard feelings if not, at least I got to have Wagamama.

My day grew steadily busier, with Chelsea and Arsenal playing this afternoon, everyone wanted to make a bet. At lunchtime, I took my lunchbox, with my cheese and tomato sandwich, apple and Dairy Milk to the park, and finding a free bench, I sat myself down to enjoy my little homemade snack and peace from the gambling den. The sun was warm which was especially strange for England at this time of year. Normally we had rain, sleet and gusty winds...all in the same day. As I finished off my food, packing my rubbish away into the bag, a shadow covered me, a shadow cast by a woman who stood right in front of me and stared - this staring thing was becoming an issue, I'll start getting a complex soon, that or I have some lunch left on my face?

She was young, probably a bit older than me, with short blonde hair tied into a ponytail so that the stub of her hair stuck out horizontally; and she was dressed like a grandma; that was the main thing that I noticed about her, that her dress looked like Jackie's mum's curtains before she died. A dress that hung off her petite frame making her look ten times bigger. It was a drab beige colour with large mustard colour flowers printed all over it, it was not an attractive look. What also wasn't attractive was how she then sat down next to me, practically on top of me with how close she sat, her curtain-dress billowing out to land across my legs.

"I've been waiting for you Zoe."

"Oookkaaayy." I leaned away from her, the scent of Ylang Ylang wafting towards me. I didn't mind all of that essential oil stuff, but it smelled like she bathed in it, brushed her teeth with it and then ate it. It was *intense*.

"You need to come with me now, you're in danger, I can help you,I can keep you safe."

Right lady, I think you've had too much of the strong stuff, I'm gonna go as I have to get back to work. See ya." Picking up my now empty lunch box, I stood to leave only for her to grab my arm. She had some strength in her skinny little hands.

"This isn't a joke, they know where you are now, you practically pin-pointed your location last night you bloody ammature." She raged. But at the mention of last night I went still. She couldn't know what happened last night...unless this was a prank and someone put her up to it.

"Very funny guys, haha, good one" I looked towards the bushes dotted around the park, expecting a 'Punk'd' to be shouted out at any time...but it didn't happen. "Look, I don't know what you think happened yesterday, but you've got the wrong girl now let.go.of.my.arm" I punctuated carefully, in case she didn't understand. Her fingers slowly released their tight grip on my forearm, and she straightened to her full height - which wasn't much, this bitch was tiny - and then straightened her granny frock, brushing her hands down the front of it.

"Tonight is a new moon. I would suggest running far away, but clearly you're too stupid so I'm guessing you will just go about your business like everything is normal..."

I tuned out her tirade, because what the hell was she on? This woman should be locked up somewhere...I tuned back into her little rant to hear her carrying on about how I was a let down, and she couldn't believe I was the last of my line blah blah, yea I'd heard this bit before from social workers, teachers, foster parents. I wasn't gonna stand around and listen to it from a stranger. Turning swiftly away, I started walking back to work,

only to hear her shout "Beware the moonwalkers, they're hunting you."
Yea ok mate. I'm outta here.

      After locking up the shop, I was knackered. My tiring night, lack of sleep and busy day made me regret telling Lucian that we would meet tonight. I had received a text from him saying he would meet me outside the restaurant at 6, but I debated whether I should rearrange for another night, I couldn't be bothered to change and then get a bus all the way there. Walking down the street towards home and seriously considering cancelling my date, I felt a shiver down my spine, that feeling of being watched. I wrapped my jacket around me tighter and walked a bit faster, hoping that it was just my imagination that had me spooked; but the crazy lady from earlier telling me that I was in danger had me paranoid, so I stepped a bit quicker hoping to get home in record time and put the door between me and my anxiety. I made sure I peeked into every shadowed crevasse that I walked by to make sure there was nothing sinister hiding in wait. Damn, this woman had me shook. The sight of my familiar red door had me relaxing just a little bit, but I wouldn't stop until it was closed behind me with the chain on. Yea, I was gonna call Lucian and rearrange, I just wasn't in the right frame of mind for date-night. If he was really interested in seeing me, he'd be ok with doing it another time, if not? Well then at least I knew what type of person he was from the get-go. Slamming the door on my worries, I leaned my back against the heavy wood and relaxed the rest of the way. Walking to the kitchen for a drink, I called out to Nathan to let him know that I was home, but I spied a note stuck to the door that said he had gone upstairs to Sarah's, she's cooking and to come up when I get home. The idea of Sarah's home-cooked food sounded fantastic right now, and it sounded just like her; finish her shift of taking care of people, then come home and take care of everyone else. And because I was still so paranoid, I made sure I peeked through the peephole to make sure the coast was clear before re-opening my door and making my way to the stone stairs that led up to the walkway housing the upper floor flats. Sarah's place - pink door - situated directly above mine had been mine and

Nathan's second home for years; I didn't have a key for it like Lissa had for mine, because Sarah worked weird shifts that changed all the time, and I didn't wanna risk waking her up. I could see her silhouette through the window, moving around in her kitchen, so I tapped my knuckles against the glass, and when she saw it was me, she yelled out "Lissy, door!" at the top of her voice. I think the whole row heard her.

Kicking my shoes off at the door - you did not walk on Sarah's nice clean carpets with shoes on - I picked a pair of fluffy slippers out of the tub by the front door; a box of indoor shoes for guests and went into the front room. The layout was exactly the same as mine. Kitchen on the left as you walk in the front door, stairs behind it, and front room spanning the width of the flat, which is where Nate and Lissa were sitting at a dining table, tucked into the corner of the room. Coming up behind me, my pseudo-mum placed a steaming plate of oxtail and white rice on the table, laying a fork next to it for me. "Sit down sweet'eart, eat your dinner." Pulling out a chair next to Nathan, I sat down and filled my belly with hot food, whilst the company filled my soul with love.

"Are you working again tonight Sarah?" I asked around mouthfuls of food.

"Yes darlin', I'm actually leaving now, I was asked to cover a double shift and Lord knows I could use the money."

Kissing us all on the head, and giving Nathan a final "be good", she left us to finish eating, knowing that we would tidy up after ourselves.

Nathan was the first to finish, and while he was in the kitchen washing up, Lissa turned her chair to face me so that the interrogation could begin. I knew she wouldn't wait long.

"I thought you had a date tonight? It better not be with Dickhead!"

I was horrified that she thought I would even go there after what he's done. "Hell no. Some fit guy came in the shop today, he seemed nice and I thought why not? Besides, he had the sexiest beard, and I read recently about a scientific study that mentioned that men with beards are more likely to be kind, courageous and trustworthy - all the things that Dickhead isn't."

"Oh my God I read the same thing! It said they were supposed to be more dominant too." Chuckling at the thought of that article, I hoped it was true, not so much the dominant part, but of course that's the part Liss would focus on. She always says she likes a bossy man.

"What's his name? What does he do? What size shoe does he wear?" She threw these questions at me like she expected me to know all of this. "Lucian. Don't know. Massive. That's all I got for ya, the rest will have to wait."

I needed a shower, my pj's and my bed. In that order. "Sorry to eat and run, but I'm so tired and I'm working again tomorrow. Come on Nate, home time" Swapping our borrowed slippers for our own shoes, we stood by the door.

"Are you seriously leaving now? You haven't even told me anythin' juicy about 'you know who'."

"I will give you all the deets once I know all the deets, fair?" She was actually thinking about it, like she even had a choice, I didn't have anything to share.

Looking confused, my little brother scratched his head, asking "are you talking about Sean?"

"Why does everyone think it's about Sean! What type of pushover do you think I am?" How annoying, that the two people who knew me so well clearly didn't know me very well. I wouldn't touch him anymore with someone else's dick! Pulling open the front door, I put one foot over the threshold, gearing up to turn left towards the stairs, when I froze. Right at the top of the stairs, its front paws resting on the landing, was the biggest fucking dog I had ever seen. And it was staring straight at me.

CHAPTER 4

Slamming the door and running to the kitchen, I lifted the nets so that I could see outside. It was still there, it's nose in the air sniffing at something...or *for* something.
"What's up babe, what are you looking at?" Both of them had followed me, and were now shoving me out of the way to get a look outside too. "Holy shit, that's a big dog. That's like a Pitbull and a doberman's love child but uglier." Peering over Lissa's shoulder, we all watched as Cujo pulled the rest of its body on the landing. "Did I say a Pitbull and a Doberman? I meant a Mastiff and a Great Dane. That is the biggest mutt I ever seen."
"How do you know the names of all these dog breeds?" Nathan muttered to her beside me.
"Discovery channel."
And as we watched, the ugliest dog I'd ever seen let out the loudest howl I'd ever heard. The sounds of multiple feet were like thuds through the glass pane, and as we all watched, large dark heads appeared at the top of the stairs and made their way across the landing. Similarly to the first dog, they stuck their snouts in the air and moving their heads from side to side, they followed a scent....straight to our door. I could see them clearer now, their shaggy fur unkempt, their fangs too long to be kept in their closed jaws and so the tips of the sharpest points jutted out, the sound of their claws scraped against the stone walkway, it sounded like nails on a chalkboard and made me clench my teeth in disgust. Their snouts sniffed at the banister and against the door frame of Sarah's flat.
"Dude, they're not dogs!" Liss grabbed my arm, "they're wolves, like, really fucking big wolves. And what the hell are they doing? They sniffed out Mum's oxtail? That's it, that's what they're after. I know she cooks real good, but this is mental!" Lissa's words

came fast and without a pause in between, "If her food can bring a pack of wolves..."

"Big dogs." Nathan interrupted "There ain't no wolves in London dude!"

"Oh yea? Well what the hell are those!"

"Lissa's right Nate, I've never seen dogs look that big...or scary." Their eyes were too intelligent, I mean I know dogs were smart and stuff, but these...things, looked like they calculated your demise, they glared at us through the window, their heads clearing the bottom window pane, they were that fucking large. Yep, definitely not dogs. I counted four of them taking up the 6 foot wide walkway outside the front door, blocking our way out. We should have gone downstairs, at least we'd have a back exit to escape from, but this was the top floor - the only exit was being guarded by what looked like hell hounds.

The breath of one of them fogged up the outside of the glass as it leered through the kitchen window. It completely ignored Nathan and was passing its gaze between Lissa and I, flitting back and forth like it was trying to make a decision, a choice. "Is it thinkin' about which one to eat first?"

"Not gonna lie Zo, but I'm all skin and bone, I wouldn't fill him up at all." I glared at her, because now wasn't the time for her jokes - at least I hoped it was a joke.

The sound of clanging turned my attention to Nathan rummaging in the drawers, he pulled out a rolling pin, a carving knife and...a machete? "Why does your mum have a machete in her kitchen?"

"Protection innit. This is London, never know when you might need it." She looked pointedly at the glass where the wolves still lay in wait for us, then turned to grab the weapon but Nathan pulled it out of her reach before she could grab it.

"Nuh uh, you can have this one little lady" He gave her the smaller carving knife, while holding the rolling pin towards me. "How come I get this one?"

They shared a look, smiling like there wasn't an animal attack waiting to happen, "Sis, you cut yourself on a can opener and you want us to trust you with a massive knife?"

"Uh fine" Checking to see what White Fang was up to, I pulled my mobile from my back pocket, googling a number for the local animal shelter.

"Are you calling the police? The army? Who?" asked Lissa.

Looking at her like the crazy person she is, I told her "I'm calling the animal shelter." Muttering under my breath, "the bloody army, seriously."

"What the hell do you think they're gonna do with their cages and leashes! Have you *seen* them...and all of their teeth. Animal control ain't controlling anything here babe."

"Are they waiting for us to come out? Because you know that ain't happening right! Right?" Nate was getting worried, but I didn't blame him, I was worried too.

"What if they have rabies?" They must have heard my comment because as one, they all glared through the glass...at me. "Oh shit!" Why did I have to open my big mouth. "We should move away from the window, go upstairs or something, they're freaking me out."

"Did you call animal control?" Asked Lissa

I looked at her sheepishly, "They're ummm closed for the weekend"

"Brilliant. We'll all get eaten because them selfish twats wanna have a weekend!"

Nate grabbed my arm, getting my attention, "Uh guys, something's happening out there." He was peering out the window, trying to see around the corner towards where the stairs were. The dog/wolves were excited about something, their tails thrashing madly, growls and yips showing their enthusiasm. A man appeared at the top of the stairs, he was well dressed in a smart navy suit, a crisp white shirt open at the collar showed just a small amount of tanned skin, and his golden hair was slicked back to highlight his stark face, his cheek bones the envy of supermodels. He was stunning - male perfection.

But that was where his beauty stopped, because his eyes were as black as midnight showing the absence of a soul. They were filled with malice and evil intentions. He was a walking contradiction: an angelic face but the essence of unholiness...and he scared the shit out of me.

He calmly walked towards the door, the animals swirling around his hips begging for any scrap of attention from him; he ignored them, stopping right outside and ringing the damn doorbell.

You know those people in films who see a gigantic monster coming toward them so they just stand there watching and maybe videoing it on their phone? I hated those people, they were so dumb; I just wanted to shake them and shout 'run the fuck away you idiot', and then inevitably they get eaten, dying horribly because they just wanted to watch….yea that was us right now. Because we were still standing in the bloody kitchen…watching things unfold. And Satan's sexy brother had leaned around the doorframe and was looking straight at us through the window. His grin was devilish, and he had a dimple in one of his cheeks, but all I could think of was Heath Ledger's legendary portrayal of The Joker and I half expected him to shout through the window "Why so serious?"

"Which one of you lives in the apartment downstairs? I'm looking for Zoe Ward, daughter of Delilah Ward." His voice was like honey, trying to lure us into a false sense of security, I knew it, I could feel it. He was not a good person, I'd always been a good judge of character (Dickhead excluded obviously) and right now my instincts were screaming at me "Get the fuck away Zoe" And how the fuck did he know my birth mother's name? "I'd just like to talk, maybe you could let me in and I can tell you what I'm doing here."
"Sorry dude" I told him. "but I've never been interested in playing Little Red Riding Hood, I'll have to pass on your invitation"
"Does this make me the Big Bad Wolf?" He said, grinning widely.
"Pretty sure the wolf died in the end so I wouldn't be so quick to laugh about it"
He placed his hand against the pane of glass and leaned towards me, only the window separating us. "Zoe, Zoe, Zoe." He repeated my name like a mantra, "You have your mum's eyes…and her mouth."
That made my whole body jolt and my eyes widened. I could see the other two sharply turn their heads to gape at me. But there's

no way he knew my bio-mum; it had to be a lie, a ploy to get me to open the door - besides, he was far too young to have known her, he only looked a few years older than me.

"What do you want from me? I don't know you. Just leave, and I won't call the police and have you arrested; they'll take your pets away too. So just do everyone a favour, and go home."

His face hardened at my order, his obsidian eyes like flint, "I tried being nice Ms Ward, but you are being quite difficult." He disappeared from view, I couldn't see him through the glass anymore.

"Did he leave?" Nate whispered to me.

"I don't know" I needed to know that he was gone; on the tip of my toes I crept to the window which was situated above the sink, and leaning over the stainless steel appliance, I could see him standing at the front door. His head was bent to the wolves at his feet, it looked like he was telling them something...and did that wolf just nod it's fucking head?

He gripped the handle of the front door, and with an ease that frightened me, he wrenched it towards him and the lock mechanism fell to the floor.

I shoved Lissa and Nathan through the kitchen doorway, pushing them towards the stairs, it was the only place we could go. Maybe if we block ourselves in Sarah's room - which was at the back of the flat - we could set up a barricade with the furniture until help got here? It was the only plan I had right now. Still carrying our kitchen-weapons, we sprinted, taking the stairs two at a time. The sound of the front door hitting the wall and footsteps - or pawsteps - clambering past the threshold in our pursuit made my heart race. The crazy lady hadn't been so crazy after all. She had said I was in danger; I wish I'd paid more attention to her words and not her outfit.

At the top of the stairs, I paused to look back (I was that idiot again) 'Evil Eye' man stepped slowly into the hallway, the wolves moving about him in a sea of fur. In what was the most fucked up thing I'd ever seen, his face started to contort, his flesh seemingly melting from his face. His jaw popped and dislocated, making way for fangs that shredded through his gums, his tongue elongated in his mouth, pink and grotesque with saliva. His hand slammed against the wall near his head, his fingernails extending to resemble hooked claws as long as my own finger, they were black and thick and looked ready to slice flesh from bone. What the fuck did I just watch? This isn't real right?

Piling into Sarah's room, we all got busy shouldering the double bed, bedside drawers, and free-standing wardrobe in front of the door, hoping that it would buy us a bit of time. "Did anyone see what I just saw?" I could feel the hysteria rising, I wanted to be sick. I wanted to go home. I wanted this to not be real.

"Did we see a random guy break down my door, really easily, and chase us with his pet wolf-dogs up the stairs? Yea we both saw that." Lissa panted. Obviously it was just me, maybe the fear had got to my brain and I hallucinated it. Yep, that sounds far better than "a creature from hell started warping in the hallway." I went to take my phone from my back pocket, only realising that I'd left it on the kitchen worktop. "Shit, does anyone have their phone on them?" With wide eyes, they searched frantically through their pockets, patting themselves down in the hope that they had one. Turns out Nate left his at home and Lissa's was in her bag downstairs. "Why the hell don't you carry your phones with you?" I shouted.

"Pot meet kettle." Liss stood there with her hands on her hips, her leg cocked to one side in a pose that was meant to mean 'fuck you too'. "What did you do with yours?" I pointed to the floor, in the universal term for 'downstairs', hoping she wouldn't make me speak my incompetence out loud. Her eye roll came at the same time as the crashing of heavy bodies against the wooden door made the furniture shudder, making us all jump; it wouldn't hold them for long. Their excitement was palpable, and the crashes just kept coming.

"They're playing with us."

Nathan had sat with his back against the wall facing the door, his knees bent and his arms resting along them; the knife he carried dangled carelessly between his fingers. "Did you see how big those animals were, and there's 4 of them. They could break past this barrier in no time...but they don't want to. Listen." Straining our ears, we heard them taking it in turns to try and break the door. It wasn't all of them trying to bash the door down. They were playing, one after the other they had a go at slamming against the door; their barks like a conversation between them, almost saying, 'damn, I didn't get through this time, your turn Fido'.

"You're right Nate, I don't think they're normal wolves." Looking at me with a 'duh' expression, we went back to our vigil and watched the door, waiting for its inevitable fall.

A deep growl sounded outside, and I saw a shadow appear, motionless from under the crack in the door. The deep guttural words that flowed through the door were hard to understand, the harsh-sounding speech was grating in my ears, but I knew what he said. "Little pig, little pig, let me come in." He was speaking around his row full of jagged teeth. I definitely didn't imagine it then. "Or I'll huff and I'll puff, and I'll blow your door in."

"Wrong wolf story moron." I shouted out. "I'm Little Red Riding Hood, remember." His throaty laugh ended on a choke, because I'm pretty sure dogs couldn't laugh. I put my arms around my brother and my best friend, pulling them tight to me - I had to reach up that little bit higher for Nate as he was taller than me, and it put a little sprain in my armpit, but I needed to hold them both close. "I'm sorry I got you into this." I said to them both, squeezing them to me.

"How the fuck did you get us into this mess? Do you know this dude?" Said Lissa.

"No but...she told me today that I was in danger" I hung my head, shame coursing through me. "I should have ran when the curtain lady told me to."

Nate turned to me, "You never leave, do you hear me. Promise me that you won't leave." Nate had been left by everyone, and the thought that I would have left, left him, devastated him. And I felt worse. "I won't leave you Nate. Promise."

"Awww that's so sweet." His slurred, grating voice resonated through the bedroom, and I dreaded the moment he decided to open that door; because based on his display from earlier, it wouldn't take much for him to get past our make-shift blockade.

"I'm being patient with you Kitten, but I won't wait much longer. If you make me open this door, your friends will pay the price." Gasps of panic erupted around me, scrambling to our feet with our backs braced against the wall, we stood shoulder to shoulder, our weapons braced in front. "Listen to me, I won't have either of you hurt ok, just stay here and I'll talk to him." I made to move away from them - my family - I needed to make sure he didn't hurt them. I'd seen his face, and I'd glimpsed the evil inside him; I truly believed that he would hurt those I loved the most to get what he wanted...me.

      A whispered sentence from behind me made me stop, "You promised you wouldn't leave me Zo." He sounded like the small abandoned child he'd been 10 years ago when the social worker brought him to the flat, and my heart shattered, because if I walked out that door, I didn't know if I would make it back. And I couldn't leave my little brother - I'd promised. I tilted my head back and looked at the white painted, wood chip ceiling that resembled my own bedroom and tried to think of a way where we stayed together, unharmed by feral wolves and black-eyed weirdos.

"Time's up Pet, I gave you a choice." Heavy breathing sounded right outside the wooden door, we had to move quickly, speed was our element of surprise. Without wanting to give the game away, I turned to face my best friends.

"Do you remember last year when Curry's announced that they had loads of PS5's available for sale?" My mind was spinning now, because it was feasible, and we could get out of here, the taxi stand was down the street, jump in a cab, go to the police station. Safety. I pictured it in my mind so clearly.

Nate immediately knew what I meant, and his eyes glittered with remembered glee. Hundreds of people had queued up outside Curry's for hours, waiting for their chance to purchase a much anticipated computer console - I didn't get it personally, why waste all that money on a computer when your old one worked fine - but Jackie's boyfriend at the time had saved money to buy one, and he was desperate. He promised us lunch if we helped him get through the crowd, and I was always up for a free meal. 4 people had been better than 1 in that mass of impatient

shoppers, and so when the doors had finally opened, we'd bum-rushed to the front, forcing our way through. Nate had played on that thing for a month until Jackie dumped the guy for a dude that owned a Ford Focus.
We were gonna bum-rush our captors. Speed and force was our friend, as soon as they opened that door, we'd be ready to run. They wouldn't expect it, and so the element of surprise would ensure that we had a head start.
Lissa grinned next to me. "It's always fun with you babe."

The oak furniture was shoved forward leaving indents in the carpet, and the door cracked open allowing a canine head to poke through. It licked it's lips and tried to force it's shoulders through the gap. Banging and thuds preceded the widening of the gap where the hairy beasts were trying to get through, and then fingers with those disgusting claws curled around the edge of the door...and thrust it open.
"Get ready," I murmured. I didn't want them to hear that we even *had* a plan. Before I could even utter 'go', a loud bang cracked through the air, and black-eyed guy flew to the side, a gunshot piercing his waist, blood splatter coated the wall where he had stood. The wolves went insane, growling with their hackles raised and fangs glistening. They ran into the hallway where the bullet had come from, and then the boom of more gunshots echoed around us. Whimpers and growls could be heard amongst the shouting and swearing of feminine voices.
We huddled in the corner, our plan for escape thwarted. Charging towards the animals with only knives and a rolling pin seemed ok at the time, but trying to maneuver between them *and* bullets? Wasn't gonna happen. Hopefully they all killed each other off and we could just wait here until that happened.

A womanly figure outfitted in all black with a balaclava shielding her identity appeared at the doorway, a handgun held tightly in her grasp; the barrel was pointed towards where 'scary-guy' had fallen, and her free hand gestured to us, waving a 'come here'.
Lissa stood up and I followed, our bodies shielding Nathan who still sat huddled on the floor, she threaded her hand around my

waist, stating that "the enemy of my enemy is my friend" and tapped Nate on the head to get up. I suppose she had a point, we didn't really have many options right now; it was 'stay here and maybe die or go with them and maybe die.' hmmm tough choice. But for Nate, for Liss, I'd take any chance.

"Don't just stand there for Goddess' sake, move your arse" G.I Jane sounded mighty familiar right now, but I couldn't place her voice. Running hand-in-hand, Nathan in the middle so we can keep him safe between us, our free hands still gripping our knives (and rolling pin) because no way was I taking them into an unfamiliar situation with no way of defending them.

The wolves had been pushed back and were standing guard over their fallen leader, his body was writhing beneath them so I knew he was still alive, but they were protecting him, sheltering his body. Another woman - her face hidden from me - stood watch, a rifle pointed straight at our attackers, holding them back and clearing a path for us to get downstairs and outside.

Our first saviour led the way outside and to a waiting grey van. She pulled the sliding door open and ushered us all inside before calling out to her comrade to "hurry up." Pulling herself in beside us, and her friend jumping in the passenger seat, we sped off. The sound of squealing tyres overshadowed the howls of anger that came from Sarah's flat.

But we weren't going in the direction of the police station, I didn't know where they were taking us, or even who they were. "We need to go the other way, we have to report this to the police."

"The police cannot help you with this," She pulled her balaclava off, her short blonde hair falling to just below her chin in waves. I gasped, because I knew she sounded familiar, "You're curtain-dress lady." And then mentally slapped myself on the forehead, because I'd said that out loud, I'd probably just insulted the woman who tried to warn me, and who saved my family tonight. "I'm so sorry, I didn't mean that." Cackling came from the two women in the front seats, with the passenger-seat lady slapping her hand on her thigh in hysterics. She couldn't even speak properly as she was laughing so hard, her cackles surrounded each word.

"She" laughter "called" laughter "you" snort-laughter "curtain-dress lady" cue the hysterics at this point.

"My name," she said snottily, "is Amber. And that dress is my favourite."

"Soooo, where are you taking us then?" Lissa piped up from the seat along the van panel. I was sitting opposite her, and I could feel the vibrations from the engine under my bum. I really wanted to know the answer to that question too.

Even though Lissa had asked, Amber stared at me to tell me the plan, completely ignoring my friend. That was rude. "We will take you somewhere safe, and then we will try and answer as many of your questions as we can."

"Are you going to tell us who or *what* the fuck that was back there?" Amber cringed at the use of Lissa's eff word, like we hadn't earned the right to swear right now. Still looking at me, Amber-curtain-dress-lady went to reply...to me...again. Lissa's face was mottled with rage, because I knew my friend well; if there was one thing she hated more than anything, it was being ignored. Clicking her fingers in front of Amber's face, Lissa repeated her question, but ended it this time with a glare.

"If you can all be patient until we reach our destination, it should not take longer than an hour, and our...boss, can provide you with details." Amber spoke so eloquently, so precise, that every letter was sounded out so perfectly; she sounded like one of those prep school girls whose parents had to pay for them to attend - weird.

It also sounded like our night hadn't ended, and wouldn't end any time soon.

CHAPTER 5

Lucian

I stared at the carnage around me. The chairs and the sofa had been ripped to shreds, their broken pieces littered the floor, and the walls looked like they had been used to sharpen their claws; large gouges had torn away the plaster and the wallpaper. The carpets were covered in blood, piss and shit and the smell was nauseating...but I was used to their stench by now so I carried on - looking for a clue as to where my Zoe had been taken. I walked upstairs, careful not to tread on anything, and saw the blood splatter across the walls. I didn't need to worry about whose blood it was, I could tell it was Jacob's from here - the stench of him was everywhere.

I loathed Jacob and his pack, they were the embodiment of everything that I hated about lycans. Disgusting animals. They thought that because they could turn into animals that they had to act like ones too, that it gave them the right to perform the most immoral and vile acts; and Jacob was the worst of the lot. The self-appointed leader that all the other 'sheep' followed, because that's what they all were, followers of a tyrant who thought he could take what he pleased. He had taken enough from me, I wouldn't let him take the one woman who had made me *feel* in almost five hundred years.

She was nothing like Caitlyn. Caitlyn had been kind and sweet, but selfish too; she had wanted everything at her fingertips, taking everything that her station had afforded her. I had not known another blood witch was out there, I thought that they had all died with Caitlyn and the child during The Great Purge. But then I felt it, the other night, the spell; it was as if she had been calling out to me. I had walked out of my house - barefoot - and driven for hours, following my gut instinct, until I had a lead - until I had a name. Zoe Ward. I had not meant to walk into her at the coffee shop, I thought I had blown my chance with her, especially as I had been speechless when I saw her. "I can buy you another coffee" Terrible, Lucian, just terrible. Taking that drink to her was the best idea I had had in so long, that she had agreed to dinner with me despite looking like I had just woken up, not having shaven in weeks - and with no shoes on - thank god she had not looked down.

But god she had been stunning, tall and luscious with enough curves for a man to hold on to. Her skin had been a warm, flawless golden brown but it was her eyes, a hazel with the perfect mix of russet and emerald, and when the light hit them, I could see striations of red...a perfect demarcation of her lineage. I had wanted to confess everything to her right there, but she did not trust me yet. I needed her trust before I told her the secrets of her past...and me. But I could see that my task would be an uphill battle; her look was that of a warrioress, a hardened look in her striking eyes that spoke of a difficult life and so I had chosen to take things slow with her. Something that I wholeheartedly regret after seeing the chaos surrounding me. Bullets laced with Aconite scattered around the floor proved that it was not just the lycans that had been here, the Hecate witches had been present too; their signature tool of choice for dealing with us, and they'd hurt Jacob, it must have slowed him and the pack down enough for Zoe to escape. If that was the case, then they had her and I didn't have much chance of reaching her now, not once they had gotten their hooks into her - but at least she would be safer with them. I needed to see her, hear her voice, and make sure she was unharmed. I would be unable to rest until I knew if they had touched her in any way, I'd heard rumours of what the pack did to their women, and that would not be Zoe. She was now mine to protect, mine to care for; no one would get in my way.

I walked out of the ruined apartment, the police 'Do Not Cross' tape hanging on either side of the door where I had ripped it on my entrance, they were long gone, not spending much time examining the scene, there were no bodies so they had put it down to fighting kids - foolish humans, but yet I envied their naivete. Not knowing what went bump in the night.

I walked to my Mitsubishi L200 and started her up, turning the vehicle around in the middle of the road to head in the opposite direction. I was guessing they would take her to their coven, and I knew exactly where that was.

Jacob

     I hissed as Jones extracted the slug that had penetrated my torso. I could feel the poison affecting me, I felt like I'd been on a week's bender; my head was spinning and my limbs felt weak. Them fucking witches sticking their noses in my business. Now that the bullet was out, the flesh started to knit together and pretty soon there wouldn't be any evidence that I'd been shot full of lead a couple of hours ago. Luckily Jones had been a doctor back when he was human, struck off for sexual assault, apparently fingering your female patients when they were unconscious was illegal...who would have thought it. He'd been given the choice of paying his victims off and going quietly or going through a lengthy public court case - he'd chosen wisely - but then he'd been broke. I found him in a dive of a bar in Soho drunk off his tits. I'd known who he was from local gossip and I liked his style so I'd turned him that night and he had been with me ever since. It's handy having the doc around, especially when those little bitches interfere. They thought they could shoot their little guns at me and there'd be no consequences. Covering their faces wouldn't work for long, I had my ace in the hole and their time would soon be coming.

Footsteps rushing towards me made me take notice, I could scent the Lynx bodyspray of Banner before he entered and my nose twitched at the affront to my senses, he did it on purpose to piss everyone off - he knew how terrible it stunk to us - but his own nose was ruined from years of snorting the white stuff, so it didn't bother him at all. You could smell him coming a mile off.

"Sir, Lucian's been spotted in the area."

Ah, so daddy's favourite pet was back in civilization, and I bet he was looking for the tasty little blood witch too. "Where was he last seen?" I needed to get to her before him, he wouldn't ruin this for me. Zoe Ward was the answer to my future, she would breed me strong sons and daughters. She wouldn't be the last blood witch after I had finished with her. And damn would I enjoy breaking her. I smiled remembering how feisty she had been; so many women cower at my feet, not daring to speak back to me. But not her, she had thrown her sass straight in my face and my cock had gotten so hard. Even thinking about it now made me hard as a rock in my jeans.

"He was last seen coming out of the woman's place"

"Get someone to follow him. Not you though, he'd smell that fucking thing you spray all over yourself." Banner looked secretly pleased at my comment, like I'd paid him a compliment. I suppose to him it was, he was an ugly fucker with a face only a mother could love. "I wanna know everything he does, even how long he shits for, understood."

"Yes sir." Banner left, rushing off to do my bidding; and I knew it would be done, because he was loyal to a fault, he'd been with me for almost a century, a deserter of the British army during the second world war. My loyal soldier had had enough of being cannon fodder, so he'd put a bullet between his commanding officer's eyes and did a runner. I seem to be one for picking up the lowly waifs and strays.

  I turned my inner musings to my soon-to-be breeder. With her power, my sons will be born strong, untouchable. No other wolf would be able to harm them; and my daughters, well...they would make me a pretty penny on the black market. Their blood would be priceless, I'd be the richest and most powerful wolf in the United Kingdom, and then no-one would ever hold me back again, I could do what ever the fuck I wanted and them weak-ars Hecate bitches couldn't do shit to stop me. I had spent decades trying to have my own children, but when that bitch Caitlyn had created the first, there had been a little clause in the contract. We were infertile. All of us. Rage ripped through me, I would have my legacy, and the little witch would be the one to do it; her ancestor had made us this way, and well...her descendant would be the one to fix it.

My cock was straining against the stiff denim and I popped the button and unzipped so that I could have some room to play; my hardness slapped against my abs in anger that I hadn't appeased it yet. "LOU!" I shouted at the top of my lungs for the wolf who managed the whores, the women who came to me begging for the chance at immortality...if they passed my tests first. I used them as I saw fit, I hurt them how I wanted and they always came back for more in the hopes that it would finally be their turn to be Changed. The ones who had outlived their usefulness were disposed of, their meat used to feed the pack; the whores who stayed behind were told that they had been turned and sent to another pack to live - they believed anything. "Get me a brunette," I told Louise.

A skinny mousy woman tottered towards me in heels she could barely walk in, her face pockmarked and her eyebrows a thin drawn on line of black pencil - but I didn't need a looker, I just needed a hole. I held my cock straight up for her, a bead of pre-cum leaking from the tip, "suck it," I ordered. She collapsed to her knees and wrapped her lips around the head of my dick and tried to suck it all daintily, her tongue flicking gently against the underside, but that wasn't good enough, and it wasn't what I needed. I grabbed her straw-like hair and forced her mouth all the way down until her nose brushed my pubic hair; her throat contracted around my cock and she gagged, coughing, I grunted because that felt fucking good. Lifting my hips from the chair, I slammed my length in the back of her mouth, not caring that she was slapping at my thighs for air, she didn't need to breathe for what I wanted from her. I pictured Zoe on her knees in front of me taking all of my cock past her plump lips and I shuddered; feeling the familiar prickle at the base of my spine signalling my impending release, I picked up the pace ramming my cock in the tight hole of her throat, feeling her blunt teeth scrape against my sensitive skin was divine and I shot my cum deep in her windpipe, holding her head to me as I released, calling Zoe's name as I finished shooting my load into the poor substitute. Finally empty, I slumped back into my seat, I didn't know when the whore had fallen unconscious - or was she dead? I didn't know, but I dropped her limp body to the ground and relaxed for the first time since I'd felt that bit of blood magic pierce my hide.

Zoe

We drove for well over an hour, I wasn't too sure, the clock on the dashboard was flashing with zeroes like they'd had a flat battery at some point and didn't bother resetting the time. We sat in silence, Nate looking over at me sporadically as if to ask mentally 'is everything still ok?' and every time he looked at me I would nod my head to reassure him that I was with him, that it would be fine, and that we were together. Lissa fell asleep with her head on my shoulder, at one point I felt a tickle under her face and I thought it was her breathing, only to see that she was drooling and it was sliding down my arm - gross. I wiped it away with my free hand and casually swiped the spit on her leg. She could have it back.

They took us to a massive place in Greenwich, a large three story townhouse that stood alone with no other properties either side of it, just lush grass that ran the whole front and sides of the place, stone steps led to an alcove with stringed lights wrapped around it. I didn't know this area of London at all, I was a North London girl and had been for as long as I could remember, but this was the South; and I knew no-one down these ends.
Gripping the hands of the only family I had, we were led inside to a gleaming foyer, solid oak floors covered the expanse and life sized potted plants were placed strategically in corners and at the foot of the carpeted stairs that were positioned right in the centre of the hall; and coming down these stairs with thunder on her face was the most miserable looking woman I'd ever seen. I mean, she was dressed to the nines this late at night, with a powder blue pants suit on, her silver hair was cut in a straight bob and looked like it was fresh out of the hairdressers, and she probably lived in these fancy digs. I however, had been attacked

by monsters, knocked up by a dickhead, dumped by a dickhead, saved by G.I Jane and let's not forget the 'party that won't be spoken of ever again.' What did she have to be miserable about! She was still storming towards us when she spoke, "who are these...these people," she spat out.

Our saviour for tonight, Rosie, stepped forward to face 'Misog' (I'd heard someone in school once call our old science teacher that, he'd said it stood for *Miserable Old Git* and that name suited this woman perfectly) "This is who you sent us to get." Poor Rosie looked about as confused as we did.

"I sent you to get the blood witch, not pick up some street urchins on your way back." She said haughtily.

"Who are you calling a street urchin?" "A blood witch?" Lissa and I spoke in unison, yea her point was more valid - we were *not* street urchins.

"Which one is it?" Misog asked, looking between us both.

Rosie pointed her finger straight at me, and I wondered if it was the right thing to do getting in their van.

"You are not what I expected. But it is what it is. Rosanna…" Rosie winced, "take the girl to her new room, and send the others back where they came from." She turned to walk away, but hell broke loose before she could make her get away. We were all shouting over each other, because no way was I staying here without them.

"I don't know who the hell you are lady, or what this place is, but me and my family ain't staying here. Thanks for the back up earlier and getting us out safely, but this is done." I turned around, fully intending to grab my people and exit this place.

"I don't think you understand who we are, young lady."

Turning my head to look at her over my shoulder, because I was planning on moving towards the door while she spoke. "Explain it to me, but you have 5 seconds, or we're out."

"You have felt strange lately, yes? You have been emotional and odd things have been happening that are unexplainable?" How did she know all of this? She couldn't know what happened the other night? My body locked in place, because now she had my attention. "You are a breed of witch thought extinct for generations." Oookkkaay, not what I was expecting at all.

"And you people are....?"
"We are a different breed of witch, ones that have cultivated and nurtured their magic over the centuries, and the only ones who can help you right now. The lycans are already aware of where you are..."
"And how did they know where she was? Did you tell them so that you could get her here?" Lissa said.
"I...you...of course not! How dare you insinuate such things! You should not even be here you...you...human." Misog sputtered out angrily.
I side-eyed Lissa and Nate, we clearly were missing something here because, weren't we all humans?

That miserable woman smoothed her hair with one hand and straightened her suit jacket, "Zoe is it?" I nodded. "I know lots about you Zoe. Raised in foster care from the age of one. You have lived with your current foster mother since the age of eight when your previous fosterer decided she had had enough of your attitude; never quite feeling that you belong anywhere."
She was right. I never felt like I fit in anywhere, but then I was bi-racial - too light skinned for the Black community and too brown for the Whites; I'd never felt an affinity for either side, if I spoke too posh, I was 'trying to be white'. It was a lose-lose situation for me, not being fully accepted by either; but then maybe that's because I wasn't supposed to fit in with them? Maybe I was supposed to fit in here, with others of my kind? And this is why Lissa was my only friend, because she didn't give a shit about the colour of my skin or what my parents were, or hell, I blew up a flat and she took me for a kebab afterwards. She had my back - and I had hers. Which is why she was currently involved with a game of stare-off with Karen, telling her that "we come as a package deal, we all stay or we all go."
"Your kind are not welcome here."
"My kind? My kind!" Lissa's voice was steadily growing louder. "Whatd'ya mean my kind? You mean Black people?"
"No stupid girl. I mean the non-magic kind." She looked pointedly at both Lissa and Nate, clearly meaning that she wanted them gone - now.

It was time I got involved in this conversation, otherwise nothing would get sorted, and I was tired. "Listen, it's clear that you went through a lot of trouble to get me here, so I'm gonna go out on a limb and say that you really want me here…" I paused and waited for the nod of her head that confirmed what I had been thinking. They needed me here. "I will stay if they can stay. This isn't a negotiation, I'm telling you how it's gonna be. Take it or leave it." Crossing my arms over my chest, I waited for her to speak.

"Fine. They can stay, but they have to pay their way, they will contribute to the running of the house if they want to eat and they stay out of the basement."

I looked at them with raised eyebrows, silently asking if they were happy with those arrangements. When I had their approval, I told Misog that we'd stay but that I needed answers too.

"It is late, tonight you will rest and tomorrow I will answer any questions."

I could deal with that, I wasn't really in the mood for question time anyway. "Rosanna will show you to the communal bunks, you can share until we set up more appropriate accommodation for you."

"No, we can stay sharing, thanks." With a firm nod, she turned and made her way back up the grand staircase and left us with Rosie? Rosanna? Who crooked her fingers to follow her around the stairs and to a door on the left, which led to a hall of white doors. Walking into the last door on the right, was a large room with two bunk beds pushed up against the side walls; there was a chest of drawers and a stack of fluffy blue towels piled on top. "This is your room, there's fresh towels and the communal bathroom is directly across from you. Any clothes or toiletries you need will be sent down to you tomorrow from the store room."

"Thanks…"

"It's Rosie, please don't call me Rosanna, I hate that name." She cringed. "Oh, and I thought you might need this." She pulled my mobile out of her front pocket and I gasped, because I thought I had left it back at Lissa's.

"Thank you, thank you." I clutched the phone to my chest, "we need to call Sarah and let her know that we're ok." The battery was still charged half way, and it would last me for the next day or two if I was careful. I could find a charger between now and then.

"Just keep the phone out of Agnes' sight, she's a stickler for keeping people isolated from the outside world, she thinks witches should keep out of human stuff and vice versa." She went to leave, pulling the door shut behind her and calling out before the wood closed us in, "see you in the morning."

"Her name's Agnes?" I was only a little bit horrified that her name sounded nothing like what I'd been calling her. "I've been calling her Misog in my head." A snort-laugh sounded from behind me and Rosie slapped her hand over her mouth to hide any laughter.

"I don't think I want to know what that stands for, do I?" Lissa opened her mouth to reply, but I halted her with a slight shake of my head, we didn't know these people. I don't think it's a good idea to chat shit about them to each other. "no, probably not."

I looked at my phone wanting to pull up Sarah's number, and I noticed the missed call and text message from Lucian - I had completely forgotten about him.

'Are you ok?'

I quickly typed out a reply, apologising for flaking on him, and that I'd call him soon, then called Lissa's mum. She hadn't even been home yet, still on her shift in A&E, and didn't know what type of damage had been done. I put Lissa on the phone to let her know that we were all safe and some crazy junkies had trashed the place, that we were staying with a friend in South London and not to worry. With that I collapsed face down on one of the bottom bunks and closed my eyes, I was just about done with this day.

"What's gonna happen now Zo," Nathan had been pretty quiet since the attack, but now it was just us three again, he was back in his comfort zone. He wasn't the greatest with change, he'd had enough to-and-fro when he was younger, he much preferred the places and people that he knew, never really venturing past what made him comfy.

I didn't think this massive change was the best place for him, the wolves were after me and now that I was here, they wouldn't look for me at home. At least he - and Lissa - would be safer.

"I think you should both go home, it's…" head shakes and 'nopes' met my suggestion. "It will be safer for you both, I'm who they want."

"Babe, we are not leaving you, we stick together, remember you're my BeeBee." I laughed out loud, because she hadn't called me BeeBee in a while. It had started when we were in school, she randomly called me BeeBee, and when I asked her what it had meant she looked at me with a *duh* expression and said "Beebee, you know. B and B together. Best Bitch. BeeBee." And that had been that, we were each other's BeeBees.

"Ok Lissy, but what about your job?"

"I work in Tesco's babe, they won't miss me. Besides, you need me more."

I looked at Nate, because Lissa was a grown-arse woman who could make her own choices, but Nathan was my baby brother and my responsibility.

"I'll get Rosie to drive you home tomorrow Nate…" "I won't go Zoe, I will chain myself to the radiator. Plus I'm bigger than you, you can't force me,"

"And what about school huh? You just started year 11 and you do your GCSEs this year, you wanna fail?"

"They said you were a witch, can't you just…" he waved his hand in the air in a 'Harry Potter' imitation "magic me good grades?"

"Um, no Nathan. I can't cheat for you, and I don't even know if I *can* do stuff like that. All I've done is blow shit up" A knock at the door preceded Rosie's entrance, carrying a tray with sandwiches and other snacks.

"Hey, sorry to interrupt, I just thought you might be hungry, it's just ham and cheese sarnies and some crisps." Lissa jumped up and went straight for the platter of food which was placed on one of the drawers.

"So Rosie, can you clear something up for me?" She stuffed a crisp into her mouth and spoke while still chewing, "can Zoe do her witchy shit to give Nathan good grades on his exams?"
"Well, yeah, of course! And Zoe can do much more than that, she's a blood witch, they're the strongest of all of us."
"What's the difference between me and you?" I asked.
"Essentially, we're just humans who practice magic, we worship the goddess Hecate and she grants us our power. But you….you're the stuff of legends." She was talking animatedly now, "you're literally born from the goddess Haima, you're created with the magic already inside of you, a part of you; isn't it so amazing."
"Duuude. You're a god."
"Shutup Nate, I'm not a god."
"You guys should get some sleep, the day starts really early. See you tomorrow." With a wave she skipped out, leaving the food for us to pick on. I really hoped the day didn't start that early, I really wasn't a morning person.

CHAPTER 6

My hope was short-lived because the lights came on and I felt like I'd been sleeping for five minutes. It must have been so fucking early. Groaning from the bunk above let me know that Lissa was about as happy with this wake up call as I was. Nathan was - as usual - still sleeping. A pack of wolves probably wouldn't wake him right now. A too-happy Rosie came swanning in, already washed, dressed and looking entirely too cheery at this time in the morning.
A moaned "What time is it?" was muffled from under Lissa's pillow.
"It's six o'clock, breakfast is at seven in the main hall, so you'll need to get up and ready, I'll pick you up at ten to." She put two carrier bags on the floor by my bed, "one bag has a change of clothes for each of you, and one has toothbrushes and stuff. Come on chop chop."
She skipped out - always fucking skipping - and left us to sort ourselves out.
"Let's skip breakfast." I said, and pulled the covers over my head, burrowing down into the soft mattress.
"You need to feed the baby."
I ripped the covers off and sat up, because she's right, I needed to feed my baby; I needed to get checked at the hospital too and make sure all the stress from yesterday didn't hurt it. Him? Her? I didn't care, so long as my baby was safe and healthy. I grabbed the bags and started separating our stuff into three piles. I wasn't waiting for them to get their arses up, I had stuff to do today - and answers to get from Agnes.

      I was just pulling my shoes on when Rosie came back at exactly six-fifty. They'd given me and Lissa matching black yoga trousers and white t.shirts that fit snugly; our own shoes from home completed the simple look. Poor Nathan, I stifled a laugh, because he wasn't impressed with the matching black skinny trousers; the hem was far too short, coming above his ankle, while the waist line finished high above his belly button.

"Did Simon Cowell lend you those trousers?" Laughed Lissa. And I couldn't help it, I cracked up laughing, because they looked terrible.

"Shut-up Liss," he threw his pillow at her laughing face, not happy being the butt of the jokes. "Aw I'm only joking."

The shirt was worse though, a navy blue hawaiian button-up with bright pink hibiscus flowers. "Someone's taking the piss." he gruffed.

"I'm sorry Nathan, that's all I was given for you. We can change the outfit later." Poor Rosie looked embarrassed - but not as embarrassed as Nate.

We walked back through the foyer and to the opposite side of the house. "This is the communal area; the kitchens, the dining room, the meeting room, the sacrificial chamber - all down this way." I raised my eyebrows at the 'sacrificial chamber' part and imagined a poor little bunny rabbit getting its throat slit - ugh. Not doing that! Chattering and the sounds of utensils tapping away could be heard just in front of us. It sounded like there were lots of people in there.

As soon as we walked in, all eyes turned to us - or rather me - you could hear a pin drop at how quiet it had gotten. Then the whispering started. It felt like being back in school. *"That's her" "It's the blood witch" "I thought she'd be taller"*

Thank fuck for my BeeBee. She took my arm and walked me to an empty-ish round table, only Amber sat there eating by herself. She didn't even raise her head and acknowledge us as we sat there.

"Sorry about them, we don't really get much excitement around here - and you're really exciting news." Said Rosie sitting next to me. Lissa sat on my other side with Nate next to her. Before I could even mention the word 'breakfast,' plates of steaming hash browns, bacon, sausage and beans were each placed in front of us, and my stomach let out an embarrassing growl. Everyone in the room had returned to eating their own food, the attention taken off of us for the moment.

Looking around, I could see that everyone in this room was female, and they grouped together on the other five round tables scattered about the room, with a long table at the front where Agnes and some other people sat. They must be the 'important' people. "Who are they?" I asked, spearing a bit of bacon and popping it in my mouth.

"Well, you met Agnes, she's the coven leader. Her family has done it for generations. And to her right is Jade. Supposedly she'll take over the running of the coven when Agnes retires, even though they aren't related. It will be the first time it has gone to a different family for centuries, but Agnes is childless and Jade's family have contributed money to the upkeep of this place for ages."

Amber piped up at that point, "Jade is also the most powerful magic-user here, so don't get any ideas."

I looked behind me thinking she was talking to someone else, but nope, she was talking to me and she was warning me not to try and get the 'head-girl' position. "Why're you telling me that? You think I have any interest in this place? I didn't even know you existed yesterday. To me, you were a crazy lady with a curtain dress on." Yea, I had to let my bitchy side come out and play, I wasn't about to let this woman make those types of accusations. With a huff, she shoved her chair back, leaving her half finished breakfast on the table - what a waste.

"The lady on the other side is Agnes' sister Anastasia, she's a bit loopy, she pretty much keeps herself to herself except for when she's dancing around the gardens naked singing to the goddess - now that's horrifying." I laughed at Rosie's expression, I'm guessing she was still traumatised.

A shadow fell across my plate, and I looked up at Jade. She was stunning in a snow-queen kind of way. Her hair was so blonde it looked almost white, and her skin was a pale porcelain that looked like she hadn't seen the sun since birth; her grey eyes were like ice, cold and hard and staring straight at me. "You will meet with the High Priestess once you have finished eating. Do not keep her waiting" and with that, she went back to her table.

"I'm assuming the High Priestess is Agnes?"

Rosie only nodded her agreement, "I'll take you to her after, but Jade's right, don't make her wait too long. She hates waiting."

After we'd all eaten our fill, I looked at all of the other women just getting up and leaving their dirty plates on the table and I was filled with anxiety at the thought that I would let someone else clean up after me. I wasn't used to this, for years I had always made sure I kept a clean house and tidied up after myself, and I had made sure I instilled that same conscientiousness in Nathan. Rosie got up to leave too, telling me to follow her. "Do we just leave everything here?"
Lissa was similarly uncomfortable with this scenario, her mum would have a shit-fit if she saw this level of mess just left lying around. Tissue had been crumpled and thrown all over the place, bits of food littered the floor. These people were messy! An older plump woman came over to our table wearing an apron and wiping her hands on a tea-towel.
"Who are my new volunteers then?"
"Sorry?" I said to her, what volunteers?
"Two of you volunteered for clean up duty. It's your payment for room and board remember. I know the boy is one, which one of you is the other?" Lissa stood, chucking her napkin on her plate looking pissed off.
"You don't have to do this guys."
"We do. We chose to stay so this is what we're gonna do. We'll have this place looking spotless in no time and then come find you. But you'll have to meet Agnes on your own; you'll be ok?"
"I'll be fine, I'll fill you in on everything later."

Following Rosie back to the main hallway, we went up the stairs; the carpet was soft and spongy beneath my feet. I was nervous. I didn't know what I would find out, what would this woman tell me? Stopping at a set of double doors, my guide for the morning knocked on the door and we waited for the muffled 'enter' before going through. The office was decorated in neutral colours with heavy pine furniture; a wall of bookshelves were filled with large tomes that looked as old as dirt, and in the corner was a sitting area with brown leather arm chairs around a glass coffee table; a china tea set was placed on top waiting to

be used, though it looked more for decoration than to actually drink out of it. Agnes was sitting in one of the armchairs, her leg crossed over the other sipping from a little cup, its steam feathered around her face and made it look like she was breathing fire. "Zoe my dear, I think we got off on the wrong foot", she placed her cup on the table and stood as I approached. "Please, sit with me." She indicated the chair across from her, so I sat, leaning back against the beige satin cushions.
"Would you like some tea?"
I declined, knowing caffeine and I wouldn't be friendly for a while yet.
"Are you sure? It's Earl Grey."
"Thank you but no."
"Well maybe some coffee then?" She signalled to Rosie who was still standing at the door waiting to be dismissed maybe?
Time to bite the bullet, I needed to make a hospital appointment anyway, this woman could hopefully let me know how I could sort that out. "Actually I'm pregnant."
She didn't look shocked at all, actually it was like I had given her the answer to a century year old riddle.
"That explains so much Zoe." She stood and walked over to her little library, pulling a thick black leather bound book from one of the shelves. It looked ancient, the leather cracked along the spine, the cover so old the leather had turned scaly - definitely not a romance novel then. "You being with child explains why your magic has now manifested, the mix of hormones, emotions and something tragic or you was scared... "
I thought about that night at the house party, when I had been scared for the life of my child and for Lissa, I hadn't been able to find her amongst the chaos. "Yea, I was scared."
"Did you bleed?"
I nodded at her, because someone had hit me in the face and I'd had a nose bleed, I remember the taste of it on my tongue.
"Your blood and all of those elements triggered the latent power in your blood, passed down through the female line."
"My mum had been a witch then?"

She paused, and something shifted behind her eyes, like she was going to say something but had stopped herself. "Yes, your birth mother."

I looked towards the large bay window that was draped with thick damask curtains, I wondered if my mum had known she was a witch. Did the same thing happen to her when she was pregnant with me? Is that why she gave me away, because she was scared? All of these questions were running rampant through my mind, and I wanted to know more.

Agnes opened the old book to what looked like a family tree, she kept turning page after page of names and offspring until she reached the end…

"Do you know who Hecate is?"

"We learned about Ancient Greece in school, wasn't she the goddess of magic?"

"The goddess of magic and witchcraft, yes. She was worshipped by thousands. But what people do not know is that Hecate had a younger sister."

"I didn't know that?"

"It is not common knowledge. Haima was born from the union of Asteria and a mortal man, a half-breed but a goddess in her own right." She turned to the front of the book where a pencil drawing depicted the face of a regal woman with short dark hair, beside her was an image of a large dog. "This is the only image we have of the goddess, everything else was lost centuries ago. As Haima grew so did her power, it matched that of her older sister, the power of witchcraft; but where Hecate could control the elements, Haima found she had an affinity for blood, manipulating it inline with her magic, creating and destroying. She became known as the goddess of witchcraft, blood-letting and blood-shed."

She sounded like a barrel of laughs.

"As Haima's power grew, so did her human followers, people who worshipped her above all others. And as she grew in strength, so did Hecate's jealousy. Until one day, the Goddess banished Haima to the mortal realm, sentencing her to spend an eternity with the humans that she obviously loved so much. As a half-human, Haima felt empathy for them and had sought to help them during times of strife. Being banished to their domain was not the issue, she spent most of her time amongst the mortals anyway, but Hecate cut off her link to her mother, putting a barrier between her and the other gods. At this Haima was furious."

"What did she do? Did she get her revenge?"

"In deference to Hecate, people would sacrifice dogs on her altar, hoping and praying that the goddess of witchcraft would grant them their wish. Haima began to ransack each of Hecate's temples, saving the dogs from sacrifice and freeing them from captivity. It was said that one of these dogs was actually Hecuba, a Queen who was changed into a dog by the gods, in saving her life, Hecuba offered up her own life to Haima, vowing eternal fealty. The demi-god bound their lives together through a blood spell, and thus she became the first Familiar." She ran her finger down the image of the animal beside Haima. "It was her descendents who became the familiars of the first blood witches."

"That's Hecuba?" She looked up from her perusal and nodded. "What happened next? Was Hecate angry?"

"Yes, she was livid. Hecate tried to turn many of Haima's worshippers against her by appearing to them and granting them their heart's desires. The blood goddess lost many followers because of this, but Haima had her own plan. She created her own army; women who would never betray her or be swayed by Hecate's jealous deeds."

Agnes turned back to the family tree, and right at the top was Haima's name.

"She cast a spell to fertilise a handful of women, and during the first stages of their pregnancy, she did what I suppose you could call a blood transfusion, using her magic to combine her blood with the foetus. These children were the first blood witches. Daughters born not from her body, but from the blood and soul of a goddess, and once Haima was satisfied these children would reach maturity and survive, she did it again, and again, and again. They were her children. They shared her magic, her power and her immortality. And they were loyal only to her."

"So I'm descended from one of these daughters?"

"No. Haima created all of these children, born from surrogates. But she gave birth to only one child; a daughter." Agnes' finger pointed to the book, and the name directly underneath Haima's.
"Tisiphone." I read out loud. "She was the goddess's biological child?"
"That's right. A child born with great magic like her mother. *That* is who you are descended from." She trailed her finger down the page, and turned it over, and the next one, and the next one. It looked like thousands of years and hundreds and hundreds of witches had been chronicled in these pages.
"These…these are my ancestors?"
She looked at me sympathetically, hearing the longing in my voice, "Yes dear, this is most of your family."
"Most? Not all? Am I in there?" I needed to know more, I wanted to find out everything about my family, about who I was, and more importantly, who I *could* be. I was going to have my own baby soon, they needed to know where they came from too.
Agnes pointed to the last name that was written in the book, "Caitlyn Garrick. Who is she?"
"Caitlyn is the reason that there are no more of your kind left. It is through her selfishness and the betrayal of her goddess that what we know as The Great Purge happened."
Slamming the book closed with a thud, she sat back in her chair, "Obviously we do not know the full details, many of your family's grimoires were lost that night. What I have here are what my own ancestors saved. It is said that her love for a human man cost her everything, she cast a forbidden spell, transferring the immortality of her canine familiar to her husband, but she did not anticipate the consequences of her actions. He was transformed into the first Lycanthrope that night, and through the deterioration of his mind, changed many others…"
"Lycanthropes, that's what that guy was in my house last night, I saw his face change…"
"He was at your house? Jacob?"
"Yes, he was…evil…crazy…"
"Lycanthropy does that to most, they submit to their beasts, allowing the animal to take over and forfeiting their humanity. If you ever see one, you must run as far and as fast as you can, they

will not show you mercy. They murdered every single blood witch and feasted on their remains for weeks after; women and children were slaughtered."

"Why? What do they want with me?"

"Your blood of course! It is power, it is life, and to them, it is everything - their creator. This is why Jacob is one of the strongest Lycans, it is said that he was responsible for the deaths of many and now he knows your face, has your scent; he will not stop until he has you." Seeing the stark fear on my face, she tried to reassure me, "but you are safe here my dear, as long as you are on our grounds, he can not get you, we renew the protective wards weekly."

"So I'm trapped in here for the rest of my life? And what about my baby, will he or she be raised in this house unable to leave in case the werewolves…"

"Lycans, not werewolves. They are two completely different things."

"To-may-to, To-mah-to. I care about getting my life back." I stood up from the chair and walked to the window, running both of my hands through the curls on the top of my head and smoothing down the stubble at the back. With my fingers laced behind my neck, I stared at the gardens below. Red and orange roses grew wild around the borders, with a field of green in between; women of all colours, shapes and sizes walked the rose garden, trimming and plucking, making sure the already pristine flowers remained perfect, baskets of loose petals strewn around their feet.

Agnes came up behind me and placed her hand on my shoulder, "it will not be forever, you are untrained, we will teach you the craft and perhaps you will eventually feel safer going out on your own, especially once the baby is born. Come with me, I will give you the tour."

We walked side by side, seeing the upstairs, having her point out the casting room, the potion room, communal library, prayer room and store rooms. The top floor was her own personal space, and no-one was allowed up there. "What's in the basement then?"

"The basement is where we conduct our ritual sacrifices and spells, it is out of bounds for non-magic folk and novices."

"Ok, don't go into the basement yet. Got it. I do need to make a hospital appointment though, I haven't seen a doctor yet and I need to make sure my baby is ok."

"I can arrange for the coven's physician to look you over until you can see a civilian doctor." Breathing a sigh of relief, I thanked her.

"Will you tell me the differences between werewolves and Lycan...Lycanth?" I Couldn't remember what the fucking things were called.

"Lycanthropes. Werewolves are myths created by humans to scare small children and they are beholden to the moon's phase, only changing on a full moon, which is a load of codswallop if you ask me, a full moon symbolises lunacy and diseases of the mind, they said that if you stared at the full moon if would drive you insane. Hence why the story of the werewolf was created, because stupid humans would test this theory and act like animals. Now, Lycanthropes were created on a new moon, a symbol of new beginnings and the creation of new life." She looked at me meaningfully as we walked towards the communal areas on the ground floor.

"And the first Lycan, he was created on a new moon?"

"Exactly." She said.

"Does that mean because tonight isn't a new moon, so they can't shift again for a month?."

"They do not need the moon to be able to shift, they can shift at will, at any time of the day or night; the new moon - or the dark moon - as it is called in some cultures, will influence their behaviour somewhat, they will be more in tune with their animal sides, the beast will want control over the man, and it is these nights that you must stay within the boundaries; your connection with the lycans is strongest when the moon is at its darkest, your death at their claws on that night will only make them even stronger and this I cannot allow."

Ok, I thought to myself, don't die on a new moon, got it. She took me to the common room, it had black sectionals placed in the corners, and two pool tables were filled with competitors;

a row of four vending machines took up the wall on my right, holding everything from Coke, Lipton Ice Tea, and water to snacks with crisps, chocolate and sweets - everything a pregnant hormonal woman could wish for. We walked to a group of women - two of which were Amber and Jade - they immediately stood up when they saw the high priestess coming their way. "Ladies, no need to stand on my account," said Agnes, "I just wanted to introduce you to our new initiate." They moved out of the way for us to sit down, with the two random women - introduced as Yelena and Casey - taking seats on the far end of the L-shaped settee.

"Zoe, you have met Amber before I believe." My crazy curtain lady (who was wearing a dull grey corduroy pinafore - in a large) gave me a tight-lipped smile, she was clearly still annoyed that I mouthed off to her at breakfast. "Amber is our Historian, and she has read every book in our library at least twice. Minimum. You will start lessons with her tomorrow, where she will teach you the history of our kind, and any questions you have you can ask her." I noticed Jade's little smirk, like it was funny Amber had to tutor me, but Agnes soon turned that smile hostile. She turned to snow-queen, "And this is Jade, she is one of our most proficient witches, and will be teaching you some defense techniques; obviously not advanced magics, you can't be doing strong spells in your condition." Looking at my stomach, telling every. single. person within ear shot that I was pregnant. Snickers sounded from the girls and I glared at Agnes, "Oh don't be offended dear, we have no secrets from each other here, we are all technically sisters - or cousins." Of course just my luck, Nathan was standing right behind me, a mop in his hands.

"You're pregnant?" He sounded hurt, and I didn't blame him, I should have told him sooner. His mop clattered to the floor, and he walked out of the room swiftly, weaving past the others in the room, but he towered over everyone here - even at fifteen - so he was easy to spot as he stormed out.

I got up to follow my little brother, but a hand around my wrist stopped my exit. "Leave him to cool off dear, he will be fine."

It seemed this woman, this head honcho, thought she could give me advice on my brother after knowing her for less than twenty-four hours. I don't think so. "I need to speak to my brother, thank you for today"

"Well, Amber will collect you from the breakfast hall tomorrow morning to start your education, and I have arranged for you to speak to the physician tomorrow afternoon."

With a nod and a muttered thanks, I left to track down my brother.

CHAPTER 7

Lucian

      I stood on the opposite side of the road looking up at the huge expanse of the property. The unassuming house was the haven for England's Hecate witches - they came from all over the country, even the world to study under their leadership. It was like Sandhurst for the magically inclined. I knew she was in there; I could feel her. She was the reason I had spent all of these years gaining control of my beast, for this moment. I knew I had things to atone for, wrongs that I needed to right, and that I had a purpose. When I knew there was a blood witch out there, I had thought "this is it, this is how I will pay my penance for not protecting Caitlyn all of those centuries ago.I'll protect her descendant.
But then I saw her.
And I knew that my atonement would be pushed to the back burner for the chance to be by her side.
She was perfection personified. Her scent called to me in the most base of ways. I had wanted to hold her close, stroke her soft skin and cherish her; but at the same time I wanted to devour her essence and taste every inch of her until she screamed my name. My beast writhed beneath my skin, wanting a taste of its own, but I would never let it. I had a tight reign over the animal inside me and I had not lost control in centuries...I wouldn't start now.
I stood in the shadows, hoping that I would catch a glimpse of her through the large windows, but that would be too easy. Just like it had been too easy to lose the tail this morning. That dog thought I wouldn't know he was following me. But I had spent too many years to count staying under everyone's radar and I knew how to stay hidden. I'd taken a detour through a vast

garden, the scents of the flora and fauna overpowering my own, until he had lost me, before making my way here - to Zoe.
Unlike my race who would hurt her, kill her - a growl tried to pour forth imagining her in pain, the thought of anyone harming a hair on her head filled me with a rage I had never felt before, and my claws started to lengthen - I guess I was not as in control as I thought I was. Pulling my phone from my front pocket, I pulled up her name in my contacts (there were not many, I didn't like people) composed a text, and waited from my spot across the road, hidden.
I would worship at her feet like the goddess she was, but first she needed to reply.

Zoe

I dropped on my bed exhausted, it seemed I was more tired than normal, this pregnancy was already taking its toll and I couldn't be more than eight or nine weeks along. I hadn't found Nathan to speak to him; I had looked everywhere except the places we were barred from going, and not a peep. He couldn't hide for long though, he had to eat and sleep at some point. He had clearly found his way around this place a lot better than me too, because I'd gotten lost on the second floor between the library stacks - that place was like a fucking maze. This place was deceptive, it was far bigger on the inside than what the exterior showed.
My phone vibrating under my bum pulled my attention away from my missing sibling problem - Lucian. My very normal, very sexy distraction from the crazy my life had gotten in the past few days.
They all thought that I would stay here permanently, Agnes called me her new 'initiate', I'd had to keep a straight face at that point, because no way would I become one of those cookie-cutter girls. They looked like they'd walked off of the set of a Regina George spin off show - except Amber, she dressed like Jackie's dead mum. Uh, now I sounded like a mean girl.
Looking at my phone - which Rosie had thankfully provided a charger for - I read my new text.

Good morning beautiful

A large grin sprouted across my face. Yea, this was exactly the distraction I needed.

Good morning, how R U ?

I'm better now that I've spoken to you. We should get dinner when you're free.

Still on 4 wagamama?

Whatever you want. Whenever.

I ran through possibilities in my head, I was all the way in South London, a couple of hours out in a public place wouldn't hurt - especially considering I was nowhere near home. Besides, I wasn't a prisoner here, I would come and go as I pleased - within reason, I wouldn't be entirely stupid. But I'd been independent for years, there was no way I was gonna sit around and let everyone do shit for me. Plus, I had about seven months to be a bit selfish, because when this baby got here, he or she would have to come first - no more outings to meet handsome cavemen. I quickly texted him back telling him that I would meet him on Friday for lunch; that meant I had three days to get Nathan back on track, meet the doctor and find an outfit that would impress a sexy guy that I had exactly one conversation with - easy.
His reply came swiftly like he'd been waiting.

See you there beautiful.

"Eeeeeek." I let out the most girly squeal of excitement, because I had a fucking date!

     Later that evening, I made my way to the dining hall; I hadn't seen Lissa or Nathan all day and hoped I'd meet them there. Sitting at the same table I was at this morning, I waited. Two plates of lasagna heaped with salad were slapped on the table, almost unloading the leafy greens. Lissa plopped down next to me, her bright braids swinging loosely around her tired face.
"Where've you been?" I said to her.

"Cleaning this fucking place, these people practically live in a pig sty."

"You've been cleaning all day? What the hell Liss!"

She put her hand up to stop my tirade, "It's not your problem, I'll deal with it"

"Deal with it, how? Let me speak to Agnes."

Her mischievous grin let me know that she was already sorting it out in her own way, and I groaned, "What did you do?"

"Nothing they didn't deserve babe. That trampy bitch over there kept calling me 'slave',"

"WHAT?!" I screeched.

"Right. Like, is she for real? Firstly, I'm not anyone's damn slave and secondly, what a racist cunt."

"What're you gonna do?"

She threw her head back and laughed, and I wasn't in on the joke. "What *haven't* I done. They kept laughing about how I should be used to restocking their towels in the communal bathroom because it was like restocking shelves in Tesco."

I sucked in my breath, because that was fighting talk right there. "So I figured I would show them exactly who they were dealing with!"

The thing about Lissa? Everyone underestimated her. They saw her multi-colored hair and and

bright personality and immediately assumed that she was on drugs, or she was a wild party girl, she didn't have a proper job...I'd heard all of the stereotypes; they thought she was stupid. I can't wait for the day they find out that she graduated with honours in Computer Science from King's College London, she only worked at Tesco part time as there were no available positions in the field she wanted to work in; but my girl was always coding, and one day, I knew she'd change the world.

"I can't wait to find out what you did!"

She cackled maniacally, I would *love* to be a fly on the wall when she gave them a taste of their own medicine.

And finally my missing brother shows himself. His eyes were red-rimmed like he'd been crying, and I felt immediately guilty that I'd been annoyed with him; he was hurting and I hoped that my baby news wasn't causing this reaction - or the women had been shit to him. I would cut a bitch if they'd treated him like they treated Lissa, he was a child.

His smile wobbled, like he wasn't sure if he should smile or cry again. It was easy to forget that Nate was still a kid because he had been taller than me since he turned twelve, he was now a six-foot tall gangly mass of a teenager.

"Your day been ok?"

"Yeah, I didn't do much, I mopped the floors and dusted a bit, then they let me play in the computer room…"

"There's a computer room?" That's why I didn't find him. "I looked for you earlier."

"Sorry, I just needed a bit of quiet time."

"I'm sorry I didn't tell you straight away - about the baby - it's still early and I haven't even seen a doctor yet, I just needed to get things straight in my head."

"It's Seans?"

"Yes, but he's not in the picture."

"Ok."

That's it? Just ok? He must have had something else on his mind. He looked down at his own plate that had just arrived and picked at the cheese on the top of his meal. Definitely had something on his mind, it's not like him to play with his food.

"What's wrong Nathan, you know you can tell me anything right?"

He was silent for a time, I could see the gears turning behind his eyes, thinking about exactly what he wanted to say.

"Will you still want me…"

I must have looked confused, I didn't know what he meant.

"When the baby is here. Will you still want me around, you'll have your own family and…"

Now I was just angry, how the hell could he think I would ever replace him?

"Nathan, you are my little brother. I love you, it doesn't matter that we don't share parents, you're the brother I would have picked above all others; you were given to *me* and I'm keeping you forever; and I also know that you'll make the best uncle to baby Ward."

I shuffled my chair around to be closer to him, pulling his head down to my level, our foreheads pressing together. "Is that what you were worried about? That I'd replace you?"
He nodded against me, his eyes were squeezed tightly shut but a lone tear traced down his smooth cheek - and my heart cracked open, I should have known this could be a possibility; his bio-parents had replaced him with a baby girl, they had never wanted a son, so they'd had him taken into care - where he found a place with me, and I wouldn't ever replace him.
"You're one of a kind little boy, and no returns allowed. We're stuck together."
Sniffling from beside me brought my attention back to Lissa who was dabbing a tissue at the corner of her eye.
"That's so sweet dude."

"Anyway, I'm being tutored in all things witchy by Amber and Jade starting tomorrow, and I'm meeting their doctor in the afternoon."
"So you believe it then? This witch thing?" Asked Nathan. I knew that he and Lissa were a bit sceptical, but I knew it was real.
"When we were attacked at home, by the lycans, I saw that guy's face; it wasn't normal, it was unnatural. Unlike anything I'd ever seen, even in films. And then today when I met Agnes..."
They leaned forward as I lowered my voice to a hushed whisper, conscious that we had wagging ears listening in. "She showed me this family tree and told me it was mine, they were my ancestors. You guys, I've never known anything about my family or why my mum gave me up. What if this is real? What if they have answers about my mum and I have to be here and play along to get them."
Nathan was nodding his head in agreement, "She's right." He whispered back, "we should stay, even for a couple of weeks and see if you can find anything out. I know who my parents are and why they gave me up, you don't know anything. It's worth a shot."
"Mmmhmmm Beebee, we'll stay for a little while, you find out what you need to know, and I..." she rubbed her hands together

in glee "will play with my new frenemies." We shared a grin, because we all knew Lissa's payback was going to be epic.

      We'd all eaten breakfast the next morning - the most amazing blueberry pancakes - when a shrill scream echoed throughout the whole house. Every single person in the room jumped up from their tables looking around wildly, some of them looking absolutely terrified, the rest of them running to find out what was happening. It sounded like someone was being tortured - the high-pitched shriek sounded again, and I seriously considered getting up to find out what the hell that was. Had I found myself in a mad house after all? But seeing Lissa and Nate calmly drinking their tea and sharing looks of amusement made me keep my arse in my chair.
"What's that noise?" I said to them suspiciously. Their snort-laugh around their cups immediately filled me into the fact that this was Lissa's work.
Lissa was almost hysterical at watching the bewildered women try to figure out who was screaming. "I rewired their doorbell."
"That's their doorbell being murdered?" Lissa was holding her side as she giggled and Nathan was trying to hold back his belly-laugh so they didn't look suspect. "Found out yesterday that they get a delivery every morning of fresh fruit and veg - that's the fucking delivery man ringing the 'doorbell of death'." And burst into fits of hysterics. I cracked up with her, because this had her name all over it; and watching these people, who had treated my girl so shabbily yesterday, I couldn't help but think 'shame'. Then I imagined the Cersei walk of shame, picturing Jade in the evil queen's position, food thrown at her face and I laughed even harder.
"What are you doing today Bee?" Lissa asked me, finally in control of herself
"I'm meeting with Amber, should be right now." I shrugged, because I wasn't in a rush to get talked down to. "I have an appointment with the coven doctor at two this afternoon, wanna meet?"
"Hell yea, I'm there, I get to meet my niece or nephew; or maybe it's both?" She grinned.

"No way! It better not be twins." One was enough for me at the moment. "I've also planned something for Wednesday that I need your help with..."

"You planned something like what?"

Shoving a bite of leftover pancake from the plate, I chewed and let out a muffled, "A date."

Cupping her ear, she leaned towards me, "What?"

"I have a date with that hot guy I told you about, remember. Coffee guy."

"WHAAAT!" Jesus she was loud, she'll let everyone here know what we're talking about.

"Sshhhh." I slapped my hand over her mouth, "what's wrong with you? Keep it down."

She pulled my hand away until I could see the dirty smile on her face. "You're sneaking out to meet a guy? You're bad Muriel."

"That was the worst Australian accent I've ever heard." a pfftt was her response, "I need an outfit, you have access to their stores right? It might look a bit weird me rummaging around for something to wear, but you could grab me something."

"Something sexy? Slutty? What are you looking for?"

"I dunno, nice jeans and a top or something, it's just lunch, but I can't turn up in fuckin' yoga pants." I mean, they were comfy, but I needed to make an impression.

"Ok babe, no probs, I'll kit you out."

"Thanks." I told her, relieved that I wouldn't be turning up looking like shit.

"But in return you gotta tell me *everything*. I'm talking shoe size, schlong size, manscaped or bush? *Everything*."

I couldn't help but laugh at her, "dude, you know this is our first, and maybe only, date. I'm not going out to get dick. Besides, I'm pregnant, remember."

"Yesss. Which means you can't get pregnant again." Her eyebrows raised, like she was making a really valid point, which I suppose she was.

"Can you just get the clothes ready please."

Sighing heavily, like I was doing her a huge disservice by not going out, getting laid and dishing the dirt, she gave me a sulky "fine."

Amber came running over eventually looking harried, apologising for being late for our 'lesson', though she didn't really look very sorry. Apparently there was an 'incident' that needed dealing with; I looked at Lissa smiling, because that 'incident' made my morning. Following my new teacher to the library, she told me to sit at a little table shoved in the corner of the room and wait for her...

I was sat there for maybe ten minutes bored out of my mind and humming the tune to 'Why Are We Waiting', before she slapped a book in front of me titled *A History of Witches - Then and Now*'

"Read that, then come and find me, I'll be in the computer room next door."

"What all of it? Now?" Our lesson was me sitting here reading this big-arse book? Was she having a laugh?

"Yes. All of it." She punctuated carefully, like she was talking to a toddler. Then she just walked out. Brilliant, I thought sarcastically, this is going to be fun.

I looked through the contents page until one chapter caught my eye: *The rise and fall of the Blood Witch.* Ok, should be interesting.

At the height of their power, blood witches were revered and feared equally for the magic each woman was born with; each daughter was nurtured and their power cultivated until they became a distinguished contributor of the coven. Due to the increasing animosity towards witchcraft and the sorrow that many felt due to the longevity of their lives, many blood witches forfeited their magic and immortality, choosing to live a mortal life.

I paused...I was immortal now? I didn't have to practise magic, could I live a normal life? I quickly read more, hoping for answers to my new existence.

At the start of the sixteenth century, it is thought that only one thousand blood witches remained, they were isolated, and it is believed that their secluded village, based in Scotland (exact location unknown) was self sustainable, many of the occupants only leaving their land to seek out male companionship; though many high ranking blood witches chose to perform magics for humans - who sought them out - for monetary gain.

Not to be confused with Hecate Witches. Please see page 76.

So what was the difference between them and me? Quickly flicking through to page 76, I started reading.

The Hecate Witch: an immemorial community.
The original magic users, and weaker cousins of the Haima line, the Hecate witches have worshipped the goddess since their inception, being granted the ability to cast spells through ritual sacrifice and daily prayer. Initially a canine would be sacrificed to appease the goddess but this practise was abolished due to the complications caused by Haima the Blooded's desecration of the sacred temples. It is now more appropriate to offer a more disfavoured creature - namely rabbits, foxes or fowl.
Mostly generational, the secrets of the Hecate witches are passed down through the matriarchal line, creating a family-like coven; only infrequently recruiting outsiders to widen the gene pool. Although human, some magic users may be efficient enough to lengthen their lifespan, but they have an average life expectancy of approx 80 years.
The coven has a strict social class that is dependent on lineage, wealth, occupation and education.

Not to be confused with the Blood Witches. Please see page 51.

Ahhh, and now it all makes sense. The treatment of Lissa and Nathan, the condescending stares where they look down their noses at you, the snickering behind your back.
They're all snobs.
Except Rosie, she was different - and nice.
But did this now mean that I would live forever? And what about my baby, would they be immortal too?
I figured my teacher had the answers to my questions, and she was only next door, so I did what any normal person would do…
"AMBERRR" I yelled as loud as I could.
"You rang." She said in her best Lurch impression.
"Am I immortal now?"

She sat in the chair opposite me, "You will not age as long as you continue to practise the craft, it doesn't mean that you can't die."
"Will my baby be the same?"
"Your daughter will. If it's a boy, he'll age as normal." A flash of sympathy crossed her features before her usual staid countenance took over. "Is that all?"
"Um, yea thanks." She walked back to whatever she was doing in the computer room.
If I had a son, it meant I would have to watch him - and Lissa and Nate - grow old and die, while I remained the same. I couldn't do that.
"AMBERRR" I yelled again. This time I could hear the huff of her annoyance before I saw her.
"What now?"
"If I don't practise, that means I can live as a human?"
"Yes, but why would you want to? Do you know how many people would kill for the opportunity to live forever and you'd just throw it away!"
"Why would I want to watch all of my family die? Hmmm good question. Not to mention that I have gigantic witch-eating monsters chasing me; if I never learn how to do magic, then my blood isn't magical and they will leave me alone."
Rubbing her forehead, she explained, "that's not how it works, your powers have been triggered, and your blood is still always a part of you regardless of whether you cast magic, the lycans have your scent and know your face, I'm sure you have heard this part too. Only death will be your escape now. You may as well accept it and learn as much as you can about being a witch, at least so you can protect yourself - and your child. Can I go now?"
I slouched in my seat defeated, and she went back to her own work. But it was like a lightning bolt hit me, and I reared up in my seat. "AMBERRR!" she was gonna hate me.
A crash of a chair hitting the floor preceded her entrance. Boy, she must be in a bad mood.
"What if I get a blood transfusion? Will I be normal then?"
She looked at me like I'd grown a second head, and that second head was trying to eat the first head. "A blood transfusion does not change your DNA, it will not alter you genetically; your blood

may be different for a few days but eventually you will return to...you."

"Bollocks."

"Now I'm going, don't call me again. I actually have important things to be doing." And again, she left me sulking in my chair.

I thought I *was* the important thing she was supposed to be doing? Now, I was just going to do it to be a bitch. "AMBERRR."

She practically flew back into the room, her brown and green spotty dress swaying around her calves; I noticed that the brown polka dots looked like ticks had latched onto her - I should get Lissa to sort her wardrobe out.

"What the effing hell do you want now?" She actually said 'effing', couldn't even bring herself to say 'fuck' when she was angry.

"Blood witches had to cut themselves to cast a spell?" I asked, I was squeamish just thinking about it. I hated pain, and stubbing my little toe on the end of my bed was the worst pain imaginable - I couldn't even fathom willingly cutting myself.

She gave me that 'duh' look again, like she couldn't understand I was that naive - or stupid.

"You're a *blood* witch. How else would you do it?"

"Well, I'm not really sure? Women bleed right...you know...that time of the month." I was gonna hazard a guess and say that menstrual blood was blood so...why not right?

Her face contorted with a look of disgust, but then she smiled and nodded, "You're absolutely right. Your kind used to do that all the time. They would share it with the other witches too."

Eww, I thought, "Really?"

"Mmmhhmmm" she hummed, confirming the most gross thing I'd ever heard. I pictured women rubbing their periods all over each other; blood clots dangling from their fingers and almost heaved, bile starting to work its way up my throat. Nope, not going there! I slapped my hand across my face trying to delete that image; the pain brought me back to the present - a period free present, and I looked at this smug light in Amber's eyes as she stared at me. I'm not sure I was liking this magic thing after all.

CHAPTER 8

Lissa was leaning against the wall waiting for me when I got to the office, she was practically bouncing she was so excited. We hugged, that one arm side-to-side hug that's quick but that tells the person you missed them because you can squeeze them tight to you. They were expecting me so I didn't bother knocking, so when I saw Agnes and an older woman in a heated discussion, arms waving around in the air, I was a bit worried that I was early or they'd forgotten I was coming.

The high priestess' face morphed into one of welcome, "Zoe, we have been waiting for you. Forgive us, we were just discussing some coven business." She indicated for us to sit, and I glanced at Lissa to check to see if she was following, her eyes were narrowed and staring at Agnes with suspicion, I pulled her attention back to me and gestured with my head for her to sit next to me.

We were introduced to the physician, a sixty something year old woman by the name of Doctor Janette Marchain, she'd apparently helped the women give birth here for years. Dr Marchain set up her treatment table alongside the large desk, and started unpacking one of those stereotypical leather bags that they all seemed to have, placing a stethoscope around her neck. She asked me to lay down and raise my shirt. Liss was like my bodyguard, coming to stand on the other side of the doc so she could watch what was going on, and see the rest of the room from her vantage point.

"I'm just going to check all of your vitals, no need to worry." She then did all the normal stuff, blood pressure, heart beat and all that jazz. "All looking good." She pulled a syringe from her pocket, "I'm going to take a blood sample so I can check..."

"Nope." Lissa piped up, "no need for a blood test, the hospital does all of that, right Zo?" She was giving me the 'eye', that meant 'follow my lead'.

"She's right doc, thanks for the check up, but I have an ultrasound booked for Friday." I didn't have anything booked but they didn't know that. But there was only one person in this room that I trusted wholeheartedly and she was giving me the red light, so I did what I always do, I trusted my BeeBee.

Sliding off the table, I righted my top and turned to Agnes, "thanks for setting this up for me, I'm relieved that everything seems ok, I'll find out the rest at the hospital."

The two women shared a look that I couldn't quite decipher, but at that point, I just wanted to go and eat something and then lay down, my head was hurting from all the thinking today; and I needed to talk to Lissa privately.

Rushing from the room and making our way back to our dorm room, we shut the door. I heard Lissa's sigh of relief next to me. "What was that about Liss?"

"I don't trust them Zoe. That woman wanted some of your blood! That seems dodgy to me, I mean, here's you with this super-blood inside you." I reared back in horror, because I hadn't thought of that.

"Shit, you're right babe, I don't even know what I can do yet, what would this stuff do in the hands of the wrong people?"

Lissa sat on my bed, "Did you find anything important today in your research?"

"Not really, just that I can't change anything," I sighed, "I need access to that library when Miss Goody-two-shoes isn't right next door."

"Well, I have a bit of good news for you." She was bouncing her bum up and down on the soft mattress, and I perked up at that, because I really needed some good news right now.

"I called mum earlier when I was sorting your outfit, and she spoke to her friend who spoke to *her* friend who arranged an ultrasound for you at ten am Friday morning."

"Shut up, you didn't!" I wrapped both arms around her and we toppled to the mattress, "I really have an appointment booked?"

"Yep!" She said, popping her 'p'.

I squeezed her to me, I was so fucking excited. I was going to meet my baby on Friday. Squealing, I peppered kisses all over her face, "you. *Kiss.* are. *Kiss.* the. Bestest. *Kiss.* friend. *Kiss.* ever."

We'd waited long enough for Nathan and we were starving, so we went to get dinner together, hoping we'd find him there. He was, and he'd already eaten by the looks of it. Turns out the chef - Mandy - has a soft spot for my little brother, and has been feeding him whatever he wants, whenever he wants. All day.

Sitting in our usual seats, Amber and Rosie came and joined us at the table, Amber with her laptop, and Rosie with her normal beaming smile. Which was good, because I needed to ask her something really important, and hopefully she'll be on my side.

"Rosie," I waited for her attention before I made my request. "Can you escort me to my hospital appointment on friday? Agnes made it clear that I should have protection, and well, you protected me, us, the other night."

She looked gobsmacked, "you want me? I mean, you want me to protect you?"

"Yea, sure, you seemed pretty capable at shooting dog-boys with lead, it seems natural that you would come with me." I hadn't told her that I also had a lunch date but that could wait until we were on our way, then she couldn't say no. It was better to ask for forgiveness than permission; best motto to live by in my opinion.

Amber's murmured "damn its" and her slapping at the keys on her laptop changed the subject and took all the attention away from me, she was stabbing at that keyboard like they'd offended her.

But one look at Lissa's face, and she was trying really hard to hide behind her hair, ducking her head down and studying her vegetable risotto that had just been placed in front of her like it had the answers to world hunger; I knew this was all her.

"What's up Amber?" She was clearly trying to remain composed, and not lose her temper, but it wasn't working.

"My laptop is broken." She went to shut the lid.

Liss stopped her, pulling the computer towards her. "Let me see." she made a few (deliberately) awkward taps on the keyboard; what was she playing at?

"I do not think you have the ability to fix my computer problem, thank you very much!" Amber was irate and she really failed at trying to get her laptop back from Lissa, before she could gain possession, my devious bestie pissed herself laughing. She shoved the laptop around so I could see, while the poor owner tried to grab it back from her.

Amber was clearly trying to write an essay about a potion but between each word was the word 'moist'. Lissa wrote a sentence on her word document, and every time she pressed the spacebar, 'moist' was typed out; *someone* had altered Amber's settings and she was mortified. Her face was as red as my front door back home.

My friend was having the time of her life here, and no-one had any clue it was her.

"How did you get to her computer?" I asked Lissa later on. We were in bed - Nathan already sparked out on the other side of the room.

She leaned over the top bunk, her braids swinging, "when you told me how she just brushed you off earlier, I was annoyed, and I noticed she leaves her laptop in the computer room, so....."

It felt like old times when we stayed at each other's place, having a sleepover. "So you changed her spacebar. I love it!"

"I also love how they haven't figured out it's me yet. I uploaded a virus to all of the desktop computers upstairs. When they click on updates, this gay porn video starts playing..."

I laughed so hard, they were gonna have a fit when their updates started. "Yea, a video called 'King Dong', and one of the guys was wearing a wizards hat, I couldn't resist."

I sat up as far as I could without knocking my head above me, "You watched it?"

"Just a little bit. I needed to see if it was appropriate." She laid back down on her bed, but I could still hear her quietly chuckling to herself. It *was* funny. Miss 'Moist' was gonna have a heart attack, I bet she'd never seen a dick in her life.

"I heard on the grapevine that Amber doesn't wanna tutor you anymore. Heard she complained to Agnes about it."
"It's not like she actually did anything, I just sat reading all morning."
"Heard Jade was gonna take over your education from tomorrow."
I groaned from the safety of my mattress, she was such a dick. "I'm just gonna stay in my room all day tomorrow and Thursday, then Friday I'm going out, I'll deal with Jade on Monday." We hadn't been here long enough to grasp the routines of the place yet, but I wondered if they worked on weekends? "Do they do lessons on weekends?"
"Only the higher ups do anything on weekends, they do their sacrifice and prayer crap, the rest of the newbies are left to their own devices."
Relieved, I relaxed back in my bed and snuggled under the covers, content that I had a few days off, they just didn't know that yet.

      I spent the whole next day in my room, with Lissa or Nate bringing me food, I only left the room to go to the bathroom across the hall. I deserved a 'do-fuck-all-day', plus I was tired and I wanted to be well rested for Friday's excitement. Then I thought, screw it, I was gonna text Lucian, I wanted to confirm the timings for our date anyway.
It was the first time I'd reached out to him, and I didn't know if he would text back straight away.

Looking 4ward 2 our date.

Turns out, I didn't have to wait long at all for him to reply.

I've been looking forward to it all week.

1pm still ok?

Most definitely beautiful girl.

I loved how he wrote out every single message properly. No abbreviations or text speak, he typed the way he spoke, properly.

And it was such a turn on knowing that this guy, this hot man, found *me* beautiful.

I'd only ever dealt with 'Dickhead' or wasters chatting me up on the street before, a wolf-whistle to get my attention and a "oi babe, send me your number," ugh.

But this was a whole other ballgame. Lucian was educated, he was cultured, and he was a gentleman; and I wondered what the hell he was doing wanting to have lunch with me.

I was a nobody, a foster kid from the system who had no education, no money and a baby on the way. Why was I wasting my time with a guy who would just up and leave when he found out I carried another man's baby? And why was I wasting this poor guy's time either, making him meet me for food and then telling him my news, what's the point? I should just cut my losses now, while feelings weren't involved.

We'd had one conversation face to face, and the rest was over a phone, but I already knew that he could be someone important. It was the way he looked at me like no one else had mattered, he had looked in my eyes the whole time, not just talking to my boobs.

He *saw* me.

The more I thought about it, the worse I felt, this was such a bad idea; I didn't know why I was even considering this stupid plan in the first place. Guys like him didn't date girls like me.

And I needed to fix this.

I'm sorry. I need to cnx.

Is something wrong? Tell me how to help you, but please don't cancel on me.

Jesus, this guy was too much, and now I felt like crying because he was willing to help me and he didn't even know what was wrong.

I'm pregnant. It's not fair to meet tmrw.

I don't want to waste your time.

I need to focus on the baby. I'm sorry.

I stuffed my phone under my pillow and buried my head in the soft cushion. It was just my luck that I met a nice guy and I couldn't have him.

The buzzing under my pillow pulled me from my misery. He was calling me? Shit! I hesitated pressing that green icon, knowing that things were going to change, and not sure if I wanted them to. I pressed the green button.

"Hello?"

Heavy breathing met my greeting, did he butt dial me by accident? "Lucian?"

"Where is the father?"

His voice was exactly as I remembered it. Rough and deep but smooth like honey. His words flowed through my ears like the sweetest nectar, and I wanted to hear more.

"He's…not in the picture." I told him. I needed him to know that there wasn't another man anywhere in any picture.

"Good. He doesn't deserve you. Any man would be thankful that you had chosen them to be the father of your child, clearly he is not worthy of you."

Woooow. "Oh." Good job with the flowing conversation Zoe. I said to myself mentally, but then, that had to be the nicest thing a guy had *ever* said to me.

"We will still have lunch in two days. I'll feed you and the baby, you need to keep your strength up, pregnancy is tough on a woman's body."

Does that mean he has kids? Not that that was a problem for me, I loved kids. But I wanted to know everything about him. "Do you have kids of your own?"

"Not yet." He replied.

"So…you want kids?"

"Very much so, I just…never had the opportunity." His voice grew melancholy, and I imagined his face from memory, picturing his beautiful eyes filled with sadness and I wanted to hug him. His question "how far along are you?" brought me out of my daydream.

"I'm not sure exactly, I have an appointment Friday morning to find out, but about eight-ish weeks?" That was by my estimation anyway.

"Then I have thirty-two weeks to prepare, is that correct?"
Silence followed that little statement, because what.the.fuck?
"Zoe?"
"Ummm I'm still here. But I'm not sure what you mean exactly?" Did he mean he was going to be my new baby daddy? After meeting me once?
"There is nothing that will make me not want to see you. You feel it too don't you. That connection. I knew you were mine the moment I saw you, the fact that you are carrying a baby just means I get a two-for-one offer. To me, that child is *yours* and now *mine*."
This was not what I expected to happen when I told him my news. Yea, I feel that fluttering in my stomach like butterflies on steroids, but that didn't mean I was in the cards for a new man. Even if he was built like a sex-god. "Lucian, this is moving really fast; like Roadrunner fast, I think you need to take your foot off the gas for a minute ok." I took a breath, because I needed to slow this down too. My heart was racing at the thought that this man wanted this with me, but that was letting the excitement get the better of me, and I knew better than to reach those exciting highs - because inevitably it comes crashing down.
"Beautiful girl. You may not understand this yet, but I have waited a lifetime for you; this child is a blessing given to us, to me. I will protect you both and provide for you, and you will want for nothing. Ever again."
"I think we should talk about this face-to-face, we need to take this slow. I just got out of a long relationship, and I need to know *everything* about you."
"We have seven months to go slow, deal?" He said.
"And then what?"
"And then all bets are off. When the child gets here, you can both live with me, and you have seven months to get to know me. I promise, you will not regret it."
Well, seven months is quite a long time, I know of people who have got married in way less time than that. "Ok Luc, you have seven months to convince me, but if I say it's not for me, then you have to promise that you will not try and push this on me. I've had enough of being bossed around to last me a lifetime." I

smiled to myself, because he was gonna have to earn a place in our lives, I was not just going to trust any random guy to raise my child. Who did he think I was? Jackie?.

"Where is your appointment and what time?" He asked.

"I'm not telling you that, I'll meet you for lunch, that's it." I stated.

"My seven months starts now, beautiful girl. I'll meet you there, and we can eat afterwards." He tried to convince me, but I wasn't a pushover, besides, this was too personal to have him come.

"You need to understand something if we're gonna do this." His intake of breath on the other end of the phone was all I heard as I continued. "You don't push me into doing things, I'm going to the hospital. On.my.own. I need this time with my baby, to meet him or her, to speak to the doctor and make sure everything is ok for *my* peace of mind, not yours. Understand."

He exhaled, clearly accepting my way of things - I hope. "Aye mo ghràidh. I understand."

I released the breath I hadn't known I'd been holding, and focused on what he'd said. "What does that mean?" I asked.

"It's Gaelic." He replied. "I'll tell you what it means when you have moved in with me."

"Ohhh that's mean." I laughed. "You know we have things like Google Translate now."

"That takes all of the mystery out of it."

Yawning despite hardly doing anything today, I put the phone on speaker and relaxed, still able to hear him beside me.

But he'd heard the sleepiness in my voice, "you should rest."

Yawning for a second time, I groaned. "I'm just gonna take a nap, this pregnancy is tiring me out already."

"The baby is taking what it needs to be healthy and strong."

Closing my eyes and picturing a certain golden eyed man, I let the honeyed tone of his voice lull me to sleep.

      Pounding on my door had me jolting awake, and for a minute I was back in Lissa's flat watching the lycans beat down the door.

Shouting through my door drew me back to the present, and Jade's voice yelling through the door had me wishing I *was* back in front of the monsters.

"You have five minutes to sort yourself out, Bleeder, we have a meeting."

And there goes my dreams of having a free day to do nothing. Dragging myself out of bed, I heard a low voice from behind me. Oh shit! Lucian was still on the phone. I picked up my mobile that was resting on my pillow, the time read 15:12. I'd been asleep for an hour...and he was still on the line. I dug the heel of my palm into my eye, my life couldn't get any worse right now. Picking up my phone, I considered just putting the phone down, but that felt wrong. "Lucian?"

"You're awake. Do you feel better?"

"You've been on the phone the whole time?" I asked him.

"I've been doing some paperwork while you slept, I just put you on speaker. It was...relaxing listening to you sleep." He said.

I didn't know what to think, was this sweet or stalkerish? "You know that's a bit weird right."

"Staying on the phone while my woman slept so I could speak to her when she woke up? That's not weird. What's weird is how such a beautiful girl can snore so loud."

"I DO NOT SNORE!" I shouted at him. His husky laughter soothed my irritation, and I melted at the fact that I'd made him laugh.

"You *do* have a sense of humour then."

"Not really, I'm not a funny guy."

Offended, I said, "So you're just laughing at me?"

"No mo ghràidh, I'm laughing because you're perfect, and only you are able to lighten my day."

The rattling of the door handle outside reminded me that Jade was waiting. She could wait a bit longer for calling me 'bleeder.'

"Go on now, beautiful, I will get to see you soon."

And then it went dead. He'd put the phone down.

Cunty-Jade (this was her new name in my head) walked me to the casting room where some of the other witches were waiting for us in what she said was an 'experiment', and if I wanted to see some real magic, I should just 'do what she says'. Well, I wasn't really one for following orders, especially from Cunty-Jade but I thought it was about time that I saw something juicy.

The door was open waiting for us, and the more skillful witches in the pecking order - including Agnes and Amber - were standing against the padded walls; the large space looked like something from an insane asylum, and I half expected them to wrap me in a straight jacket and shove me around.

Agnes opened her arms wide, "Welcome Zoe. We thought you would like to see some of our more proficient witches practise some spells this afternoon. It's nothing too big, just some protection spells that some of the girls have been working on."

This sounded way better than staying in my room, so I took up a spot near some random and watched the show.

Cunty-Jade stepped forward and stood in the centre of the room, a pedestal with a large, stone flat top held small glass bottles sealed off with brown wax, and indecipherable words were written down the sides, but clearly Jade knew which ones were which.

She picked up one of the jars, breaking it's seal and poured a drop onto her hand; rubbing her palms in a circular motion, she began to whisper. *"His verbis, conjuro te rogamus vos et solstitii temporis sens."* She kept repeating over and over, until within the palm of her cupped hands, a speck appeared; a spot of pale blue light that grew to the size of a tennis ball within her hands.

She aimed the ball of magic at the far wall, where I realised everyone was staying away from, and on the wall was a large target with scorch marks - though none in the centre - whoever it was that had been practising didn't have very good aim.

Cunty-Jade pushed her hands towards the target, releasing the ball of energy; it flew towards the wall and sparks exploded outwards, then melting before they hit the floor.

Magic was real. I'd seen her make that ball in her hands, whisper a spell and bam! I couldn't believe it.

It was crazy. It was unreal.

It was...anticlimactic.

Rounds of applause went up from the people around the room. She hadn't even hit the target, the new mark on the wall was to the left of the whole thing, and now she was bowing like she'd won a Nobel Prize.

As the clapping died down, Cunty-Jade - or CJ for short - started packing up her potions, and Agnes stepped forward to quieten the few stragglers still making noise.

"Thank you Jade, that was beautiful; and a great new spell to share with the coven."

I raised my hand, waiting to be noticed in a sea of sycophants. "What did she do exactly?" I asked the room.

Jade turned to me, arms crossed and hips cocked, "It's a repellant, it's designed to keep enemies away or keep them back, whichever."

I nodded my head, because it didn't seem to me that it would repel anyone. It looked more like a light show from Disney; but what do I know?

"You think you can do better?" She said, "Come on, everyone's dying to know what the blood witch can do."

Choruses of "yea let's see." and "come on Zoe" echoed around the room, and I wished I'd never opened my big mouth.

CJ grabbed my arm, pulled me to the centre of the room and handed me a pocket knife. Slapping it in my hand, she then went and stood next to the high priestess, leaving me standing there with not a bloody clue.

"You know what to do now, use the knife, and just a small incision in your hand will do the trick. Then concentrate, imagine what you want your blood to do, and your power will manifest it." Instructed Agnes.

"You want me to cut myself?"

"Yes, it's high time you started practising, not much though remember; a small spell will not harm the child." She said.

Holding the blade, I told her, "I thought I'd just wait until after the baby was born, and use *that* blood."

She looked confused, "What blood?"

"You know, the menstrual blood, I could just save it…" gags and heaving surrounded me, and Agnes and Jade looked disgusted. "I'm guessing I can't use that?" That fucking Amber, she played me. I looked around the room and saw her standing in the corner, an innocent expression on her face; I glared at her. Oh, it was on bitch.

Flicking out the blade on the pocket knife, I held the sharp point to the meaty part of my hand and dug it in, "ow ow ow," nope, this wasn't gonna work. I let my hand fall to the side, still gripping the knife. I couldn't cut myself, me and pain didn't go together.

I was officially the worst blood witch. Ever!

"Tut, for goddess' sake," Jade took the knife in one hand, and pulled my other hand towards her. "On three."

We counted together, "one, two..." she stabbed the knife into my palm, "FUCK. That wasn't on three!" There was a reason I was calling her Cunty-Jade in my head.

Blood welled from the half inch gash in my hand and pooled in my palm. "Now what?" I said.

"Now just like I explained earlier, picture what you want to happen in your mind." Agnes announced.

I recalled what Jade had done, imagining the little blue ball in my hand swell, but the glow started within the drops of my blood, a gleaming pinprick that undulated within the tiny puddle and rose to hover within my cupped palms. I slowly moved my hands away from it, keeping them straight so my blood didn't drip everywhere.

A red smouldering fireball floated in mid-air. "Holy shit, I did it." I laughed excitedly. "I fucking did it." The fireball flickered and wavered, and gasps filled the room as people tried to move even further away from me.

"Keep your concentration Zoe." Cautioned Agnes, "You are in control of the magic, do not forget that."

Where Jade's ball of light was the size of a tennis ball, mine was the size of a melon. And it was beautiful. It was almost like tiny fireflies flitted away inside of it and I stared intently, enamoured with the dancing flames that I'd created.

"Release the energy Zoe," shouted Agnes.

I dared not take my attention from the magic to look back at her, so I did what she asked, and I imagined the ball hitting the target, right in the centre of it.

I just wasn't expecting those results.

The energy ball crashed into the target - and the wall - creating a gigantic hole where I could see into the next room. Bits of bricks and debris littered the floor beneath the gaping hole in the wall. Well, I definitely hit the target.

Some of the women closest to my mini explosion were coughing dust, while the others just stood there gaping at me.

"No applause?" They all just stared at me, varied expressions of shock, awe and....fear. They were scared of me? I turned my attention to Agnes who looked excited at my display; except Jade and Amber who looked annoyed. Sorry Jade, my spell beat your spell.

One of the other girls brought me over a wipe and a bandage, and indicated my hand that had stopped bleeding, the blood starting to congeal around the edges already.

"That was fun," I said, sticking the bandage on my cut, "we should do that again soon."

"Yes, well, we may have to continue this outside next time." mentioned Agnes.

I figured now was a good time to leave considering everyone was gawking at me, but this is what they wanted wasn't it? They wanted to see me in action, and yea, I was curious to see what I could do too. I had no idea it would be so...intense.

I thought I would have found a place here with the witches, people who were like me and somewhere I could fit in, finally. But I guess they were just like all rest, and I was still the weirdo on the outskirts looking in.

CHAPTER 9

Jacob

      I flipped the coffee table roaring my rage to the occupants of the room. "How the fuck can you not track one fucking lycan!" I swiped my claws across the shelves lining the wall, smashing the figurines that Louise collected. I heard them smash to the floor, but my attention was on the useless fucks that still hadn't found my witch.
"I'm sorry Jake, we followed Lucian but we lost him in Dalston Market, there were too many people and…"
I growled my discontent at Cam, "Stop making excuses for your fuck ups." I turned to Reggie, another waste of space, he cowered before me and lowered his eyes to the floor. Good, he knew who his master was at least. "And you. What's your excuse?"
"He…he…went….to the public gardens and…and the smell was overwhelm…" with a backhand across his pathetic face, I sent him crashing into the wall. I didn't pull any punches either (no pun intended) I put the whole of my strength behind it, feeling his jaw crack beneath my fist.
"Excuses excuses." I wiped my hand on Cam's shirt, the first useless dog in my arsenal, smearing Reggie's blood on the white cotton. "I don't understand how hard it is. I asked you to follow Lucian to the witches, that's it; and you keep failing. I should just get rid of you both." My claws unsheathed, and his face paled before dropping to his knees in front of me."
"Please Jacob, please." he begged, "We will not fail you again, let us try one more time. Please."
Maybe I was putting too much faith in these two, I'd given them a job to track another Lycan; one who was far smarter and older than either of them. I'd probably underestimated Lucian too, he wasn't stupid, and he'd know I was after the little witch. "Stand up and have some self-respect." I spat at him. "You're a lycan, we

don't beg." Grabbing his Tee and pulling him bodily up from the floor, I wiped the creases from his shirt and smiled, "don't worry, I probably just put the wrong guys on the job; I should have given it to Ty from the start."

"Ty? You're going to send Ty? But he's…"

"Crazy?" I interrupted. "Yes, I know." I walked through the long hallways of the converted care home I'd bought a few years back; it had enough space for the pack to have their own rooms and space to roam, it was set on three acres of land, so they had space to run around in their lycan form too.

The room I was after had been set up in the basement, where they used to keep all of their store rooms, and had been converted into a large room with an en-suite; he had wanted it because it was pretty soundproof - and Ty liked to have company over. Of the non-consenting type. I walked down the stairs and banged my fist on the door, hearing some muffled screams inside; really I was just letting him know I was coming in, it wasn't because I respected his privacy - this was my house after all.

A human woman was tied up on all fours on his super king, arms spread out wide in front of her and her legs spread as wide as they could go and shackled to the sides of the bed, hitched to the metal frame, a ball gag in her mouth that didn't mute the sounds of her pain and distress; tears flowed down her face freely and she stared at me with hope in her eyes that I was there to save her…but I wouldn't. I never did.

Ty was - as usual - in his lycan form, his large canine body curled over the female and fucking her like she was the last girl on earth. She looked like she came from money, her shoes in the corner had the legendary red bottom, and her ruined dress looked expensive. She'll probably have people looking for her at some point, but as long as it wasn't traced back here, it wasn't my problem.

With every plunge she grunted in agony, his massive cock not meant to fit something so small; but that was the beauty of it, wasn't it. Taking something that doesn't belong to you and ruining it. It was the most delicious gift making something your own, moulding it into your very own masterpiece. Blood covered the sheets where his claws had nicked her, and I could see more blood underneath her where the amorous wolf had ripped her pussy open.

I took a seat to the side of the bed to watch the show, Ty's dick had certainly done a number on her, she looked like ground mince-meat down there, but I knew it was his preference to fuck in his wolf form; like our animal counterparts, our dicks knotted the female when we orgasmed, tieing the body in place beneath us. Which is why we all called him 'Ty', I couldn't even remember what his real name was. I knew he was close to knotting the woman, because he growled and held himself still inside her; she tried to scream around the gag, her eyes rolled into the back of her head and she passed out. Probably for the best, she wouldn't want to be awake for the next part. He'd be stuck inside her for at least an hour while he was still cumming, he'd have a snack in between…a finger, an arm. Depends what he was in the mood for?

"I have a job for you." I told him, I wasn't expecting a reply right now, but neither was I expecting him to say no. "Track Lucian, have him lead you to the blood witch. Do not under any circumstances touch the witch. She's mine, do you understand?" His big body shuddered over the unconscious woman and he tilted his head to look at me, his yellow eyes were crazed with lust. He would normally use them three or four times before getting rid of the body…alive or dead, didn't bother him.

But I needed him lucid to complete this job, he was the best tracker I had, but he was volatile; it's why I hadn't chosen him in the first place. He couldn't always be trusted not to touch the merchandise. "Make sure you're sated, and then get ready to go. Remember my words." I glared at him. His answering tail wag told me all I needed to know. He was excited to start the hunt, and I would have my witch soon.

I stayed where I was, getting comfortable in the arm chair to watch the rest of the show. Maybe I'd take my turn before she was disposed of, no use in wasting posh pussy.

Zoe

I sat next to Rosie in the passenger seat of the van, the same van that they had 'rescued' us in. I was stewing on the events of Wednesday, not in a talkative mood, but Rosie didn't seem to get the memo that I wasn't interested in conversation. All she was talking about was the magic I had done in the casting room, and she wished she could have seen it and apparently *everyone* was talking about it. Brilliant. Just what I needed. To be the centre of attention where everyone looked at me like I was the freak. I had spent yesterday holed up in my room, and even when CJ banged on my door again for another one of her 'lessons' I had pretended to be asleep; I wasn't in the mood to be gaped at again.

I cranked the music up louder to give her the hint that I did not want to talk about my 'explosion fiasco'. I didn't know who was playing on the radio, but the lyrics resonated with me, some guy singing about a saturday night.

Hey, man, I'm alive I'm taking each day and night at a time
Yeah I'm down, but I know I'll get by

It was good advice, the way I was feeling now, I was feeling like a Monday, but hopefully after my date with Lucian, I would be feeling like a saturday night too. Once the song finished I turned the volume down a bit so Rosie would hear me. "Who was that singing just now?" I asked her.

"You don't know who Bon Jovi is? Where have you been living, in a cave?" she laughed, she took her eyes off the road long enough to shoot a smile my way.

"No, it's just not normally my style," I replied. I smoothed the maxi-dress down my legs that Lissa had picked out for me, it was perfect for a lunch date, sexy but casual, the capped sleeves showed off my toned arms and the peach colour contrasted perfectly with my bronzed skin. I'd only used a bit of clear lip gloss and mascara on my face; the only eyesore was the ugly white bandage on my hand from yesterday's 'explosion-gate'.

"Zoe?" Rosie grabbed my attention, she sounded unsure, and I wondered why. "Please don't take what Amber did to you seriously."

"Are you for real? She embarrassed me in front of everyone, she made me look like a mug, and you want me to just…ignore that." I hissed back.

"Not ignore it, it's just…" she paused to think of how to explain why she wanted me to let it go. Let's listen to this excuse.

"Everyone in the coven was raised to know their place, their mums are judges and doctors and lawyers. Amber's mum was the cleaner before she died, it's the only reason she even got a place. She used to just read in the library everyday so she didn't get in the way of all of the other girls who used to make fun of her for wearing hand-me-downs, and they used to order her around thinking because her mum was the 'help', then Amber had to be too. It only stopped when they realised that Amber was smarter than them, and that if they wanted help with tests and information on literally *anything,* then she was the one to go to. Just…take it easy on her ok?"

I could empathise with that, I suppose our upbringings weren't so different - still a shit thing to do though, and she won't be getting off easy just because I felt a bit sorry for her.

"She's struggling with her place in the coven," Rosie continued. "Now you're here, and you're the most powerful witch in the …well…world," she explained, "I think she's starting to feel a bit useless, like maybe she won't be needed anymore?"

I heaved a sigh, "fine, I suppose it wasn't all that bad anyway. I mean, she probably won't do anything now. I think they're all scared of me."

"They really are, you should have heard them last night," she cackled, "they were saying how you nearly blew their heads off."

I rolled my eyes, "that's a slight exaggeration, they weren't even standing near the fireball when I let it off."

"They said it was red?" she side-eyed me.

"The fireball? Yea it was red, is that significant?"

"It's red because you're a blood witch, we've just never seen it before." she explained, "ours, which are waaayy smaller, are normally blue or green." She pulled up at the hospital and put the handbrake on, "do you want me to come in with you?"

"No, it's fine, I'd like to do this on my own." I released my seatbelt and opened the door.

"Ok, I'll park up and wait out here, just text me if you need me."

Two hours later I walked out of the hospital with a sonogram, it was too small to notice much at the moment, the size of a kidney bean. I was a bit further along than I had expected, eleven weeks, I'd heard the heartbeat and it was strong. The doctor had given me some pre-natal vitamins to start, and a date for my next check-up.

I kept staring at my photo, not paying attention to anything around me, so I didn't hear Rosie come up beside me and startle me. "Jesus woman, you walk stealthily."

"Time to go."

I waited until we were in the van to let her know about my other plans. "We need to make another stop."

"Where? I can pick up anything you need if you give me a list or something?"

We sat side by side, the engine running, "I have a date in town and I'm meeting him at one, can you drop me off?"

Her hair flicked me in the face as her head whipped around to frown at me. "Are you kidding? I'm supposed to take you straight back to the house."

"Rosie, I'm a grown-ars woman, and I won't be held prisoner in a house with a bunch of strange women. You can take me there and wait for me...or I can get a cab and you go back to Agnes and complain that I made plans." I scowled at her, no way were these people stopping me from having a life. I didn't even need a babysitter but I couldn't drive so it was convenient for Rosie to just take me, especially because I didn't think I had enough money to even pay for a cab.

"Why didn't you tell me earlier?"

"I thought I would tell you when I knew you couldn't really say no." I said triumphantly.

"Fine, but I'm coming in with you," she put the van in gear and pulled out of the car park to hit the main road.

"No you won't," I exclaimed, "You are not ruining my date. You can wait in the van or go for a walk." I'm not having anyone scare Lucian off.

"I'm supposed to protect you."

Holding up my bandaged hand, I told her "I can protect myself just fine."

Lucian

  I sat in the corner of the restaurant with my back to the wall so I could survey the whole room, only a glass of water in front of me. I'd been there for over half an hour and the waitress was annoyed I had not ordered anything else yet. But I wouldn't until Zoe was here. I ran my hand over my jaw, not used to the lightweight feeling; but I finally had a reason to trim it and not walk around like I had just woken up from a ten-year coma.

A ripple of awareness danced over my skin - and there she was. An angel basking in the afternoon glow with her short curls a shining halo. In the few short days since I had first met her, My memory had not dimmed her beauty, nor had it deceived me. She was as perfect as the day I had met her.

Her floating dress did not hide her curves from me, merely accentuated them. Her full breasts were cupped by the material, a shadow hinting at her cleavage before it fell to her ankles, the dress curled around her shapely legs as she stepped into the restaurant.

She looked around the room and, spotting me, she did a double take before slowly approaching me. I stood from the table to greet her, and before she could say anything, I wrapped my arm around her tiny waist and pulled her body into me, her head only coming to my chest. I hugged her to me and rested my chin on top of her head. "You can hug me back, beautiful girl."

It was equal parts ecstasy and agony when she wrapped both her arms around me. Ecstasy because I finally had my queen in my arms, and agony because I could feel her breasts pressed against me; I could smell her unique scent of magic and cocoa butter and my cock sprung to life, eager to feel her and make her mine.

But I was a patient man, and this was more than I had hoped for; more than I had ever dreamed I would have.

Holding on to her, I considered all of the things that had happened to bring me to this spot. I had thought for a long time that I had feelings for Caitlyn, I kept them hidden because she was my best friend's wife, but that was nothing in comparison to this. Zoe fit perfectly next to me, and if I had my way, she - and the child she carried - would stay by my side, permanently.

Zoe

I rested my head against his firm chest and closed my eyes, with his arms around me I felt safer than I ever had before; it felt like no-one or nothing could get past him. He felt like home. With my arms wrapped around him, not able to meet on the other side because he was so big, I tilted my head to look up at him, "Hi." I whispered. He only smiled at me, flashing his perfect white teeth in my direction.
And in the most sweetest gesture, he placed a gentle kiss on the tip of nose, and stepping back, he took my hands in his and kissed each one; he paused as he came to my bandaged one. His entire body stiffened as he turned it palm up and ran his thumb over the padding. "What happened here?" He asked, "You hurt yourself?" His nostrils flared as he bent closer to my healing wound, running his nose along the covering. I could have sworn I saw his eyes flash molten gold.
"It's just a scratch, I fell over." I pulled my hands from his, "it's fine. Shall we sit?" I moved around him to our table and sat at the seat opposite his own.
"How did you fall over?" He asked gruffly.
He really wasn't made for these small wooden benches, his massive body dwarfed the bench seat. I pulled the sonogram from my bag and slid it across the table to him, it certainly drew his attention away from my hand.
He carefully picked it up like it was the most valuable of treasures and studied the grainy black and white image. "This is him?" He was in awe of the picture, he didn't take his eyes off of it once as he addressed me. "Everything is ok? He's healthy?"

"*She* is perfect and growing at the expected rate. I'm eleven weeks along, I have another appointment in four weeks to make sure the baby is all ok. They said I might be able to find out the gender by then…if baby is cooperative."

There really wasn't that much to see at this point, a tiny little blob, but he was enraptured with the image. Even as the server came over to take our orders, his attention remained on the picture, his thumb rubbing over it softly.

"What are you eating, Luc?" I asked him

"I don't know, you order something for me, none of that Tofu crap though."

I laughed, he really didn't look like someone that lived on Tofu. More like protein on top of protein. I ordered us both the Teriyaki Steak Soba with a side of Duck Gyoza; my mouth watered as I waited for our meals to arrive. I was starving, but I also wanted to know everything about my date. Especially as he was adamant that we would live together soon.

"How old are you?" I questioned.

His eyes shot to the sides as if he was thinking how to answer. With a smirk on his face, his gaze found mine, "much older than you."

"How much older?" I said suspiciously.

Holding his fingers about an inch apart, he murmured, "a little bit."

"What do you do?"

"I invested in some properties a while back, so now I just manage them, collect the rent as needed, fix them when required. That sort of thing."

I raised my eyebrows in surprise, property in London was expensive and his clothes weren't the cheap kind that I bought for myself from Primark. He must be doing alright for himself. Selfishly, this made me feel better about my decision to accept his proposal. After living in council housing my whole life, having a decent home for my child would be fantastic. A proper home that didn't have damp stains all over the walls and broken boilers in the winter.

"I need some assurances from you."

His eyes found mine, "anything," he replied.

"You said you want this child, and I'm not sure why, but I need to know that if anything happens to me, my baby will be well cared for….money wise."

He rested his arms on the table and leaned towards me, "I can't…" his shoulders hunched forward, "I can't have children of my own. There was an…accident years ago."

"I'm sorry," I laid my hand over his, was this why he wanted me? Because he couldn't have children of his own so this was a ready made family for him? "and that's why you want my baby?"

"No. I wanted you first, the minute I saw you I knew you would be mine. You already being pregnant is just the icing on the cake, because it's something I can never give you." He growled. His face flushed as if he was embarrassed by his confession.

"What happened?"

"It happened a very long time ago…" his hand turned in mine and grasped it, holding it firmly in his, "I have longed to be a father, and I do not want you to think me strange."

Well, I did think it was strange that he was so ready to claim my child as his own, but then, I was a witch, would he think that was strange too?

"I was raised by very…old fashioned people. I need to take care of you both, it is a drive inside me. I felt drawn to you from the moment I saw you; your beauty, your spirit. If this child is anything like you, then I would be honoured to have a hand in raising him…or her."

Squeezing his large hand between both of mine, I halted him.

"You don't *need* to take care of us. I want you to spend time with me because you *want* to." I thought about how it felt growing up with no parents. This baby would at least have one parent, but maybe, I could give my child *both* parents?

Besides, what would he do when I made my own confession? When he found out I was a witch would he still feel the same about me *and* my baby? That was a problem for future Zoe, if I made him love us enough then that would be a moot point. I had six months. Less time than we had initially planned.

Our food was placed in front of us, and conversation became lighter as I told him the ideas for names that I had been thinking about for the baby. I had decided on 'Saxon' for a boy, a good strong warrior name, but I was undecided on a girl's name. Luc was throwing ideas at me, but they were all very old fashioned, and I had to veto them. Kids were cruel, I couldn't imagine sending my daughter to school with a name like 'Agatha', she'd be picked on her whole life until she reached the age of eighty. True story, that's one of his recommendations.

He had me laughing as he regaled me with tales of some of his tenants and the stuff he had seen. There was a man who liked to answer the door naked, every single time. And I nearly choked on my food when he told me of the seventy year old grandma who tried to seduce him by spreading whipped cream on her saggy tits and asking him to lick them clean; he said he'd never run that fast in his life.

My phone vibrated in my bag with an incoming text. Rosie was letting me know that we needed to leave soon; I didn't want this day to end, I had completely forgotten that my life outside this place without Lucian still existed and I wish it didn't. I wish I didn't have lycans chasing me and shifty witches watching me, I wish I wasn't even a witch at all and I could go back to my boring job and accept a date with a sexy man who brought me coffee. But that's not what my life is about, and it won't ever be like that again.

"I need to leave soon."

"Stay, I can give you a ride home soon." He grabbed my wrist and ran his thumb along my pulse point, "Don't leave."

"I have to, my friend's waiting to give me a ride."

"Tell her to leave, I'll make sure you're safe." His eyes were intense as they stared at me. I really wanted to take him up on his offer, but how would I explain where I was staying?

"Rain check?"

"Then you'll let me kiss you before you go, to tide me over before I can see you again."

"Oh I will, will I?" I sighed, I didn't realise I'd leaned towards him over the table unconsciously wanting that kiss more than anything. His large hand slid behind my neck and pulled me towards him, he didn't need to lean that far over, his tall frame only needing to bend a bit further towards me so that our lips met over the wooden table.

His lips brushed mine tenderly back and forth, and rubbed his nose along mine before laying claim to my mouth; enclosing my mouth with his. His tongue brushed the edges of my lips before conquering my own.

I couldn't move, my head was being cradled by both of his hands now, and my arms were holding me off the table as his tongue plundered my willing mouth. He licked and tasted everywhere and it was the single most sensual experience of my life. I groaned as he sucked my tongue into his own mouth and I tasted the chocolate cake that he'd ordered for dessert. Lucian and chocolate together? A sin that no mortal woman could ever survive...good thing I wasn't mortal then.

His answering groan caused goosebumps all over my body as I returned the favour, sucking his tongue and running my own along it, imagining myself on my knees and doing the same thing to his dick. His hands tightened around me as he tried to pull me closer, like he wanted to meld us into one being.

"Ahem." The throat clearing next to us broke the spell he had weaved over me, and I half wondered if maybe he was a witch too..or Wizard? Whatever men were called. "You can not do that here," he said with a condescending tone, "this is a family establishment."

I was mortified as I ducked my head down, hoping that not many people saw our public display since we were tucked in the corner, but looking around I could see people staring and a young mother covering the eyes of her small son and glaring in my direction. It wasn't that bad was it?

A snarl from next to me showed Lucian glaring at the waiter who had interrupted his second dessert. One of his hands was still wrapped around my neck, and he leaned over to rain kisses over my cheeks and forehead trying to kiss away the flush of embarrassment with his affection. "Apologise to my woman." He growled, "now!"

The poor guy looked shit scared of Luc, and he stammered an apology before dashing off, probably to find the manager.

"We should leave."

"We will in a minute, I can't get out of my seat right now." His head nodded towards his lap, and because I was obviously a glutton for punishment, I ducked under the table to get a look at his 'problem' and stared in amazement, because that thing was massive!

"You're really not hiding that thing at all, it's huge." I cried out. His answering smirk was steeped in male satisfaction, "I know." It was long and thick in his grey slacks, resting along his thigh, and I wondered how the hell that *thing* would fit inside me when I eventually had all of him. Because, I would have all of him, there was no way a man could kiss like that and be lousy in bed; it would be phenomenal. My pussy clenched at the thought of that monster dick stretching me open, these damn pregnancy hormones had me horny all the damn time, and it didn't help that I had a man right there willing to make me feel better.

"Don't worry, beautiful girl, we'll take it slow," His heated gaze was locked on mine, "when I have you, I will fit all of me inside you. And you will be begging for more."

"Phew," I waved my hand in front of my face, trying to get some air, "is it hot in here? I need some air."

He stood up and pulled me with him, his cock still prominent in his trousers, it didn't look like it was going down any time soon. "Walk in front of me."

"Yea, I don't think that's gonna hide your trouser snake, handsome." I laughed. I was right too. Women oogled him as we walked by, and I relished in their desire, because he was mine and they didn't have a chance.

Once outside the restaurant, we walked to a small alcove where we wouldn't be in the way and I could wait for Rosie to swing by and pick me up. He crowded me against the wall, both arms blocking me in while keeping prying eyes out, and leaned his forehead against mine; his eyes looked haunted as they stared into mine, "promise me that you'll never hate me."

"What?" I was confused, how could I ever possibly hate this man who had done nothing but treat me like a princess since I first met him.

"Promise me Zoe," one hand stroking over my curls and down the side of my face, touching his fingers reverently over my lips, "that you will never hate me, no matter what."

His eyes pleaded with me to give him that vow, like he needed it more than his next breath.

I brushed my fingers lightly over his own lips, the lips that had already promised me and my child so much, and I vowed that I would never hate him. No matter what.

The honk of a horn alerted me to my ride, and I saw the familiar van idling at the side of the road just passed where we had eaten; giving Lucian a soft kiss at the side of his mouth, I skipped towards Rosie, knowing I needed to leave straight away otherwise I would find other reasons to stay - namely, a third leg with my name on it. Climbing into the passenger seat with a massive grin on my face, I buckled in.

I tried to spot him through the window but the angle was all wrong, and I think he was keeping himself hidden in our little spot, which was ok with me; I didn't need my friend drooling over my man, she'd just keep talking and talking about him until I shut her up.

"Have fun?" She asked.

Letting out a satisfied sigh, I replied, "Yea. I really did."

I didn't know that the next time I saw Lucian, the vow that I had made never to hate him, would be seriously called into question.

Lucian

I watched from the little alcove as my woman climbed into the van with the other witch, making sure she got away safely. It pained me to see her walk away from me, but it was not time to spill everything yet. I needed her to promise me that no matter what I did or what she found out about me, nothing would change between us.

I hoped that it would make us stronger, knowing that she didn't have to keep her magic a secret from me. But time would tell; I just hoped that those old hags at the coven were not filling her head with bullshit about lycans that would turn her against me. It's true what I had told her, I couldn't have children of my own. Robert had stolen that privilege from me when he'd turned me. We were all infertile, every single lycan; the only way of creating new life was to turn someone, and even that wasn't guaranteed. Most men transitioned successfully unless they were already weak and frail. Some women were turned, but that was full of uncertainty, their figures were not as sturdy as a males, and their body and organs normally gave out from stress, unable to make the full transformation; a lot of them died mid-change, a grotesque mix of human and lycan that had to be disposed of before the humans found it.

It wasn't easy getting rid of a lycan. I'd had to clean up so many of Jacob's messes over the years, but I had never been able to get him alone. I knew where they resided, but I was one man against the whole pack. What good would I do?

For years I had hounded Robert - begged him even - to sort out the mess that he had made; but he was too busy wallowing in his own self-inflicted misery, lamenting over his wife's death. Even now, hundreds of years later, he still blamed himself, and so he hid away, ignoring the problems...or leaving me to deal with them. I hadn't spoken to him in years now, the fucking troglodyte would not get a damn phone, he didn't even have phone signal where he lived. I had to write him letters the old fashioned way. This was the legacy that Robert had left me with, all of those years of friendship, and I was now his fucking clean up crew.

The kids were the worst. One of the women that Jacob had successfully turned hadn't been able to accept her new barren existence, and so every few years she would try and turn a child in her quest to be a mother. They *never* survived. She would steal them from their homes and bite them, knowing that she was subjecting them to hours of pain and torture as their little bodies tried to shift for the first time, their bones breaking over and over until their hearts stopped.

I remember the first time I found one, a little boy about four years old. His face had frozen for eternity with fear etched across his features, his nose and jaw was elongated enough to see that his death had not been merciful; his fingers were bent at awkward angles as they tried to arrange themselves into some semblance of paws.

Tears had stained his face.

I had dropped to my knees before him and cradled his tiny broken body against my chest, and cried for his lost life.
And for mine.
Finding the bodies of the women didn't phase me anymore, especially because I knew so many of them sought Jacob out hoping for eternal life. But finding the children never got easier.

     As the van holding my future sped off, I could feel eyes on me and the hair on the back of my neck stood on end. I stepped out of the nook, looking around frantically for the source of my unease.
"Fuck!" I shouted out, loud enough for the passersby to get scared and run from me, and loud enough for Jacob's attack dog to hear me from across the road. He had seen her, he'd spotted Zoe getting into the van, I couldn't risk him being able to track her from here. Crossing the road, causing cars to slam their brakes on, I sprinted towards him. His manic grin telling me that he'll enjoy the chase.
Jacob must really be desperate if he let that psycho, Ty, out. I couldn't let him get away. It was about time I put this mutt down for good.
I tracked him down roads and alleys, his deranged laughter mocking me for not catching him yet.
But I was older and faster than him and I didn't *want* to catch him yet, I wanted him to run somewhere that humans would not see or hear us. And I knew he would lead me somewhere appropriate for what I wanted to do with him, he was too proud, too stupid to try and escape. His animal instincts had always been at the forefront, leading him to make choices that a smart man would not.
As a beast, he would only be trying to make a kill.
As a man, I would be protecting what was mine. And I had made sure over the centuries that my humanity always stayed front and centre in my mind, never allowing my lycan side to hold the reins. That would be devastating for all who crossed my path.
I followed him to a scrap yard with old cars crushed and stacked on top of each other. The idiot probably thought this was the best place for him to ambush me. What he didn't know was that I

had every intention of walking out of this place without a scratch - and with his head.

And I always got what I wanted.

Moving around the side of a stack, I stripped and carefully laid my clothes and shoes on a crate conveniently placed for me to rest them on.

Then I shifted, it always hurt, but I was used to it by now. My calves broke first, bending backwards and sending me to my knees, my fingers retracted and my nails lengthened forming powerful black claws.; My jaw broke and reformed around a muzzle; each of my human teeth were pushed out by rapidly growing fangs and I spat them, and a wad of blood, on the ground before me; my ears lengthened and my eyes sharpened, heightening my senses, they were already highly sensitive in my human form but as a lycan, I could scent my prey from a mile away.

Ty was in the process of shifting too, I could smell the blood and hear the crack of his bones from beside the derelict office of the scrap yard. Shaking my thick midnight coloured fur and flexing my muscles, I reorientated myself in my new form. I kept my claws retracted so they didn't make any grating noises on the dirt floor, and I silently tracked my prey.

He was only half way through his shift when I saw him on his hands and knees, he was a lazy wolf, never training his body; relying on his love of weak victims to make him feel strong.

I'm not ashamed to admit that I came up behind him, attacking from where he could not see me coming; he did not deserve an honourable fight. Flexing my powerful hind legs, I pounced on his back, digging my unsheathed claws into his shoulders and dropping him flat on his front. My teeth sunk into the back of his neck, and biting down I shook him side to side, growling my pleasure at the taste of his blood on my tongue.

I could feel him try to finish his shift beneath me, his fur growing to replace his human flesh, but it was too late for him. I had him in my grasp and I wouldn't let him go.

I scored my fore claws down his back, ripping ribbons of skin and fur, and feeling the slick blood splash over my paws. My attack was weakening him, I could feel the fight starting to leave him as he lost more blood, but this would only render him unconscious. For him to truly die, I needed to take his head or his heart.

But I was greedy, so I'd take both.

Thrashing my head from side to side, I bit down harder trying to sever the muscles and tendons. Pinning my whole weight on top of him, I used my paws to hold him still as I pulled my jaws upwards; feeling the neck start to give way, I heard the tearing and the 'slurp' of his neck starting to pull apart; putting all of my considerable weight behind my pull, I yanked and fell back with his neck still held firmly between my fangs, his head separated from the rest of his body.

His arms and legs were still twitching and his body hadn't yet got the memo that it was dead, as it tried to complete the partial shift.

If you've ever seen a dead body on TV, all clean and peaceful looking, this is nothing like that. As the lycan's death throes ended, his muscles relaxed, falling completely lifeless; all of his bodily functions ceased working, and his bladder and bowels emptied themselves.

This was the part they never spoke about. The side of death that reeked of shit.

Dropping the head on the ground, I shifted to my human form as I needed the use of my hands for the next part. Standing naked next to my kill, I felt the blood on my human skin start to cool. I took a deep breath, not really overexerted, that had been an easy kill, he hadn't been expecting me to be able to shift that quickly; my speed and stealth had always been one of my advantages. Pushing the body onto its back, I released my claws and stuck them into his chest, gouging through flesh and bone until I had my prize. Pulling the warm organ from his chest cavity, I held the heart in one bloody hand. I wrapped it in Ty's shirt that was left in tatters on the dusty ground, and walked to my own clothes to get dressed.

Most of these places kept canisters of gas that they had removed from the vehicles before being crushed, so after searching around the yard, I found four containers holding the fuel. Pouring it all over the body and surrounding area, I used a lighter that I kept in my pocket to set fire to the remains, knowing that before anyone came here to check out the inferno, his body would be so unrecognisable, and his blood completely burnt away, that they wouldn't be able to tell what it was.

Stuffing my hands - and the wrapped heart - in my pockets so no-one could see the blood stains, I walked back to where my vehicle was parked and drove to the hotel I was staying in. I needed to call Zoe and check that she was ok, and that they had made it back to the house, then shower and change. I couldn't risk going back to the coven tonight to watch over her, it was unlikely that there was someone else watching me, but it was a risk I was unwilling to take. And Jacob would be angry that his little soldier had failed, and so easily too; he would be getting a nice little package in the post soon enough.

CHAPTER 10

Zoe

      We hadn't even parked and got out of the van before Agnes had thrown the door wide open and was storming down the stone steps towards us. "Where have you been? You have been gone for hours, don't you have any concern for your own welfare?"
"Woah. Excuse me? Who the hell do you think you're speaking to?" She may have been the reason we were saved from the lycans initially, but that didn't give her the right to speak to me, or anyone, that way. "I am not one of your witches, I am not your prisoner. I'm an adult capable of making my own *fucking* decisions," I ranted, "and while I'm on the subject, my family are not your personal *fucking* slaves." She flinched every time I swore, "Starting right fucking now, they do not clean up after you, wash your shit, or anything else you have them doing."
I had had a good day, and she thought she could ruin it by acting like she had some hold over me.
An audience was building after hearing my yelling, and some of the Hecate witches in their pyjamas were watching the show. Lissa and Nate were not trying to be discreet at all, and were standing right behind the high priestess as she squirmed under my anger.
"We don't have to stay here, we have other places we can go…"
"And just where exactly will you go? Can you be so sure that you will be safe without my wards to keep the beasts at bay?"
"Like I can't make my own wards," peeling my bandage off, I picked at the scab that had formed over my cut.
"No wait!" She cried out, her arm stretched towards me, "No need for that, I believe you, but isn't it better being here amongst your own kind?"

"Them girls have made it perfectly clear that I'm not 'their kind', they ignore me and let's face it, you're all scared of what I can do, that's why you've barred me from the casting rooms" my anger was vanishing as quickly as it had arrived, leaving me feeling tired and annoyed that she dare question my whereabouts in the first place.

I was going to be a mum soon, and I knew that if I stayed here when the baby was born, she would make my life a nightmare. "I don't think this is going to work out for all of us in the long term," I explained.

"What do you mean child?"

"I mean, that we have somewhere else to stay, we will stay for a few days while I get my new place sorted, and then we're gone." Lissa and Nate looked confused at my announcement, they didn't know about my agreement with Lucian yet. The agreement that I just moved forward by a few months.

But the more I stayed here, the less safe I felt, and I knew that I should trust my gut on this one, that I could trust Luc more than the people here; but for once I'd wanted to be around people who were like me, who could teach me about...being me.

Her face slid into its usual stoic mask, the face she wore when she didn't want people to see what she was really thinking. "I think you are making a terrible mistake that you will come to regret."

"I don't think I will, and I hope we don't end on bad terms Agnes; I would like to continue visiting the coven to practise my magic, and I think the best place to learn about my powers is here, unless you'd ban me from here too?"

"You and the baby are welcome here for as long as you want." She smiled at me, but it was as fake as her welcome; and I didn't know what she was after, but I knew she wanted something from me.

"And just so we're clear, you've done your research on me, so you know where I came from?" I explained, "I did not raise myself in a shitty council estate where I didn't take crap from anyone, to come here and take all of your shit."

"I have done nothing except take care of you since you got here, you're being ungrateful." She scolded.

"Ungrateful? What are you really after Agnes? Hmmm? Why is it that you're adamant I have to stay here? Let's stop with all the bullshit now. What do you want from me?"

She looked offended, and I wondered if I had her all wrong? "How dare you." She sniffed, "My kind have always aided yours, we were the ones you came to for potions and ingredients while your ancestors hid in the woods, scared that they may be found out." She wiped a tear from her eye, "When your people were wiped out, we mourned you, and now you're here..." sobs and sniffles rang out as she covered her face in despair.

Ok, now I felt bad that I'd made the old bird cry. CJ ran out and wrapped her arm around Agnes' shoulders, leading her back into the house, away from me, glaring at me from over her own shoulder while whispering sweet nothings to the old witch.

I decided then that there was nothing else I would rather do than leave this damn place, I was sick of being followed everywhere I go; if it wasn't Rosie playing babysitter then I had the little mousy girl that would follow me about all day with her little beady eyes watching me through her lank, brown hair. Like, she must have thought that if she covered part of her face with her greasy hair then she would become invisible? Did she think it was a spell? Because if it was, then clearly she was doing something wrong. I was tired of walking out of my room to use the bathroom and she would be standing at the other end of the corridor, peeking at me from behind the corner. Bloody weirdo. Either way, I couldn't even take a shit in peace without Stuart Little trying to eye-ball me.

And now I was being questioned on my whereabouts too? Nope. I was done!

"Well that was fun." Lissa shouted out.

"Pffft, that was a train wreck."

She waved away my discomfort at having made Agnes cry, "don't worry about her, I bet she'll be back to her normal solemn self by morning." She grabbed my hand and dragged me inside, away from prying ears and little brothers who may be grossed out by girly conversation, "tell me, how was it?"

I grinned, my cheeks actually hurt from smiling so much, "so good." I sighed in appreciation, thinking about that kiss.

"Sooo, where are we moving too?" Lissa asked.
I waited for Nate to catch up with us, where we immediately locked ourselves in our room. "We're staying with Lucian, he offered us a place, and well...I accepted."
"And who is Lucian?" Nate had sat himself on his bed, his elbows resting on his knees, staring straight at me. "How long have you known him? Where is his place?"
I shared a look with Lissa, because I knew my untrusting, worrisome brother would not like my answers. "He's someone I've been seeing, he's nice and he wants to be part of our lives; ours...and the baby."
"You didn't answer how long you've known him for. Why have I never heard of him before now? He questioned.
I...I met him at work," I paused, and braced for the inevitable fallout. "Last week."
He jumped up, his eyes wide with shock, "are you bloody crazy?"
"Calm down and let me explain, just..."
"Calm down? CALM DOWN!, you've known him a WEEK! And you want us to go and live with him?" His arms were doing the talking for him now too, waving in the air while he was on his mini rant.
"To be fair, we didn't even know these women five minutes before we moved in with them." Lissa piped up, and she made a valid point that I hoped Nathan would listen to.
"That's different Lissa, this is different." He started.
"No it's not babe." she put her hand up to halt his next words, "your sister has always done what's best for you, if she thinks this is it, then you need to listen to her. Now quit the attitude."
His shoulders sank in his defeat, and he turned to me with an apology in his eyes, but I didn't need it; I offered him a smile and he took that as acceptance that I was ok with his semi-tantrum.
"Besides," Lissa carried on, "if she wants to go out and fall in love, who are you to stop her."
"Love?" My whole body jolted at that word, because that wasn't what this was. "I don't love him, I've known him for a week!"
Nate smirked at me like he'd won some kind of argument, "I don't love him Liss. I like him, there's a difference."

"Then why are we packing everything up to go and live with him?"

"You and I both know that that insta-love crap only happens in romance novels - this is reality. Could I love him in the future, yea...I really think I could. I think this could be big. But not yet."

"Then explain to me why we're leaving the safest place for us - for you. A place you can learn about your past." She argued. Her hands were firmly planted on her hips so I knew she meant business.

"You'd have to meet him to understand, but I feel safe with him, like there's this...connection between us; I feel it every time I see him and when I hear his voice, I get butterflies. I just feel that I should be there with him." I sat on my own bed facing both of them, "when I left him today, I felt like I was leaving a piece of myself behind..."

I heard gagging from Nate's side, "Shut-up loser." Throwing my pillow at his head, I continued trying to explain why us uprooting our lives - again - was the best decision. "I mean, I didn't want to leave him, and I knew that being next to him, I felt invincible. Being here is like...trying to fit a square peg into a round hole, I just don't fit. But with Lucian, everything just falls into place." I looked at them to gauge their reactions, they weren't shouting at me so that was a plus. "Do you think it's insane?" I asked them

I had expected Lissa's words of wisdom, but it was Nate that put my mind at ease.

"This whole thing is insane, my sister is a witch, she's being hunted by shape-shifter things that want to eat her and oh, she's descended from a goddess...you telling me that you fancy a guy after a week and going to move in with him, I suppose it's not so crazy after all."

I threw my arms around him, thanking him over and over, because if they'd said they wouldn't go, then I wouldn't go either. We're a team - a family - and we stick together always, just like we've always done.

"Ok, I'm gonna call Luc and ask him." I pulled my phone from my bag.

"What do you mean *'ask'* him? I thought he knew we were moving in?" Questioned Lissa.
"Ah yea, about that, well...I said I'd move in with him...in seven months, not yet."
I grinned at them, because they'd agreed now, there was no take-backs. "Go and make yourself useful and give me privacy for my phone call."
Both of them left the room grumbling about crazy sisters and bossy women. Flicking to Lucian's name, I hit the 'call' button and listened to it ring, waiting for him to answer.
"Zoe? Are you ok? The baby?" His voice was low and slightly out of breath, like he'd been running.
"I'm fine. We're fine. Are you ok? You sound...like I interrupted something."
"No, beautiful. I was just taking out the rubbish."
"Ok, well I have something to tell you - or ask you rather." I started, "I know we had a deadline of seven months, but..." My mouth was dry, I don't know why I was so nervous, we'd agreed on this earlier; I swallowed the spit in my mouth, feeling it slide down my throat like razor blades.
"You can ask me anything, you know that." He professed.
"Can we move into yours now instead of in seven months I promise we're all house trained." I figured spewing it all out in one go was the better option, now it was out to him, I just had to wait for his response. And it felt like it took longer than it should have. It was silent on the other end, and I had to check I hadn't accidentally ended the call. "Lucian? Are you still there?"
"What changed your mind?" He enquired.
"If it's a problem then we'll wait, I just thought that..."
"No!" he interrupted. "Stay. I had thought you wanted to wait to get to know me first, what changed? Not that I'm unhappy you changed your mind."
"Our living situation is slightly...precarious. We can't stay here anymore, and we have nowhere else to go, and well...You said that we had a place with you...if we wanted?"

Lucian

      I had forgotten how much hard work it was getting rid of a body - especially a lycan one. Their bones were thicker than the average human, made more dense to account for all of the shifting back and forth to support our unnatural forms. The fire had burned through enough flesh and fur that I could dispose of the rest of it a bit easier, but that still meant dismembering the remains and burying the evidence.

I wasn't staying at my normal residence where I could just dig a hole on my land and shove him in without worrying that it would be found by humans, so I'd had to improvise.

What was left of Ty was now buried at Streatham Park cemetery, hidden inside a burial plot that had yet to be filled in. I'd been lucky that time to find the recent burial, although it probably was not very lucky for the poor soul that now had to share his grave with a psychopath for generations.

But it was not like he could argue.

I just needed to be better prepared next time.

I had let Zoe and the baby fill my thoughts too much, and Jacob had gotten even more bold in sending Ty out. I needed to be extra vigilant if I wanted to keep them safe.

That's why I was in the hotel in the first place, it was just a coincidence that I was in London at the time I felt Zoe's call - or maybe it was fate after all.

I was initially just having the appliances and electrics updated in the old house, but when I had asked her to move in with me, I called my contractor immediately to make everything child-friendly, and to create a nursery that every parent would be envious of.

Of course, I also needed a safe room for Zoe to practise her magic - if she chose to use it.

That's why everything was taking so long and I was stuck living out of a suitcase. No matter how luxurious this place was, I wanted to be home; being away for so long was making me antsy to be back on my own land and behind the safety of my borders where I could better protect my new family.

The vibrating of my phone in my pocket brought my thoughts back to the present as I ran up the stairs to my hotel room - it was too risky taking the lift, in case nosey people saw the state of my clothes. I didn't know how I would explain away the blood and smell of burnt dog. Seeing Zoe's name on the screen had me worried that I was too late and something had happened to her...to the child that I longed for with every fibre of my being.

Fumbling with the small contraption in my hands, I quickly brought it to my ear, "Zoe? Are you ok? The baby?"

Hearing that they were both safe settled my nerves. But that she wanted to move in earlier was a surprise. My heart beat quicker in my chest knowing that I could have her here in a matter of days; I looked around me at the hotel room that I was currently calling my home, housekeeping kept it clean and tidy, but I was a mess, and there were some books that I would have to hide. I had wanted her trust, clearly the witches had ruined their chances with her - now it was my turn.

"You said that we had a place with you...if we wanted."

"When should I pick you up?" I told her firmly. I could get them another room for now, although I hoped that she would want to stay in my room with me. That kiss was on constant replay in my mind, and I had to keep adjusting my length in my trousers, tucking my hard-on in the waistband of my slacks to keep it from rubbing against the material when I walked - it was fucking uncomfortable.

"A couple of days maybe? We need to pack our stuff plus also it's quite late and I don't want to bother you, you sounded busy?" Her hesitancy had gone, and in its place her natural inquisitiveness took over.

"You don't have to fish for information from me mo ghràidh. Ever." I told her, "what's mine is yours now, always." Except for a few minor little details.

"If we're going to try this out, then you need to know that I won't accept anything less than complete commitment. There can't be any other woman except me...and your mum. That's it. I've been cheated on before, and it's pointless, if you want to be with another woman and you decide you don't want me anymore fine, but if you're gonna be a part of this baby's life then you need to understand that I won't have any other woman around my child." She paused to catch her breath, "Just be honest Lucian, I can take it."

"You got all of this because I answered the phone out of breath and you thought I was with another woman?" I growled.

How could she possibly think I would even want another woman after seeing her. Kissing her. Did she think I reacted like that to every woman who crossed my path? It had been years since I had taken a lover, and even then it was only to scratch an itch; it wasn't to form any kind of connection, I couldn't even remember her face. "Beautiful girl, you are all I think about, no-one could compare to the fire you hold inside, no other female could make me burn the way you do, and I can not wait until you are here with me so that I can taste you again. And this time I will not be stopped by some scrawny little servant in a pinny." Her laughter on the other end of the phone caused my own smile to form, and I wondered if it would always be this way, that just the sound of her laughter could ease me, and fill me with happiness - I hoped so. "Although, you may wish that someone would interrupt us, because I do not plan on stopping once I have you beneath me. I'll have you begging me to give your sweet little pussy a rest." Her sharp inhale let me know that she was just as affected as me, and I laughed out loud. This must be a new record, I have not laughed this much in so long.

"How about tomorrow?"

"You want us to move in tomorrow? She replied.

"Why not? You have already committed to moving in, no take-backs allowed my sweet Zoe."

"Okay, tomorrow. Let's do it."

I sighed in relief; tomorrow she would be mine, and then no-one would ever be able to take her from me.

Zoe

His sweet talk soon turned into dirty words, and with it my imagination went into overdrive, I was pretty sure my knickers were now soaked, and I wasn't really in a position to do anything about it, especially because I shared a room.

"That's another thing, where will we all sleep?" I asked, "because you know my brother and best friend are coming with me."

"Of course they are, I wouldn't have it any other way," he replied. "I'm currently staying in a hotel. I hope that's ok with you? It will not be for much longer. I am having some...renovations done on my house that should be ready shortly, and then we can move there. I will book them a room, pick you up tomorrow morning and bring you here to get settled; I'm sure your family can make use of the facilities while we get to know each other better."

"You don't have to pay for our rooms, we can book one, just tell me where you're staying and I'll call them." I wouldn't be starting this relationship with him paying for all of us. We had enough saved up between us to stay for a couple of weeks, although I hoped it wouldn't be that long, I wanted to save some of my money to get the baby some bits.

"You are my guests darling, I would not have you pay to stay with me here, especially when I have asked you to live with me." he explained, "if my house was ready, then we would not even be here."

"Alright, how about you pay for one week and we pay for the other week?" I bartered.

"Unacceptable."

"Well you don't really have much of a choice buddy, you want me to come there, that means you don't get to make these types of decisions for me. I'm used to paying for myself, and I will not be reliant on you or anyone to pay our way." I told him, "I need to be financially independent, Lucian, I want...no, I *need* to work." I told him, "Once the baby is born and old enough, I'll find a job to help pay my way." He was silent on the other end, I hoped he wasn't angry with the fact that I wanted to do things my way but, well...tough. I had been taking care of myself and Nathan for years now, I wouldn't stop just because I had a sugar daddy who wanted to pay my way.

"Ok Zoe, You can book for one week." He said smugly, "I'm staying at the Shangri La."

"You're an arshole." I scolded, his laughter sounded through the phone, "you know full well I can't even afford one damn night in that place, let alone a week. I thought you were in a Travel Lodge or something, but noooo, you're in the damn Shangri La, London's most luxurious hotel"

"Listen to me darling. I have...my family rather...have spent many years making money on the housing market; I couldn't spend all of it in one lifetime if I tried."

Wow. I knew he had money but I never expected that level of wealth - and I didn't know how to feel about it.

"Let me take care of you Zoe," he continued, "let someone finally carry the burden for you, and you concentrate on staying healthy."

That part was definitely right. I needed to focus on staying sane and safe, especially now I was in this weird-ars predicament with wolf-men chasing me. And a hotel of that calibre would definitely have the best security. "Let me speak to my family about the hotel, I'm not sure how they will feel about you putting us up, can I call you back?"

"Call me anytime, I'll be waiting." He replied. The phone went dead, and I realised he had actually meant for me to go and ask them *right now* and call him straight back.

I pulled the door of my room open, only to find my nosey people shoving at each other to move away from the door.

"Were you listening to my conversation?"

They both pointed, each blaming the other, "he started it."

"What? She had her ear to the door and everything. Even tried to find a glass to hear through the door better." Replied Nate indignantly.

"You're such a snitch!" Cried Lissa.

"You started it, blaming me and I didn't even do anything, I was just following you."

"Yea well, snitches get stitches mister."

"Yea? And skanks get shanked."

Her screech pierced my ears as she tried to slap him around the head, but he was too tall to reach, they kind of reminded me a bit of that old cartoon Pinky and the Brain, where Brain was always hitting the dimwitted one. Groaning and rubbing the skin between my eyebrows to stave off a coming headache, I tried to get them to stop. Man, parenting was hard work. "Children." I called out, but they kept on trying to hit each other in this silly slap fight where their hands were flapping about in each other's general direction. "*Children!*" I yelled, "Jesus Christ, pack it in." They turned around to face me, still sending glares each other's way, they were acting like five year olds. I didn't care that they had heard my conversation really, it saved me time having to relay the information to them, what I couldn't take was this stupid behaviour, especially from Lissa, she was old enough to know better - although sometimes I wondered if she was mentally still a teenager with the way she often acted.

"Both of you." I pointed to the room with the sternest expression on my face that I could muster, "get inside now."

They filed in and sat opposite each other, which was good since I didn't really trust them right now to sit next to each other. "I'm assuming then that you heard what I was speaking to Lucian about."

Their faces cleared of their annoyance, replaced with some fake innocence; they both shook their heads, denying that they had heard anything, that the walls were really thick. Nathan even tried to say that Lissa was breathing too loudly to hear anything. Such lame excuses.

"Guys, it's ok if you heard, I needed to talk to you about it anyway."

"You mean about the hotel stay?" asked Nathan.

Didn't hear my conversation huh! I side-eyed him and he flushed with embarrassment, giving me this sheepish smile because he knew he had just admitted to spying on me; Liss just covered her face with a palm.

"Yes I mean about the hotel stay." I sat next to my brother and looked at both of them, "I'm not sure how I feel about staying somewhere that...extravagant. We can't afford that place guys and I don't want...

"We're in." they shouted together.

"What?"

"We wanna stay at the posh hotel sis."

"Lucian would be paying, you know that right?" I looked at them both, but they each had excited grins on their faces.

"Cool, let him pay, he obviously really wants to take care of you Zo." Said Lissa.

"Yea Zo," started Nate, he took my hand in his large one, "people like us don't get to stay in places like that. Ever. Please can we go?" He begged.

Lissa's hands came up in prayer form, and she waved them in my face, "Pretty please with sugar on top, call your man and tell him we'll be there with bells on."

"Looks like you've both made up your mind, I'll call him now and give him the news." I told them, "but you can't act the way you did out there when we arrive; both of you better be on your best behaviour, otherwise I'm kicking you out myself."

They made the sign of the cross over their hearts, and I sighed, hoping that they actually meant it, "and no tricks from you Lissa."

Shock covered her face, her hand flew to her chest in mock outrage, "me? Play tricks? Never!"

Tutting at her theatrics, because I knew it was her who had ordered three dozen extra large glittery dildos to be delivered in place of the herbs that should have turned up today. I'm pretty sure the girl who signed for the order almost had a heart attack when she opened the boxes.

"I just wanted them all to relax a little bit," she announced, "they're always so uptight here."

We all cackled, because she was right, they could all use some good dick around here. Maybe I should get Lissa to order them some clitter bombs next.

"Right, since we have this all sorted, let's go and tell Miss Trunchbull that we're outta here tomorrow." I declared.

Traversing the hallways at the coven had always been interesting; they were lined with photos and portraits of the past and present. Some of them were clearly old - oil paintings of dames and sepia toned faces stared solemnly along the halls at the newest recruits. Some had names and titles embossed in gold underneath stating their lineage, of course, they were all the families of the current ruling-class; the elite of the Hecate line.

There were so many pictures of Agnes, she had looked different back then, an unlined, smiling visage posing in front of the manor, her arms linked with others in their matching polo shirts and knee length skirts. She was easy to spot amongst the other smiling faces - always in the middle, the tallest, the prettiest - and her hair was exactly the same style.

I looked at each one as we made our way to find the high priestess. The matching mahogany frames of each image lined up perfectly along the halls and up the stairway, taking up every available inch.

Generations of women watched the comings and goings of the current cohort.

It was freaky as shit!

One photo made me pause my perusal. Another photo of Agnes, she looked to be in her early forties in this one, with one other woman. A pretty petite - very pregnant - brunette was hugged to the woman's side, her arm wrapped around Agnes' waist. I don't even know why this picture made me stop in my tracks, but the woman looked familiar, like I'd seen her somewhere before; I stared hard at her face, hoping that it would ring a bell and I would remember where I had met her but there was nothing. She was pretty in a cute, girl-next-door way, her dark hair was long and straight. The photographer had caught her picture when the breeze had blown her hair forwards, her long tresses wrapping around her sides and partially obscuring one eye. She was smiling as the hand not wrapped around Agnes tried to brush it aside, frozen in the air and reaching for the mess of wind-swept locks .

She looked happy, her joy immortalised in the photo.

"Come on slow coach." Called Lissa, who was already at the top of the stairs looking down at me. I hurried up my steps to catch up, and silently thought that somewhere, I hoped that woman was still as happy as she was in the photo.

As I walked up the rest of the stairs, two acolytes were walking down. They looked at me with narrow eyes, distrust evident on their faces. As they moved swiftly passed me, they began whispering behind their hands at each other - obviously about me. It was the same everywhere I went around here, even when I

left my room earlier, all the women I saw glared at me or whispered to each other, like I couldn't hear what they were saying. And it was the same thing over and over, *"there's the blood witch, thinking she owns the place." "That's her, I thought she'd be prettier, can't she magic herself up a new face."* Yea, she actually said that. Rolling my eyes at the stupidity of ignorant children, I caught up with my BeeBee, who has told me repeatedly that they only act this way towards me because they're jealous that their power is so weak.
I just think they're all cunts.

    We paused at the door to where the newbies practised their incantations, and knocked. And waited. But they must not have been able to hear us. Lissa leaned over me and knocked hard with the side of her fist - still nothing. Trying the handle, the door swung open easily, and a waft of incense stung my nose. It's acrid smell made my eyes water and when I breathed through my mouth, it felt like the taste had pasted itself to the back of my tongue, leaving a bitter tang behind. Nate's big hand waved in front of my face trying to dispel the horrible stench as we walked in. The smoke from multiple burners clung to the walls and ceiling, its writhing tendrils like swaying cobwebs.
Nathan stopped beside me, pinching his nose and rubbing his watering eyes, "Oh my god, it stinks like Gwyneth Paltrow's vagina in 'ere."
"How do you know what Gwyneth Paltrow's vagina smells like?" I questioned.
"Um," Lissa started, "How do you know what *vagina* smells like?"
His flushed face turned to Lissa, and with the straightest face, he replied, "your mum."
Laughter bubbled out of me, and Lissa's followed.
"That was a good one, very funny." she chuckled.
"No, I'm being serious." He grimaced, "your mum came over about a year ago and gave me a massive bag of condoms, and started telling me the whole 'birds and the bees' talk and what STD's did to you, *then,"* he stressed, "she gave me that candle that Gwyneth made called 'This Smells Like My Vagina' and told me if it smells this bad, don't touch it."

Holding on to Lissa to stop myself from falling over, we cried with laughter, tears streamed down my face, a combination of that wretched stink and hilarity. That really sounded like something Sarah would do in her blunt, straight forward way; just imagining Nate's horrified face when she gave him The Talk made me feel grateful and horrible in equal measure. He should have had his mum to do those things for him, not some shitty drunk foster mum who still hadn't noticed we had left, she hadn't even tried contacting us.

And just like that, my mood soured.

I only hoped I was half as good a mum as Sarah was to Lissa - and us. And if I had a son, I was gonna damn well buy him a vagina candle too!

Our hysterics had apparently disturbed the chanting because now all eyes were on us, with Cunty-Jade's scowl aimed right at me. I put on my best smile and aimed it right back at her, "is Agnes here?" I asked sweetly.

Her resting bitch face wasn't something new to me, and I wouldn't let it bother me either, but maybe someone should let her know that if the wind changed, then her face would stay like that.

"What can I do for you Zoe?" Agnes asked as she stepped forward from the edge of the room; I hadn't seen her initially, the vapour hiding her from view. But now she walked through the smoke like a wraith, her pale suit blending in with the fumes to make it look like she had just appeared out of nowhere.

The foggy air dissipated as she waved her hand and whispered *"Patet"*, the air swirled around her to lift up to the ceiling so that her way was clear; her magic blowing the rest of the vapour away to clear the room. Which left us standing in front of the door, and the occupants of the room - Agnes, CJ and some trainees - to stare back at us.

"You have interrupted an important session, it better be important." snapped CJ.

I ignored her, because I called her Cunty Jade for a reason. "Could I speak to you privately, Agnes?"

"Well, as Jade has just told you, this is a very important time for the younger witches, and we must get back to their test." she declared, "so best not to keep us all waiting. Tell me here and then we can continue...unless you *want* them to fail their Incant assessment?"

The younger girls looked at me suspiciously, like I'd deliberately disturbed them; there really wasn't anything I could do here to make people think better of me. There seemed to be a stigma attached to my bloodline, and only the negative aspects were looked upon. They didn't see *me*, Zoe Ward - just what I could do. And I didn't even really know what that was, no-one would teach me anything. Yea, they told me about my lineage, about the massacre, what the blood witches were like. But did they *show* me? Like fuck did they!

I know I've only been here a few days - even though it feels like weeks - but I was gonna do some of my own research; I had no idea how I would do that, especially if Agnes wouldn't even let me read her precious books, but I would find my way...eventually.

"Just tell her now." Lissa's whispered words in my ear reminded me what I had come here for.

"We're leaving in the morning." I stated, "we don't want to take up any more of your time."

Her eyes widened comically, "leave? And go where?" she scoffed, " Jacob is still looking for you, do not be silly girl."

I shared a look with my family standing to each side of me, and they both wore similar faces of confusion. Did she not remember me telling her yesterday that I was leaving?

"I told you that I had somewhere else to go..." "Pfft." she interrupted, "And just who else will put you and your...friends up?"

"Family. They're my family." I argued, "And we have already found somewhere to stay." I took a deep breath to calm myself down, it wouldn't help losing my temper with her. Besides, I still wanted access to her library, so this meant playing nice with her.

"I heard she had a new boyfriend." Snickered Jade.

I glanced at her smirking face, obviously Rosie had been talking. "And does he know that you carry another man's child?" quizzed Agnes.

"She probably won't tell him." Jade spat, "she will spread her legs for him and then let him think it's his."

Snickers from around the room assaulted my ears, and Agnes just stood there with her usual stoic mask on neither denying it nor shutting them up.

I had thought at the back of my mind that she wanted me here for a reason, and although I hadn't figured out that reason yet, I had come to realise that she liked me about as much as everyone else in this place - which was on the 'barely tolerated' list.

I swear I could feel Lissa's and Nate's rage beside me, the tension was palpable; I held my hand up in the universal sign for 'wait', asking them to hold back and let me deal with this.

    I stepped towards the priestess and her lackey until there was just breathing distance between us. It pleased me that they both had to look up to make eye contact with me. Satisfaction filled me knowing that they were uncomfortable right now; I could see the wariness in their eyes as they watched me. "My child is not your business." I kept my voice low but I knew it would carry around the room to the other girls who were watching with avid interest. It was good that they were listening, they could pass the message on to everyone else in the coven. "My personal life and who I fuck is not your business." Agnes flinched at my crudeness. "Where I live is not your business." and with each item I listed to my audience, I grew more resolute. I didn't need these women, I didn't need their animosity or hatred or distrust. They could keep their little parlour tricks with their ignorance and shove it up their tight arses.

I knew in my mind that I was stronger than everyone here, their reactions proved it even if I hadn't felt my magic grow within me with each passing day. That spark, that little speck of light that I had always felt inside me had been a warming balm these past few days, since the party on Saturday night when all of this shit had started; that speck had grown and spread throughout my body, a constant reminder of my power and my new position in this life.

"You can be a participant in my life and help me grow into the witch that I want to be...into what I should be, or I will leave in the morning and you'll never hear from any of us again. It's your choice." I laid out my ultimatum to Agnes, already sure of what her answer would be.

I knew she didn't want *me* here, she wanted my magic and what prestige it would bring her should the other covens find out she had a blood witch on tap.

Having Nate spend his time in the kitchens had been really handy, turns out the old cook likes to talk...a lot.

What was once the most prestigious school for aspiring witches in the UK, was slowly dwindling to nothing. They had been losing sponsors for a while apparently, and barely had enough money to keep the place afloat. Girls didn't wanna come to soggy old England when the newer, more modern Academy had opened up ten years ago in sunny California.

Parents were paying to send their daughters to America to practise under a high priestess who still practised the art of Sashiat - or seduction.

Agnes had found this practise 'distasteful', and had banned everything to do with sex magic.

But the Californian school was thriving, one of their graduates was apparently in power in the White House; her skills of seduction had allowed her to wheedle her way in where she - and her coven - now had the ear of the president.

That, if you ask me, was forward thinking. Agnes had prohibited so many of the spells that the women could have used to help elevate their status in societies, in positions of power where they could use their voices to make change; but clearly Agnes had other plans for the future of the coven here, and no one knew those plans but her.

But my chatty little chef hadn't stopped there.

Agnes wanted me here to gather new recruits, she wanted me to help train them, and eventually, my daughter would help too.

So, I knew that she only wanted me here for my magic and what my title could do for her, but my child would not be her tool to help get her foot back on the proverbial ladder.

I watched her as she considered all of her avenues, I envisioned all of the cogs in her mind turning around and around trying to find the route that would benefit her the most.

Her gaze wandered down my body, and I instinctively placed my hands on my still-flat stomach. Narrowed eyes turned to me, and she must have made her decision.

"Despite what you may think of me, I have always done what is best for this coven and all of my girls here." She started, "you seem to have come to the conclusion that you are not included in my best intentions, and that I have some ulterior motive for trying to keep you here."

I didn't want to get the cook in trouble for talking about things she shouldn't, so I didn't mention how I knew the things that I did, plus I didn't want the younger ones to worry that their beloved home was in trouble, so I didn't say anything that could cause issues amongst the masses. So I just hinted that I knew why she wanted me there, and I wouldn't play her games.

Her face didn't change at my knowledge of their financial ruin, but her hands, which were clasped in front of her, tightened enough that I could see her white knuckles; Jade looked confusedly at Agnes, clearly not important enough to be kept apprised of the coven's situation.

"What is it that you want Zoe?"

Ah see, now I was getting somewhere. She needed something from me...but I also wanted something from her. Win-win.

"Let's make a deal." I told her.

I felt Nate's hand curve over my shoulder and turn me to face him, "what are you doing Zo?" he whispered harshly.

I had kept this part from him, not deliberately, it was a plan I had been thinking up whilst walking here. A spur of the moment thing that actually made sense. I looked at my best friend, but we had known each other long enough that she knew what I was planning without even asking. Her head nodded in acceptance, and she pulled Nathan towards her gently.

"It's ok, just trust her." I heard her mutter softly to him.

"You want me to help you out here right?" I asked the high priestess.

Her head jerked once up and down, like she didn't want to admit it but that she had no choice. Her features were pinched with the knowledge that I currently held all the hands, and she clearly didn't like not being in control of the situation.

Things had turned on its side for her in a matter of minutes, and she came to the conclusion that she had to give me what I wanted if she wanted to - in her words - have everyone's best intentions at heart.

"I will help you out in the coven, and meet with other priestesses on your behalf; you can tell them all that you have a blood witch staying with you." Agnes' eyes glittered with triumph at the thought that she could rub her new status in everyone else's faces. "In return, I want complete unrestricted access to your libraries."

"Of course, you may read to your heart's content." Agreed Agnes, "but in return you will stay on the premises, and you will have all of the access you desire."

"No dude, I don't think you're understanding me." I huffed. "I'm still leaving tomorrow, I will visit two or three days in the week, depending on what I'm doing, and in return, you can use my face as your unofficial mascot or whatever."

She waited a breath before silently nodding her agreement, "This means I want access to your personal library too." I added.

Her mouth opened to dispute my demands, but she quickly closed it, she didn't have anything else to barter with.

"Very well. I agree to your terms. But you will not show up here willy-nilly. We will have an agreed upon schedule that you will keep to," she said, "we can rearrange any days you cannot make, so long as you give me notice. In return, I will make sure you have access to my personal collection at certain times of the day."

"Done."

"Good, I will arrange your first meeting with the southern coven. Lily will let you know when it is." Her hands relaxed by her sides, "if that is all, we must return to our lesson. The Autumn Equinox is coming upon us swiftly, and the girls must be prepared for the ceremony."

She turned her back, effectively dismissing me and walked towards the other end of the room, CJ following right behind.

I turned back to my people, giving the room my own back, and brushed my hands together. "Sorted." I told them.

CHAPTER 11

We stood in the forecourt of the huge property, our bags packed and waiting on the stairs for us. Lucian had said he would pick us up at ten AM, and - looking at my watch - it was five to ten now.
Agnes and her posse exited the front door and stood at the top of the stairs, the shade from the porch casting shadows across her face.
"Come to wave goodbye Aggie?" Said Lissa.
Her eyes shifted to my BeeBee, her glare as hard as stone, "do not ever call me that," barked Agnes. "Your boyfriend is not here yet."
"He said ten."
She looked at her own watch, and turned to Cunty-Jade, a small smirk lifted on the other woman's face.
"I told you he would have changed his mind. He clearly decided that taking on you, another man's spawn and your Null family was more hassle than it was worth."
"Null?" Questioned Nate.
"Yes, Null." confirmed CJ, "You...non-magic humans." She said this with a curled lip, like talking about people who didn't do magic were disgusting.
"You do realise..." started Nate, "that you're human too."
An unladylike snort left her like she couldn't believe Nate was speaking to her. Either that, or she thought she was more than human?
"It's bang on ten o'clock." I heard stated from a voice above me.
CJ's trade-mark snide smile took over her face once more, obviously happy with the fact that no one had shown up yet.
But for once in my life, Fate was wrapping her silken thread around me and giving me the chance to give them all a big 'fuck you!' because a long, black limousine - yes, he sent a fucking limo

- pulled up in front of the house. The driver got out, dressed in his all-black suit and little cap, and walked towards us.
"Miss Ward." He enquired.
We grabbed our bags and moved towards the driver, with Lissa leaning towards me to whisper, "babe, it's a fucking limo!"
Said driver took my bags and proceeded to the trunk where he carefully placed my meager belongings in it like it was priceless. All we had was our clothes that we had arrived in and the stuff that had been donated to us by the coven: two extra sets of clothes, a pair of pyjamas, slippers and some toiletries.
That's it. That's all we had.

     Nate was in awe of the luxurious vehicle, his mouth hung open like he was trying to catch flies; I very gently put my index under his chin and pushed his gob shut.
But the women on the raised porch? They were openly gawping, with the exception of CJ who looked set to explode because now she had to eat her words, and Agnes, who had a contemplative look on her face. Obviously she was wondering who my beau was, but she could keep guessing because I wasn't telling her shit.
The chauffeur ushered us into the limo and shut the door with a thunk. Even with the three of us in the back, there was still plenty of space to stretch out; I'm pretty sure it was bigger than my bedroom back home.
The seats surrounded me with their soft buttery feel, and I ran my hands across the soft tan leather. The other two made it their mission to push every single button and lift every single lid to hunt for goodies. There was an 'ooh' and an 'aah' every five minutes that they found something interesting. They pulled out champagne, little pots of caviar, bottles of sparkling water, and initialled napkins. That wasn't even all of it. This vehicle was a treasure trove of trinkets that seemed wasteful.
There are people back home struggling to put food on the table, and he had a mini fridge full of fresh fruit that wasn't being eaten.
I counted the minutes until we got to the hotel because anxiety was setting in the closer I got. I wondered if this was for real, and if Lucian still wanted me. Why didn't he come and meet us

himself but he sent a driver to collect us? Was that an omen? A sign that he wasn't truly invested in this relationship despite the fact that we had known each other for days, not weeks or months.

He had money. Wealth that I could never have imagined, I mean, who the hell had their initials inscribed on their paper napkins? The gold embossed 'L' and 'G' glared at me with their ostentatiousness.

And it occurred to me. I didn't know what the 'G' stood for. I was literally moving in with a guy and I didn't know his surname!

Lissa must have noticed the horror on my face, because she scooted next to me, a worried look on her own.

"What's up?"

"I don't know what the 'G' stands for." I whispered, "I don't know what Lucian's last name is, and we'll be at the hotel soon."

She just shrugged her shoulders, "so what," she replied, "you know he's rich and that he can afford to take care of you both." She started ticking things off on her fingers, "you know that he's hot. You know that he clearly likes you despite the fact that you snore."

"I don't snore."

Her eyebrows lifted in a 'really?' gesture, and I had to admit, I wasn't entirely sure if she was right or not.

She continued, "you know he has a massive knob, so what does it matter what his name is."

"So, him being hung is more important than knowing his name?"

"Hell yea sister." She nudged me with her shoulder, making me rock in my seat, "you gotta try before you buy. Imagine moving in with him, and then you get down to the nitty gritty and he has a clitenis. What would you do then?"

I belly laughed, "what the fuck is a clitenis?" I asked her, still laughing.

"You know, when a clit is so big it looks like a little penis. Clitenis."

"Do you make this stuff up yourself?"

"Sometimes," she shrugged again, "or Urban Dictionary."

I considered the things she had listed - except the dick part - yes, he was obviously loaded, and he seemed to like me. No normal guy would waste all this time and money, especially knowing I was pregnant and it wasn't even his. Did it matter that I didn't yet know his last name? I mean, I would find that out pretty soon anyway.

"Listen babe, people have got together before and known far less about each other. You remember that Sherry from school?"

"The girl who did all that online dating and moved to Italy?"

"Yea, her. She met the guy online, didn't even know if the guy was real, packed everything up and moved to another country to be with a dude that she had been talking to for a couple months."

"Oh yea, I remember now. What happened to her?"

"They got married, just had their second kid and celebrated their fourth wedding anniversary." She looked at me pointedly. "At least you know your guy is real. She took a chance and moved to a whole other country after only speaking to him on the phone. He could have been some sixty year old, overweight weirdo living in his mum's basement.. You only moved to a different borough!"

I sighed, she was right, we haven't gone far; not that we have lots of options. It's not like we can go home, the lycans know where I live, and we definitely were not going back to the coven; if it came to it, and Lucian and I didn't work out, we could move to a different city outside London where it was cheaper, hunker down for a bit while I practised my new calling. Hopefully if the time came when they found me again, I would have had my baby and be prepared to defend us.

I wasn't even going to try and convince Lissa and Nate to go back, because I knew they wouldn't leave me. Especially now. We were in this together for the long haul, and if Lucian wanted to join the ranks, he was more than welcome.

A voice came through the speaker - the driver - announcing that we would be arriving in ten minutes. And immediately, that anxiety that I thought I had control of came bombarding back. It felt like moths had made their home in my stomach, attracted to the speck of light which was my excitement at seeing Lucian again. But it was just a speck. My nerves were the most prominent emotion right now.

"Calm down, it'll be fine. We'll be there too, remember."

I relaxed slightly at Lissa's words, knowing my family would be there made me feel a bit better about all of this. I'm not sure what I would have done if I was doing this all by myself..

The limo came to a slow stop outside a colossal glass building; a single block of black marble stood outside the entrance, its gold lettering spelling out the name of the prestigious hotel. I didn't even feel us stop, neither did I feel the driver exit the vehicle, but he must have, because he had come around to the passenger side and opened the door, patiently waiting for us - for me - to get out. *Ok, you can do this Zoe, you're independent, strong, and a bloody witch too, woman up.* I gave myself the mental pep-talk as I shuffled inelegantly out of the low-lying car. My yoga leggings - not the most classiest of attire to arrive in - allowed me to slide across the leather to the open door.

Stepping out with the guys following at my back, I smiled at the driver, whose name badge read 'Brian,' he tipped his head at me, and with a quietly murmured "Ma'am," he shut the door behind us, leaving us standing on the sidewalk outside the hotel while he went to collect our bags.

"Wooow." Lissa whistled as she stared up at the towering wall of glass.

Yea, definitely wow. This place was way out of our league. Men and women dressed to the nines walked in and out, not paying us any attention, but I felt like we stood out like a sore thumb. The sound of wheels rolling on the pavement had me turning my head towards Brian, pushing a small trolley with our bags loaded on top. Everyone else's designer cases with their clear logos filled up trolleys without an inch of space left, you could barely see over the top, but our bags only covered half of it, and they looked like the hand-me-downs they were.

I had never felt so self-conscious in my life.

With Nate still standing there gawking as usual, I quietly asked Brian if there was a back way that we could use.

He looked confused as he stated clearly, "Mr Garrick has already been informed of your arrival, he is on his way down now."

A hand slapped at my shoulder, "there you go, now you know." Stated my annoying best friend who was now leaning her head over my shoulder.

"Thanks for that, Captain Obvious."

Garrick. His name was Lucian Garrick. A sexy name for a sexy man. And I was glad I didn't have to embarrass myself by asking him, or worse, nosing through his papers until I found out what his name was. I shivered at the thought of being caught red-handed snooping. I was one of those people who cringed at awkward moments, even TV shows where something uncomfortable happened, I had to cover my eyes. Nope, couldn't do it.

Brian had started moving towards the entrance with our luggage and gestured for us to follow him. With a shared glance at my people, we followed.

It was like walking into another world. Marble, glass and leather surrounded me; my shoes squeaked as I walked across the gleaming expanse.

Brian was standing at a lift, the doors being held open by an attendant. "We're going upstairs?" I asked him.

"Yes Miss Ward, it's this way to the hotel."

"I thought this was the hotel?"

"This is The Shard, the hotel starts on the thirty-fourth floor."

Right. Of course it does.

If I thought the ground floor was beautiful with its sleek design…then the actual reception area was stunning. The marble theme continued across the room, with two large desks, veins of gold threaded through the black and white pattern where a man and a woman - smartly dressed in pressed uniforms - were checking people in.

Spotlights were arranged in symmetry on the ceiling that left a reflection on the tiled floor as I walked towards the receptionist. She looked down at my outfit of plain clothes and looked behind me at the others. They hadn't noticed the hostility in the woman's gaze yet; too busy looking at the surroundings…but I had. I plastered my most fakest smile on my face as I approached her. "Hi, we're here to see Mr Garrick." I told her in my most politest voice. No need for her to stereotype us even more.

She looked shocked for a second, clearing her throat, she replied in a sugary voice, "I am sorry, Mr Garrick is very busy. If you let me know your name," she said, taking out a pen and a pad of paper, "I can leave him a message."

Her smile was frozen in place as she cocked her head to the side, condescension oozing from her. Nate leaned one arm on the counter and leaned over, peeking behind the desk. The unhelpful receptionist leaned back slightly, her eyes taking on a familiar wariness that I'd seen before on the faces of strangers when they looked at Nate's size, and automatically assumed he was a hooligan; not knowing that my big, friendly giant of a brother wouldn't hurt a fly. But his curiosity often led to scenarios that I had to help him out of.

Like the time when he picked up someones puppy on the street, because he wanted to stroke it and cuddle it, he'd only been eleven at the time but already way bigger than most boys his age; the owner had almost cried and begged Nathan to put his precious dog down, and not to hurt it. I had been there that day, and I had seen the crestfallen look on his face as he had realised that the stranger thought he was a bad person and that Nate would harm his dog, just because of the way he looked. When we had gotten home, he'd asked me why, and it was at that moment when I knew I had to explain some things about the world to him. Because people like us would always be stereotyped by certain people, they would always expect a typical behaviour. So I had sat my little brother down and told him some home-truths; that even though he was light skinned, people would still see him as Black. And because he was a Black boy, growing up into a Black man, and growing up where we lived, people would think he was a particular type of person...not the sweet, caring boy he actually was.

The postcode war was a real thing where we lived, boys and girls who grew up and got mixed in with the wrong people. But poverty often led people to join in with certain crowds. Crowds that helped put food on the table and keep the heating on. Even if those ways of keeping a roof over your head and your belly full were less than ideal. I'd seen the other boys in the area eyeing

Nate up like he was prime rib. A candidate for their little crew. And that would not be my Nate. Ever!

When Nathan had said he was staying with me, I was glad. Glad that he wouldn't be going back to that cesspit where he could be roped into doing all kinds of nefarious things. And he was so helpful...and clueless. Which was mostly my fault. I had wanted him to stay a child for a bit longer, to enjoy being young without all the stresses of adult life that would soon creep up on him. So I was doubly glad when Lucian had asked us to stay with him, because being away from there would be good for him, and yea, I could just wave my metaphorical wand and magic him up some good grades; but I couldn't magic him up life experience.

Nathan was oblivious to the woman as he looked all around her, "Is this desk built up from the floor? There isn't a seam anywhere, it's flawless." He looked down at his feet and around the bottom of the marble desk stroking his hand across the counter.

"Could you please not touch anything." She pulled a disinfectant wipe out of a packet on her desk and wiped down everywhere Nate had just had his hand on. The blush staining Nate's cheeks showed his shame; clearly this woman thought we were dirty, thought that we would spread our 'common' germs... because obviously her germs are classier. Fucking moron. I wanted to hug him to me and smash this bitch's face in simultaneously. I glared at her, imagining her slicked back hair catching fire; in my head she looked like Hades from the Disney film, flames shooting up from her head, only she was running around screaming in pain in my imagination. A tingling sensation shot up from my fingers and wormed its way upwards, spreading its malice across my chest and burrowing in my heart. I knew instantaneously that if I was to bleed right now, this woman would be dead. Power writhed inside me mingling with my anger at her ignorance. It wanted to escape, I needed to keep this shit under control. I needed to keep my anger under control. I rubbed Nathan's shoulder to comfort him - and to comfort me too. I needed that touch more than anything right now, I needed to be reminded of where I was and who I was with. Lissa was standing on Nate's otherside, a constant presence that offered comfort whenever it was needed.

"I will have to ask you all to vacate the premises now."

"But..." Nate started.

The squeeze of my hand stalled him. "It's fine, I'll call Lucian and find out where he is."

"Mo gràidh."

I heard the deep voice of Lucian calling to me from across the room, the sound of his hurried footsteps followed after. I turned towards him, watching him stride across the room and turning every eye in his direction.

His emerald green dress shirt was open at the collar, his sleeves uncuffed and rolled up to his elbows, emphasising the strength in his corded forearms; it hung loose and untucked from his black jeans that fitted snugly across his thick thighs. I hadn't forgotten how sexy he was, but I stood there and looked my fill - and probably looked smug doing it too - because the receptionist was practically drooling on her newly cleansed counter.

"I am so sorry I wasn't there to pick you up." He wrapped his strong arms around me, encircling my waist and pulling me into his embrace. Bending down, he buried his face into the crook of my neck and just breathed; his whole body relaxing against me like he had been waiting for this moment all day. His hot breath was like a fire in my core, his beard scraping against the sensitive skin; that and the feel of his strength surrounding me, was lighting me up from the inside out.

I wrapped my arms around his neck and squeezed him against me, feeling my breasts press against his torso.

I could have stood there all day in his arms, but that sickly sweet voice interrupted our reunion.

"Oh, Mr Garrick, I was just about to let you know that your guests had arrived."

Without lifting his head, he replied, "Thank you Stacey."

"My name is Tracey, Mr Garrick."

His hand stroking down my spine was his only response, he completely ignored her. Lifting his head and finally giving me his pretty golden eyes, he smiled, relief shining down at me.

"You're here."

"Looks like it." I replied cheekily.

"I trust Brian got everything sorted out for you?"

"Well he got us here, I'm not sure where he went? He has our bags and everything."

"I trust him completely, he would have had your things sent to your rooms already."

Without releasing his hold on me, he turned to my brother. "You must be Nathan." Lucian held his hand out, "I've heard lots of good things about you."

Nate took his hand, shaking it. His hand looked scrawny in comparison to Luc's, despite his age, Nathan was normally the tallest person in the room...not anymore. Lucian dwarfed him, and made him look all of his fifteen years.

Not forgetting Lissa, Lucian turned to her, introducing himself and completely going up in my estimation of him; I had told him how important these people were to me, and he had listened and remembered their names.

And for once, my bestie was speechless. She was nodding her head at whatever he was saying to her, it seemed as though she was finally lost for words.

"Make sure they are given access to my rooms, and their own keys." He told the receptionist, his voice was stern and commanding, "They are to be given everything that they require. Understand?"

"Yes Mr Garrick."

She wasn't so confident now, her voice quieter than the snotty tone she had on when it was just us.

It's true what they say, money really does speak.

After following Lucian to his rooms, he gave Lissa and Nathan their own room keys; they were adjacent to 'our' room, which is what he was now referring to it as. Brian had arranged for our bags to be dropped off, so my little rucksack was already there waiting for me to unpack.

What I hadn't been prepared for, was for Luc to have this whole floor to himself. There were only four rooms on this level, and we each had one assigned to us, although as it turns out, I wouldn't be getting my own room anyway.

Lucian had shown the others to their doors first, spending more time with Nathan and showing him how to adjust the controls and order room service. Nathan's eyes lit up like a kid at a fairground when he saw the menu, and was told that he could order anything he wanted - at any time of the day or night. Leaving them to unpack, he showed me to my room.
He opened the door to a large suite with wall-to-wall windows that had views of London. The vision was stunning, showing nothing of the London that I had known my whole life. This was looking at it with a whole new perspective.
The Thames glittered below, it's ripples like scales on a snake winding its way through the city. "This is your room," he said from behind me, "I thought you might need your own space."
"I thought you said that I was staying with you? Did you change your mind?"
"You will be staying with me. Every night." His arms enveloped me from behind, and his head rested at the side of mine, "I want you with me, sleeping beside me, but I will understand if you want some privacy. Just know that I will not allow you to stay away for long." His arms squeezed me gently to him as his lips brushed against my cheek; with a gentle back and forth, he caressed the side of my face with his closed mouth. It was sweet and tender, and everything that I wanted right now, so I let him take my weight as I leaned back on his frame, somehow knowing that he would support me as I trusted him to hold me up.

    We stood there like that in each other's embrace, my arms cradling his while the little spots of people moved about on the sidewalk below, going about their day. I couldn't remember a day where I felt so content, and comfortable enough to just forget about the world around me.
And so I stood there, doing nothing except watching.
I felt one of his hands reach up and softly turn my face towards his; he looked down at me with such adoration, I didn't know what I had done to earn such an emotion, but I wanted to keep it. His other hand, still wrapped around me moved to rest on my stomach, and I pleased my hand over his where my - our - child rested.

"I will take such good care of you both." he whispered, "no one can ever hurt you here."

A thought flitted through my mind, *how did he know someone was trying to hurt me?* But it was swept away as quickly as it came. He *didn't* know that, it was just a

figure of speech.

"Come, let me show you something." He took my hand and led me towards the main bedroom, to a dark wooden door at the far side of the room - I followed him blindly. He pushed the door open to a large walk-in wardrobe lined with rows and rows of clothes: shirts, jeans, slacks. Shelves were filled with Tees and shoes and everything a girl could ever need. Probably more than anyone one person could use at any time.

I picked at a hanging label dangling aimlessly from a pair of jeans, the designer tag had an extortionate amount written on it.

"What is all of this?" I questioned. Too shocked to even consider what all of this was for.

"It's all yours," he replied, "everything in here I ordered just for you."

"But..." I looked at the tag again, "it's my size. How did you know what size I wear?"

He rested his shoulder against the doorjamb, leaning there watching me with his arms crossed over his thick chest. "I have a really good personal shopper."

There was so much stuff, I couldn't wear it all before my bump got big, pretty soon half of this stuff wouldn't fit. "You know that soon I won't fit into this stuff right?"

"I know love," he stepped towards me, his hand going to cup my cheek, "I didn't know what you'd like so I just ordered one of everything. When you start to show, I'll have the rest sent over."

"The rest?"

"The maternity clothes that I ordered."

I didn't even know what to say to that. I was half tempted to get angry because he'd taken away my choice, the decision over what to wear. It may be trivial to some but this was my first baby, and I hadn't been able to choose maternity clothes. But on the flipside, he'd bought me clothes, for everything. I didn't need to worry about shopping, especially when the baby got bigger and I couldn't be bothered to go out and buy stuff.

"Thank you, but there's so much, I'm going to grab some bits and give them to Lissa." I started looking through stuff some that I thought she might like, preparing to pull a soft yellow top off the shelf.

"You don't need to do that, Lissa and Nathan have their own supplies already."

"What?"

"I had all of their closets filled before you arrived."

"You did that for them? For me?" My voice wavered with emotion as I stared at him. He'd provided my family with clothes and toiletries and a roof over our heads and now I was a blubbering mess. These damned pregnancy hormones.

"Ssshhhh. Don't cry." He pulled me in his arms, stroking his hands up my back, "I'm sorry Zoe, I didn't mean to upset you." And I just cried. I used his shirt as my own personal tissue; wiping my tears and crying my hope and sadness into him. I hadn't allowed myself to cry once since the attack, I had just sucked it all in and carried on for the sake of my baby and Nathan. I hadn't cried when we'd had to leave everything behind - even if it was a shitty home, it was still our home. I was just so overwhelmed that this one tiny thing was the catalyst for my emotional breakdown. This man hadn't just bought me clothes, but he'd done it for *them*. That meant everything to me. I don't know how long I stood there in his comforting embrace, with just his hands rubbing everywhere, but I eventually wiped at my eyes which felt raw.

Planting my hands on his bearded cheeks, I looked up into his golden orbs, and, standing on tiptoes, I reached up and planted a kiss on his soft lips; I wanted to show him every ounce of my gratitude. His mouth parted under mine, and I traced his teeth with my tongue; our tongues met in a duel, his towering frame bending slightly to reach me. And despite him being so bloody massive, he was gentle with me, like I would break under his touch.

BANG BANG. "Open up lovebirds, it's lunchtime." Lissa's fist against the door broke the magical spell that had weaved around us in the enclosed room.

He pulled away from me slowly, reluctance evident on his face. "I thought you said they had room service?"

He laughed, "I told them that we would have lunch together downstairs in the main bar once they had settled in," his smile grew as he continued to stare down at me, "do not worry love, we won't take long. Go and change into something else, and we'll leave."

I perused the rows of clothing, looking for something nice but casual. After flicking through dresses and trousers, I settled on a pair of dark wash Boyfriend jeans and a black long sleeved Tee. They were comfortable and extravagant - not something I could ever normally afford to buy. Once I'd changed, I went to get my man. I was starving, and - after that kiss - I knew exactly what I was having for dessert.

Jacob

"Alpha, there's a package for you."
"Did you eat the postman again?"
"That was only one time."

I looked up from my desk at Louise - the only female in my pack - a bloodthirsty little bitch, she had survived the turning and had taken to packlife with relish; but she always wanted more. Greedy. She'd taken my cock a few times before, and begged for more, but it had gone to her head, and she started trying to give orders in my place thinking that because she sucked my dick, she could do what she wanted...in my house.

I'd had to take her down a peg or two, let her know who was boss. That's why she was currently collecting my mail and doing my laundry. She was my slave until she had learned her lesson. I was the boss here. I gave the orders.

"Well. Give it to me then." Her hesitation spoke louder than her words ever could, and I looked down at the unassuming parcel in

her hands, wrapped in brown paper that was the size of a lunch box.
"Alpha..."
"Give it to me." I demanded.
She stepped forward, creeping closer to me. As she got closer, I could smell the unmistakable tang of old blood. It was a scent all too familiar to me. I swept my papers to the side, they were unimportant right now, and made a space on the hardwood. Carefully placing the box in front of me, she stepped back as far as she could, her back ramrod straight against the far wall, her eyes wary as they lingered on the package.
"Who's it from?" There was no smell I could detect on it, nothing that would lead me to who had sent it, no trace of anything, just the adhesive smell that normally comes along with that horrible packing paper.
"I don't know, there was no return address."
Carefully pulling apart the glued sides, I unveiled a black plastic box. The rotting smell got stronger the closer I got to the centre of it.
And I knew. I recognised the iron smell of Ty's blood. I hadn't heard from him since I sent him after the witch. I hadn't been too concerned, there was often radio silence when he was on a hunt. He refused to carry a phone, saying it was just something weighing his pockets down, and he liked to shift without the burden of technology tracking him.
I guess that didn't matter anymore. He wouldn't be carrying anything anywhere.
His heart lay battered and blackening inside the plastic and lined with clingfilm, with congealed blood stuck to the lining. Holes punctured the muscle - claws - there was no guessing who'd done it.
"Fucking Lucian."
"Lucian's here?"
I glared at the stupid woman across the room, she'd spent years trying to get him to join the pack, constantly sniffing around his ars. He wasn't interested then, he definitely wasn't interested now he had the little witch.

That's why Ty's heart was here and not beating in his chest. Lucian had the blood witch, and he was protecting the little lady. I sat back in my chair resting my chin on my hand, I had to think. "Get rid of that." I lifted my leg and nudged my foot against the opened box, nudging it towards her.
"What shall I do with it?"
"I don't know," I huffed, "use your imagination."
Her eyes took on a gleeful hue, she loved being imaginative. Snatching the box from my desk, she walked out swiftly, shutting the door behind her.

I needed to figure out how the fuck I was going to get Zoe out of Lucian's clutches. He was always the little do-gooder. Sucking up to Robert. Master's favourite little pet.
Even when we were human, Robert favoured the bastard. The son of a maid with no idea who his dad was, he'd been the stable boy - very cliche - but he had worked well with the horses, so Lucian had quickly caught the eye of the young lord, and they'd become best friends despite Robert's father's disapproval. According to him, they were not the same class, and Robby should "find friends of his own standing."
Even back then Lucian would play the 'protector'. Pretending to help Caitlyn out when everyone knew it was because he was in love with her.
Fucking pussy. Who the fuck falls in love with your best friend's wife?
Picking up the phone on my desk, I dialled a number that I had memorised years ago. The number hadn't changed in all this time.
She answered on the third ring, "I knew it would be you."
"You owe me a favour," I started, "I didn't kill you the last time you fucked up, now you have the chance to make it right."
There was a pause, as if she was weighing up her options, but she didn't have very many. "What do you want me to do?"

Zoe

I didn't eat much at lunchtime, I was too nervous, too edgy. I couldn't concentrate on anything when Lucian had his hand on my knee through the whole meal. The heat of his hand was like a brand on my skin claiming ownership of me; and I was so ready for him to make me his in every way.

It was weird though, he would lean slightly towards me, his nostrils doing that flary thing, like he was smelling me. Could he smell my arousal? I started to feel paranoid about halfway through thinking that there was a smell to it, and everyone would notice.

I crossed my legs, trapping his hand between them; he didn't seem to mind that though, he just left it there, and stroked my knee softly with his thumb. Damn.

His smile was innocent, but the hungry look in his eyes was a message for me to be prepared for what was coming. And I couldn't fucking wait.

After what felt like hours sitting in the bar and listening to my brother and best friend grill Lucian for information, I was ready to call it a day. I wanted to spend the rest of the afternoon getting to know my new roommate; in the biblical sense of course.

Nudging him with my foot under the table, I widened my eyes at him hoping he would get the hint and end the conversation. Luckily he was a smart man.

"Do you mind if I take Zoe for a tour of the hotel?" he asked them both.

They looked at each other, amusement lining their faces, "yea sure, a *tour*." Coughed Nathan.

"Yea, enjoy your *tour* of the *bedroom*." cackled Lissa.

It was fucking embarrassing when your fifteen year old brother started laughing about your sex life.

What dicks.

Chucking my napkin - that wasn't initialled - at her head, I stood up and took Lucian's hand that was outstretched and waiting for me. His palm was rough against mine, but I grasped it firmly as he pulled me from my seat. "See you tomorrow." I said to them.

"Have fun." She called back.

I turned around just in time to see Nathan pretending to make out with his hand, and Lissa throwing her head back and laughing at him. Such dicks, both of them.

"I like your family, you're lucky to have them"

"Yea, I kinda like them." I smirked. "Do you have any brothers or sisters?"

"No."

Ok, that was shut down pretty quickly. He sighed, still not looking at me.

"I had a brother."

Oh, shit. "I'm sorry, I shouldn't have brought it up."

"It's fine, it was a long time ago." His smile was strained, and it showed that even though it was a long time ago, it still affected him greatly. I lifted his hand that was clasped in mine, and kissed the back of it, trying to ease some of his pain the way he had eased some of mine with his generosity.

    We made it back to the room without discussing dead siblings, and I kicked my shoes off by the door and reached around and unclasped my bra under my shirt. "Aahhh, damn that feels so good." There was no feeling better than taking a bra off when you just got home, and although I wanted to be sexy for him right now, I was more interested in getting comfortable.

"You may as well take it all off."

His voice was husky with need, I could see him staring at me in the reflection of the glass. Without turning around, I stripped off my shirt and threw it over my shoulder in his direction; then I shrugged off my plain black non-wired bra and dropped it to the floor at my feet and stood there with my bare back to him, in just my jeans. He looked longingly at my exposed skin and licked his lips, like he wanted to taste me.

I felt empowered. I felt the sexiest I had ever felt and it was all because of the way this man was looking at me.

Our eyes locked in the glass and held, he wanted a show? I could do that.

Raising my hands and running them through my short curls, I slowly dragged my hands down my body and over my breasts. They were fuller than they used to be - a perk of my pregnancy -

my nipples were so sensitive that just my own hands brushing across them made me gasp out loud and sent a shiver down my spine.

A growl behind me had me pulling my eyes back to his, his mirror image was slightly faded but I could see his own hand rubbing at the thick bulge between his legs. The heat between my own thighs was an inferno, and I tried to rub my thighs together hoping the friction would ease some of it. No such luck. There was only one way this was easing and that was when I had that massive cock inside me.

I lowered the zipper of my jeans and shimmied them down my legs, bending over so he had a nice view of my ars in just my thong. I was so glad that I had picked the little black lace to wear today.

After kicking the trousers free, I walked towards the bedroom, adding a little sway in my step.

I didn't need to look behind me to know that he would follow.

Lucian

Her backside in her little knickers was begging to be bitten; the luscious round globes jiggled as she walked away from me. I stalked her, following her to the bedroom and stripping my own clothes off as I went. I couldn't take my time with clothes right now, I was too wired, too ready to be buried inside my woman.

I entered the room to find her kneeling on the large four-poster facing me, her legs slightly spread. Her scent was intoxicating to the man and the beast, her thighs slick with her need.

Her eyes flared at the sight of me. I knew I was bigger than average. Long and thick, she wouldn't be able to get her hand around the width of it; but I could definitely fit it all in that pretty pussy.

Grasping my cock with my hand, I squeezed the tip, pre-cum leaking and dripping on my closed fist.

"Taste me." I gathered up the pre-cum, and, with my thumb, wiped it across her closed lips. I felt my cock jerk at the sight of her pink tongue flicking out to lick it all up and taste my essence. She groaned, and deciding that she'd had enough of waiting for me to take her, she grabbed my beard in her own fist and pulled my head towards her, slamming her mouth on mine. I could taste myself on her. The mix of both of us had me panting and ready to cum; I had to dig my claws into my thigh, that bite of pain keeping me from cumming too quickly.

Our teeth clashed and our tongues tangled, but I needed more of her. It wasn't close enough. Grasping her thighs in each hand, I dragged her legs around my waist and placed her in the centre of the bed.

She was exquisite lying beneath me, her chest heaving for breath. "You are the most beautiful woman I have ever seen." Before she could say anything back, I took her nipple into my mouth and sucked. Hard. Scraping my teeth gently against it, I listened for her moans; they would tell me what she liked the most.

Grasping the scrap of material that she called underwear, I pulled it away from her, tearing them off of her and running my fingers across her soft folds. She was soaking wet as I dipped first one then a second finger inside her tight pussy, stretching her and getting her ready for me.

"Oh please," she begged.

"Please what? Mo ghràidh" I growled against her breast.

"Please...don't stop." she whimpered. Her head thrashed on the pillow, her eyes glazed with her passion.

"Don't stop this?" I plunged both fingers inside her, pumping them in and out while I sucked on her neglected nipple, taking more of her breast into my mouth; trying to suck on as much of her beautiful tit as I could. Her pussy gushed around my hand, I could feel her wetness seep through my fingers, and she screamed, the noise echoing around the room. I sat up - her legs spread on either side of me - I wanted her to see me. I pulled my hand free and sucked her juice off of each of my fingers, making sure I didn't waste any; her taste exploded on my tongue, sweet and salty and fresh.

She watched me transfixed as I sucked my fingers free of her, until I ached for more. Dropping forwards, I caught myself and rested my arms beside her head, staring into her multi-colored eyes. I knew that everything that had happened until now, was meant to. I was meant to be here at this moment with Zoe, about to claim her as mine.

Reaching down and notching my rock hard cock at her entrance, I waited for her to let me know she was ready. She wrapped her arms around my neck and pulled me down, her tongue licking across my mouth and tasting herself. As she kissed me with everything she had, I sank my full length inside her; I swallowed her moans of pleasure, as I groaned my own bliss into hers. Our mutual cries of pleasure and the slap of our bodies filled the bedroom.

I drove my cock inside her faster and harder, feeling her nails digging into my shoulders as I gave her everything of me. Her screams filled my ears every time I bottomed out, it was like a symphony playing in my ears when my growls joined her sounds of pleasure.

My tongue mimicked the action of my body, plunging inside her mouth everytime I filled her up.

Her tongue pushed past mine, licking the roof of my mouth and catching on one of my fangs. A drop of her blood, just a tiny drop, and I was gone.

Grabbing her hips in my hands, I slammed inside her over and over, feeling her pussy pulse and clench around my throbbing length, I knew that she was about to cum.

"That's it love, take all of my cock," I commanded, "take it now."

Her thighs squeezed my sides as her body lifted towards me, her pussy spasming around me as I hammered at her sweet pussy; her blunt teeth sank into my shoulder as she tried to hold in her cries.

Her little teeth marking me sent me spiralling into oblivion, I filled her cunt with everything I had, and still I wanted to give her more.

"Fuck." I grunted, feeling her pulse around my dick; her pussy was heaven and I would die a happy man if this was the last thing I ever felt. Feeling my cock softening inside her, I continued to slide in and out of her, wanting to prolong the pleasure. Her

screams were now just faint moans as I rained kisses over her face.
Her chest heaved beneath me as she panted for breath, "That...was amazing." She gasped.
Leaning over her on my raised arm, I caressed every inch of skin I could reach, brushing my hand over her glossy curls and sliding my fingers over her soft lips. Her arms softly stroked up and down my back, the feeling of her gentle touch was exquisite and I couldn't hold back a shiver.
I place kisses at the corner of her mouth and trail my mouth down the graceful column of her neck, licking and sucking, leaving small red marks on her skin.
Marks that everyone will see and know that she is taken.
I can still taste her on my tongue, that exquisite forbidden drop that sent me reeling. I'd felt like a god inside her, untouchable and...complete. It was like nothing I had ever felt before. That one drop had filled me up inside, it had created this warmth inside me that had grown into an inferno until there was only fire remaining. I couldn't see anything except her, I couldn't hear anything except her screams in my ear. It was like my whole world had narrowed down to this one act; I couldn't stop until the fire had been extinguished. I'd been uncontrollable as I fucked her like the animal I was. And when I'd finally cum, that heat had bled through me, burning me from the inside out.
And I was ashamed to admit that not once did I think of what could have happened if I'd lost complete control of the beast. But I was selfish enough to want to do it again; even now, I could feel her warmth surrounding me, and I could feel myself getting hard again.
"Did I hurt you?"
"Hurt me? No," she replied, "why would you think you hurt me?"
"I lost control. I could have hurt you."
"If I'd said stop, would you have stopped?"
"Of course!" Fear slithered down my spine, I would neve have taken it that far.
"Then you didn't lose control."
Burying my face into her neck, I rested over her, taking a minute to get my breath back, her hands continued to make patterns

over every inch of skin she could reach. It was playing havoc with my idea of giving her some time to recover.

"I didn't know it could be like that." she whispered.

"Explosive?"

"Yea." she sighed. "I've only been with one guy, and well...it wasn't like that. Ever."

"It's not always like that Zoe." I lifted my head to stare down at her, she looked confused at my declaration.

"It's not?"

"No love. It's never been like that for me either."

She brought her hands up between us, and ran them over my head. I normally kept my hair shaved, because it was easier to handle, otherwise - along with my beard - I looked like a caveman. But her short nails lightly scraping over my scalp had my semi growing rock hard.

Her eyes widened as she felt me growing, stretching her from the inside. "Again?"

Lowering until I was just a breath away, our noses touching. Specks of brown, hazel, green and even red shone out at me from her multi-hued eyes, "Again." I told her, "but this time." I lifted her legs to encourage her to wrap them around me, holding me tight against her, "this time, I'm going to go slow."

CHAPTER 12

Zoe

I woke up to the feel of hands on me spreading my legs apart. The tenderness between my legs was more prominent in this position as my thighs were pushed open to accommodate a wide set of shoulders. I managed to crack my eyes open long enough to see a dark head lowering towards me.
"Lucian." My voice was scratchy from spending my night screaming his name. He'd woken me up twice in the night to have me. Both times he'd had his way with my pussy, fucking me until I almost passed out from the pleasure. I didn't think I could do it again, not this soon anyway. I could feel how sore I was, and I had lost count of the amount of times he'd made me cum. "I can't Lucian." I placed my hand on his head, ready to push him away from my tender centre.
"Does it hurt?" he asked, looking up at me from his prone position between my legs.
I nodded, it felt like I had been rubbed raw. His answering grin was pure male satisfaction.
"Don't worry love," he said, slowly lowering his head towards me, "I'll kiss it better for you."
His long pink tongue swiped up and buried in my folds, circling my clit when he reached the top. I was so sensitive, that just that slightest touch had me arching off the bed.
I was going to push him away, I really was; but that tongue stabbed into me, laving me up inside then licking up, flicking at my clit and licking back down again; it was heaven on my sensitized skin. His beard rubbed at my thighs, creating a different sensation and adding to the pleasure that his tongue was creating.

Our mutual moans filled the room as he slurped at my pussy; the wet sounds should have embarrassed me, but I was too far gone to even care.

He alternated between flicking at my sensitive clit and licking me from top to bottom while I told him how much I loved his mouth over and over. But it wasn't enough, I teetered on the knife's edge, wanting to cum so badly but needing more - something extra - to push me over.

"Lucian. Lucian...please." I begged. "I need more. I need to cum." I moaned, "no, what..." I pleaded, as he took his mouth from me. "Where the fuck are you going?" His eyes blazed at me, and I could see myself glistening on his beard. He pulled me to the end of the bed where he was now kneeling on the floor, leaving his hands free and buried his face between my thighs. His lips sucked at my clit, while I felt a finger tunnel inside my swollen pussy. "Aahhh, fuck."

The feeling of his mouth sucking at me while his digit curled up inside me to rub at that spot that I never even knew I fucking had, had me clutching at his head, pushing him harder onto me, begging him not to stop without words. I felt that familiar wave overtake me, and I groaned out my climax, still holding his head to me and rubbing his face and his beard between my legs trying to prolong the ecstasy.

Lucian prowled towards me on all fours, kissing his way up my body while I lay there, replete and breathing like I'd just ran a fucking marathon.

"Good morning love."

"It's definitely a good morning." I panted. The rumble of his laughter was my response. His kisses continued as he made his way to my mouth; I could smell the musk of my desire all over him.

I didn't have much experience with men, being this close to my own release didn't gross me out as I had once thought it would, in fact, I loved the idea that he smelled of me, and that I had marked him in my own way. He lightly kissed my lips, the moistness from his own rubbing off on me.

"I like waking up like this with you." He heaved his massive frame to the side, and I turned towards him so that I could look at him properly in the light. The morning had snuck up on us while we were sleeping...and fucking. And now I could better appreciate the specimen lying next to me. His broad chest was tanned, with a smattering of hair across his pectorals, scars littered his skin. Thin white lines that criss-crossed around his rib cage, "what happened here?" I trailed my fingers over the closest one to me.

His hand trapped mine against his chest holding it there, "I was scratched by a dog."

They weren't deep scars, more like permanent scratches, but still, they must have hurt, and I found that I didn't like the thought of him being hurt. At all. I continued looking my fill; he didn't have defined muscles like some of them gym goers who spend all of their time crunching abs, but he was solid. A thick wall of muscle peppered with crisp dark hair, following that trail of hair down his torso led me to that glorious dick that was like a steel rod against his thigh, it was impressive; long and thick with a patch of dark wiry hair surrounding the length. It twitched as I continued my staring contest and thickened even more under my gaze.

"Is that all for me?"

I pushed his shoulder flat on the bed, lifting my leg to straddle him. His hands rested on my hips as I lowered myself on him, his dick was trapped beneath me laying along my slit, the hardness pressing against me. I wanted to watch *him* this time. He had spent all night making me his, and now I wanted a turn to watch him go wild beneath me. But fuck, I was nervous. The only thing making me continue was the fire in his eyes as he looked up at me, he licked his lips as he stared at my breasts so I cupped my hands beneath them, lifting them towards him and offered them up for him to taste. He raised slightly from the bed so that he could reach my offering, and caught one of my nipples in his mouth, sucking and licking it like a starving man.

"Oohhh."

His groan vibrated on my breast as he sucked me, "fuck woman, what you do to me."

The pull from his mouth was sending tingles through me, and my pussy clenched, wanting to feel him filling me up. But I wasn't ready to give him that yet. I wanted him to moan *my* name this time. I rocked above him feeling his hardness between my legs rub against my clit, his fingers clenched on my waist as I stroked over him, rocking faster as he growled against my nipple.

"Put me inside you." He groaned.

Releasing my breasts, I put my hands on his broad shoulders so I had leverage, "hold it up for me." I gasped out.

Once that cock was being held at the perfect angle, I lined it up with my centre and sank onto it a little bit at a time. His hands gripping me tried to pull me onto him faster, "nuh uh." I pulled up, "we do this my way this time." I pushed his shoulders back against the bed until he was lying flat, "just relax."

"Relax?" he huffed, "I can't relax with your sweet pussy teasing me like this, love."

I grinned, then slowly, I worked my way on to his cock until my thighs were touching his. He was panting heavily now his whole length was inside me; his head thrown back against the pillow as I started to grind on him, circling my hips until I could feel his hardness pushing against my inner walls in the most delicious of sensations as he stretched me. The feel of his chest hair against my palms as I stroked him everywhere was another sense explosion, as I remembered that abrasion against my nipples from the first time he'd taken me.

"Fuck, don't stop."

I circled my hips faster, winding on his dick as his groans got louder, his eyes were clenched shut as I continued my torture. I wanted him to know who was fucking him. "Who's fucking you?" I asked him

His eyes shot open and caught me in their glare. "You, Zoe. Only you."

Resting my hands against his chest, I lifted my hips up slightly, leaving only half of him within my pussy. Before he could catch his breath, I slammed my hips down, pushing the full length of him back inside me, our shouts joining each others at the shared pleasure.

I rocked back and forth, watching him, keeping my own climax at bay until I'd seen to his. It was harder than expected considering we had been fucking all night. But I felt that pressure beginning to build again, and every time I rolled my hips, his pelvis would hit my clit sending waves of ecstasy through my whole body.

"Whose cock is this?" I demanded.

Hands squeezing my waist was my only warning as he twisted us around, the room moved so damn quickly. I had no idea he could move that fast, but before I could even blink, he had my back flat on the bed and my legs over his shoulders hammering at me like he'd lost all control of himself.

"This.cock.is.yours." And with each word ground out between his clenched teeth, he slammed himself inside me, his hips pistoning, sending me careening.

I couldn't breathe. I couldn't even scream out, the tidal wave crashing over me was too much, too intense. All of the pleasure built into a crescendo until I was milked dry. My pussy gushing as he kept pumping his thick cock past my spasming walls, until he threw his head back and yelled out his own release. I could feel the warmth of him as he came inside me; he held himself still as he spilled his seed, the only movement from him the twitching of his cock against my inner walls.

I hadn't even noticed that at some point, I had dug my nails into his shoulders, and as I slowly began to get feeling back in my body, and my heart rate tried to get back to normal, I relaxed my fingers, rubbing my hand over the crescent shaped marks I had left in his skin.

"Sorry."

"Don't be," he rumbled, "I like that I wear your marks on my skin."

"I definitely need a shower after that," I sighed. The sweat - and other bodily fluids - was wet and sticky on my skin, and I was starting to feel a bit gross after our sex-athon.

With a grunt, he pulled my legs down and around his waist, wrapping his thick arms around me, pulling me up with him.

"Aahhh. Give a girl some warning you know."

He carried me like I weighed nothing, and I know for a fact that I had some meat on my bones. More than once dickhead Sean had asked me to get off of his lap because he'd said I had made his leg go numb. I clutched his shoulders as he walked to the en-suite, "I'm heavy Lucian..."

"You weigh nothing, love. I need to feed you as soon as we are both cleaned up."

"Of course I'm heavy, look at this arse." Taking one hand from his shoulders, I grabbed one of the handles around my hips, I squeezed it between my fingers, "look." I demanded.

The sound of a slap smacking skin hit my ears before I felt the sting of his hand on the meaty part of my bum. And the realisation that he had slapped my backside like I was a child needing scolding pissed me off. "Hey!"

"Do not insult my woman." His hand was rubbing the area, but I bet I'd have a handprint there now.

"I was talking about myself."

"So? You think you can call yourself heavy? Imply that you need to lose weight?" He questioned.

"Well, no. I'm not going to lose weight, I'm pregnant. But you don't need to lie to me. Sean…"

"That useless sack of shit does not get spoken about in our home," he scoffed, "a worthless excuse of a man who didn't know the treasure he had." He lowered me gently to the floor, making sure my feet were on the soft matt by the shower cubicle, and not on the cold grey tile. The shower was big enough to put four Lucian's inside, but luckily I only had one of him; I don't think I could cope with four of him. His hand adjusted the temperature of the water before patting me - gently this time - on the bum to walk inside.

  The water cascaded over my whole body from separate shower heads positioned from three points on the ceiling. It was literally raining on me…and it was fabulous. The water helped ease the muscles that had been used throughout the night, and massaged away the strain from the past few days. My shoulders slumped under the fall and I let my head fall back against Lucian's chest behind me; relaxing against him felt like leaning against a brick wall, strong and sturdy and not likely to fall when I rested my weight on it. That this man was holding me up felt like a metaphor for my current situation, a support when everything else around me was crumbling. His hands reached around me to the soap dispenser on the wall, lathered up the sweet smelling foam between his hands and proceeded to rub them over every inch of my body starting from my shoulders.

"Mmmmmm, that feels soooo good." I groaned, "But don't get any ideas big guy, I'm sore from our sex-athon."

He snorted out a laugh whilst running his soapy hands down each arm. "The only idea I have is to wash you. Just stand there and let me take care of you."

"I'm totally up for that." I sighed, "But please don't put that soap in my hair, I'll wash that myself."

"I have a personal shopper on call, just let her know what you need and she will order it for you." He said while soaping up my abdomen.

His hands gently washed my stomach, the bubbles being washed away by the hot water falling around me, but a fluttering inside me had me perking up. "Did you feel that?"

His hands paused their ministrations, "feel what?"

"I felt the baby. I felt them move."

He moved his great size to my front and crouched at my feet, but even on his knees his head came to my shoulders; he had to bend down still to place his ear against me.

I laughed at just how cute it was seeing this gigantic guy so excited. "Is he moving now?"

"You won't be able to hear anything. The midwife called it Quickening, and that I may be able to feel the baby fluttering around soon." I cradled his head to me, glad to be able to share this experience with someone. No, not someone...Lucian. "Besides, it may be a girl."

"What did it feel like?"

"It was like little butterflies. But it's gone now." I muttered.

"Baby was letting you know she is ok." He pulled himself from the shower floor and wiped the water from his eyes. "And hungry probably. Let me finish washing you and we can find the others for breakfast. Unless they have eaten already.

  The night spent with Luc and feeling my child this morning had me on cloud 9. Not even the thought of arranging time at the Coven could dull my mood. I pulled a pair of silky Royal Blue harem trousers off the shelf in my new wardrobe, along with a fitted white V-neck Tee. I needed something soft and comfortable today that wouldn't chafe against my sensitive parts. Jeans would *not* be a thing for a good few days. The next step was hunting down my phone. I had briefly heard it vibrating earlier, but I'd been a bit preoccupied at the time. Besides, if Lissa and Nathan had needed me, I was just across the hall from them, they would have knocked if it was an emergency.

Fishing my mobile from yesterday's outfit that was crumpled on the floor where I had stripped it off last night, I found two missed calls and a text from an unknown number.

Hi, it's Rosie. Just wondering when you will be coming back? I can pick you up? Agnes said she found some stuff that you might want to see.

How convenient that she 'found some stuff' as soon as I had left. I shot off a quick text telling Rosie that I would pop back tomorrow and I could meet with Agnes about this stuff. But I didn't need her to pick me up. Lucian had already said I could ask Brian to take me anywhere I needed to go. Plus, I felt better knowing that it was Brian, and I wasn't beholden to the witches for anything anymore.

Her reply came instantly, like she was waiting by her phone for my reply. It just said *'K'*.

Uh, I hated when people did that, like they couldn't even be bothered to write the whole word. OK. one extra letter, how was that so difficult?

Sliding the iPhone into my pocket, I met everyone in the lounge of our room. Luc had called them to meet us before we all went downstairs to the restaurant together.

And even though I was wearing these silky trousers, walking was a pain. I probably walked like I'd sat on a horse for two days straight. It certainly felt like that. As soon as I hobbled into the room, all eyes turned to me. Lucian looked at me like he hadn't seen me for ages, even though I was in the other room getting dressed for about twenty minutes. I guess some girls would think it weird that we were moving so fast; I had spent countless years with the family of my own making because everyone else was a let down or non-existent. I'd tried tracking down my birth mum when I hit eighteen, but there were no details that I could track. Delilah Ward had been a nobody; no family, no previous addresses. A homeless young girl with no record. I'd been depressed for weeks afterwards. Lissa and Sarah had brought me food and forced me out of the house when I would have rather stayed in my room and sulked. It was only Sarah's words of wisdom that had made me realise that I needed to go out there and take life by the uterus. Yea, she said 'uterus' because that's where life came from she had said, not the balls, not men…women. And it was us women who had to make that life for ourselves and pave our own way forward; life was what you make of it. Family was what you make of it and if your family is a hoard of cats and budgies, well, who were anyone to judge! The great Sarah Anderson everyone.

And so I had got my arse out of bed, put aside my disappointment, showered for the first time in days and went out to find a job so that I could start putting away a nest egg for me and Nathan, so that we could leave together one day.
And this is why I was jumping all in with Lucian. I wanted that Happily Ever After and the white picket fence and the adoring husband and the cute kids who grow up in a stable home; maybe I'll have a few cats too. I thought maybe that's why I stayed with Sean for so long. I had wanted that life so badly that I latched onto the first guy and tried to fit him into that scenario, but he just didn't fit.
"Uhhmm. When you two are finished eye-fucking each other, can we get some food, I'm starving." Lissa was standing in the middle of the lounge waggling her eyebrows, while my poor embarrassed brother stood by the door looking everywhere else except at me, his cheeks bright red. Rolling my eyes at her remark, I grabbed Lucian's hand, offering him an apologetic smile, though he didn't seem to mind my Beebee's lack of subtlety; we walked towards the door all while I apologised for my friend's behaviour.
"It is ok, love," he assured me, "I quite like the jokes that you all have together, I never had that."
Stupid. How could I have forgotten his dead brother? He'd told me that, although he didn't go into detail about it. "I'm sorry, does it bother you, seeing them? I mean…"

He squeezed my hand, "no mo ghràidh, do not ever think that; I like that you had that. Have them."
His hand swallowed my small one, but I could just squeeze it enough in mine to show my sympathy, and how sorry I was that he had grown up without his brother...because I don't know what I would ever do without mine.

Finally, I got to sit down and rest, even though all we had done was walk to the lift, then walk to our table, my legs were wobbly and my crutch felt like it was on fire from all of the friction. The free-standing tub back in the room was looking mighty fine about now; soaking my poor used fanny was going to be my new afternoon task. I fidgeted on the chair trying to find a comfortable way to sit.
"You ok there sis?"
"Hmm? What? Oh, yea Nate, I'm fine."
My attention was pulled across the table by Lissa's snickering, "what's so funny?"
"Don't glare at me, I didn't say anything."
I narrowed my eyes at her in a 'don't say shit' look. Focusing fully on my family, I couldn't help but notice that they looked good. Healthy. The bags from under Nate's eyes were gone, and they had worried me when they appeared while we were at the witches' house. He'd said he was fine, but I knew he wasn't resting completely, probably too worried about the attack and having to leave home; it definitely wasn't about school. He had on a brand new dark blue hoodie and tracksuit bottoms with a familiar white tick that fit his frame perfectly; and Lissa was in form-fitting jeans and a red kimono top, her braids plaited into one big braid pulled over her shoulder and hanging down her front.
I felt tears tickle the back of my throat, gratitude for the big man who had stepped outside to make a phone call. He had said that he had bought them new stuff too, but upon seeing my family looking well cared for and - dare I say it - happy and relaxed, I knew it had almost everything to do with Lucian. The other part was that they were away from the cesspool we had all grown up in, but then, I suppose that was Lucian's doing too.
"You both look well rested?"

"Oh my god that bed was like sleeping on a cloud. It was heaven!" She gasped.

"Yea I slept like a baby," Nate chimed in, "haven't slept that deep in ages." He shoved half a bagel into his mouth and tried chewing and smiling at the same time...it wasn't pretty.

"Soooo, what are you gonna do about the bitchy witches?" Lissa asked.

"I told Rosie that I would pop back tomorrow to look at some stuff, I mean, Agnes did also promise the use of her personal library; I wanna see if I can find some stuff on pregnancy." Looking around to make sure Lucian hadn't popped up behind me, I wasn't ready to have that 'magic' conversation with him yet. Though it would have to come eventually, I figured I would wait for him to be fully invested, maybe even in love with me, before I broached the whole *hey guess what? I can blow shit up with a drop of my blood, wanna see?* Subject. Yea, no. He seemed open minded, but I really didn't think he was *that* open minded.

"Are you sure it's a good idea going back there?"

"I have to Nathan, I need to find out if it's safe for me to practise while pregnant, I have to know if there should be some spells I should be casting while pregnant? I don't know." I rested my elbow on the table and leaned forward "What if I should be doing a spell to make sure my baby is, I dunno, blessed by their goddess or something? I have no clue. You heard what cunty Jade said, we weren't human; was she telling the truth and will I have a normal human pregnancy? These are all the things I need to find out, and I'm not asking them to tell me because, let's face it, they've hardly been forthcoming with information."

"Take a breath babe," Lissa coaxed, "calm down. It will all be fine. We can go with you tomorrow…"

"Nope." I said, popping my 'p', "not gonna happen, you two are staying here, I won't be long anyway."

"I'm not really feeling that plan Zozo."

I reached across the table to rub Nate's arm, "It's ok, Brian is going to take me and bring me back, I'll be there for a couple of hours and then I'll be back in time for dinner."

"Until next time you have to go there?" He sulked.

"What choice do I have? You know anywhere I can go to find out this stuff? You think I can pop to Smiths and ask them for a book on Witchcraft?"
"Hey, hey," Lissa broke in, "calm down babe."
I heaved a sigh, "I'm sorry Nathan, I didn't mean to snap."
"It's ok, I'm sorry too, I just...don't trust them, you know?"
"Me either, and I'd much rather be here with you guys bingeing Netflix, but until I can understand what all of this means for me...and for us, then I have to go back there."
He nodded, his eyes caste with worry, he turned his hand over and clasped it with mine, his hand was much bigger than mine but soft, life hadn't roughened them yet with callouses or hard skin that denoted years of hard labour, and unless he decided that he wanted a life where he had to work with his hands, then I wanted them to stay this way.
"Just be careful."
I nodded back at him. Lucian returned then, which meant that we changed the subject completely, and ended up discussing The Walking Dead, which was Nate's favourite show, turns out Lucian had seen every episode so far; it wasn't really my thing, I didn't like the whole zombie genre, mainly because it wasn't really true to life. If there were zombies everywhere, and dead bodies littering the whole world, there'd be flies everywhere, the survivors would be covering their faces everywhere they went because of the decomp smell, and don't even get me started on the toilet issue. In every single season, not one person had to have a number one or number two, no one got eaten while they were having a dump in the woods, and that just seemed totally unrealistic to me.
But then, turns out witches and lycans are real, so who am I to say that a zombie apocalypse can't be that neat and tidy?

  We spent the day touring the hotel, browsing the shops and just enjoying each other's company. Lucian fit in with my crazy lot like he had been there all along; he bonded with Nate over lame TV shows, he discussed the latest technology with Lissa and me...he held my hand the whole damn time. I learnt so much about him from just listening to his conversations. He was smart, funny and patient; and I loved just hearing the rumble of his voice. Sometimes when he didn't notice, a lilt entered his speech, a sexy little accent that I couldn't quite place.

It was the most relaxed I had been in a long time, I didn't worry what Nathan was eating for dinner, or making sure there was money on the electric to keep the lights on or what the lycans were doing. And my family, they were happy, and as I watched them both walking ahead of me and Lucian, their laughter carrying towards me, I couldn't help but think that I had made the right choice in coming here.

"You're ok that Brian is taking me to the school tomorrow?" It was the only thing I could think of, and not really a lie. The coven was advertised as a private school for 'gifted young women', and so I had told Lucian that I was a mature student there, studying cosmetology on weekends - ok, a little lie.

"I was actually thinking that I would ride along with you," he looked down at me and must have seen the worry on my face, "I will not be a nuisance, I can make some calls and work on my laptop from the car."

"It might be a few hours, you'll be just waiting in there."

"And when you are finished, we can get dinner somewhere. I can wait for you Zoe."

I smiled up at him as we continued our walk through The Shard Parade. Company would be nice on the journey.

Lucian

I wasn't about to let this woman out of my sight; she was here with me, safe, and I would keep her that way. And if that meant shadowing her every step - at least until I could fix the Jacob situation - then she needs to get used to having me around. I had spent days since I had got rid of Ty trying to sort out the Lycans, and so far I had no luck. The witches were no help, they wanted no part of the problem of beasts, and so I had been trying to contact every lone lycan I had met over the centuries, in the hope that they would help me protect Zoe, but they were selfish and stuck in their ways, and most of them had decided to stay far away from Jacob's pack; I was still waiting on a few that had not got back to me, but I was starting to lose hope that any of them that I had considered trustworthy, would not help me.

Contrary to what humans thought and what myths abounded, most lycans were loners, the ones who retained any sense of their humanity and wanted to keep their compassion and morality, stayed far from packlife; because living in a pack meant giving in to the hierarchy and submitting to an alpha, it meant giving in to the beast inside, and the longer they lived together, the more animalistic they became, and the fewer fucks they had to give.

But unfortunately, Jacob's pack was notorious for its size and cruelty, and so no-one wanted to deal with them. Least of all was the loners who thought that Robert might take issue with them handling Jacob, considering he was one of Rob's first progeny, and no matter how many times I told them that Rob wouldn't care, because, well... Robert didn't give a shit about anyone but himself and his misery. So unless they heard it directly from him, they wouldn't lift a finger.

So I was following Zoe everywhere she went so that I could keep her safe myself, and if that meant my secret got out, then so be it. I didn't trust them bloody Hecate witches, I didn't trust them nearly five hundred years ago when they were fleecing poor unsuspecting humans for their last coins, I certainly didn't trust them now.

But I would wait in the limo, and if she needed me, I would be there.

Until then, I would spend my time showing my woman how good our life could be together, and when all of this was over and she was safe, I will take her - and her family - back home, where we can raise our child free from all of this, and if the baby was a girl, then she would have plenty of space to practise her craft on my lands.

When we were finally alone in our room after dinner, I saw how tired she was. I had kept her up for most of last night, which had been the best night of my life; her reaction to my touch, and the way she tried to take control had driven me crazy, and I had taken her, giving her everything I had. Just remembering had me growing hard, but I tucked that away for another night, she

couldn't take me again so soon; besides, I was content to just spend the night next to her and learning everything I could.
She yawned and stretched as she walked towards the shower, carrying her PJs in her arms and shutting the door behind her. I undressed and stepped into my own lounge bottoms, a soft grey cotton that was comfortable to move around in, and lay on the bed. I had bought her a gift today while we were browsing and she wasn't paying attention; I had wanted to surprise her, but as I hear the shower turn off, I felt irrationally nervous that I was overstepping.

Overstepping? I'd practically moved her in after a matter of days, she would not think I was taking liberties by buying her this would she?

I held the wrapped package in between my hands, swirling it and wondering whether I should save it for another day. She stepped out surrounded by steam, the glow from the bathroom light seemed to halo around her, her cheeks were flushed from the heat and her curls were falling over her forehead in a riot of ringlets - and she was the most beautiful woman I had ever seen. She only had on a pair of red cotton shorts, and a matching white vest with little love hearts on, a simple ensemble for bedtime, but it was sexier than if she had walked in wearing silk and lace. Her nipples stood out under the cotton and I could see the faint outline of her areola beneath the thin material. She stood there trying to pull the vest down, but all it did was stretch the cotton even tighter over her plump tits. A growl worked its way up my chest, my beast rising at the luscious sight before me, clearing my throat to hide it, I shoved the gift towards her. "I bought you a present, I hope you do not mind."

"For me?" She cradled the wrapped parcel between her own hands, her eyes shining as she looked at me like I had given her the most expensive of jewels.

"Open it."

She sat down beside me, her legs tucked beneath her while she carefully pulled apart the wrapping to reveal the narrow white box. Her eyes lifted to me curiously before lifting the lid and pulling apart the peach coloured tissue paper that delicately enfolded what was inside.

Her gasp and the tender look in her eyes as she lovingly caressed the tiny babygrow that I had purchased killed any anxiety that I had been feeling over if she would like it or not. Her finger traced the words *Mummy's little Muggle,* that was printed in gold on the little black outfit.

I couldn't resist when I saw it, the irony of buying a Harry Potter themed babygrow for a witch was too hilarious not to pass up, she would think it was a coincidence for now, but soon, our child would fit into it, and Nathan - the geek that he was - could teach his niece or nephew all about the world of Hogwarts while growing up in a real world of magic and mayhem.

"Nathan is a Potter fan, he told me today that he had read all of the books and seen all of the films…oomph" she threw herself at me, her arms wrapping around my neck and squeezing.

"Thank you, thank you, thank you."

"I think I should buy you more things if this is how you react."

I wrapped my arms around her and held on, breathing in her fresh scent.

"This is perfect Lucian."

She leaned back to give me her smile, her eyes crinkled at the corners with the force of her happiness; I vowed that I would make sure she smiled like that everyday for the rest of our lives. I reached behind me to pull back the blanket, laying her down in the middle and carefully placed her gift on the side table closest to her, then lay down beside her, pulling the thick duvet over both of us but leaving the bathroom light on so that she could see me. Stretching my arm out, I beckoned her to curl in beside me, her head resting on my chest as I curved my arm around her, holding her close. And finally, with the woman of my heart wrapped safely in my arms, I could relax.

Her fingers swirled through my chest hair making patterns and her breath was warm as it blew over me when she exhaled. The minty smell of her toothpaste was strong in my sensitive nose, but I knew I wouldn't move. "Tell me about your childhood." I asked her.

"What do you want to know?"

"Anything you want to share love, I want to know everything about you."

And so I laid there listening as she told me about growing up in foster care, and about her foster mum. I learned all about the infamous Sarah - Lissa's mum - and would thank her in person one day for all she had done for Zoe and Nathan over the years. I found out about her search for her birth mum and how she had felt finding nothing. Her voice filled my head with stories of her youth and the mischief her and her best friend got up to and I laughed when I heard about the time they had put laxatives in the foster mum's beer, only for her to make a mess of herself in the local pub, even five years later she apparently couldn't live it down, still being called Tacky Jackie.

I spent my night cradling her against me, and listening to everything she wanted to share, hoping that maybe she would touch on the subject of her being a blood witch, so that we could finally broach that subject while we were both so in tune with each other, but she did not say anything about it, and I could not help but think that maybe I should have just asked her about it, because all I could think about was that tomorrow, she would go to the coven, and I had no idea what would happen behind those closed doors, and sending her into there unprepared felt like I was making a huge mistake. But it could also push her away from me, learning about me and my secret, and I could not risk losing her right now when I finally had everything I had always wanted. And so I kept my mouth shut, hoping that tomorrow would end exactly the same as today had.

CHAPTER 13

Zoe

I woke up warm and rested but with a sense of foreboding in my gut, the thought of returning to where all of those scheming women housed didn't fill me with warm and fuzzies, so I snuggled down deeper with Lucian by my side giving myself five more minutes of peace before I had to get up and ready for the day; I wanted to be as prepared as possible, so at dinner last night, I had snuck a sharp steak knife in my bag to bring along with me, just in case I needed to make myself bleed...or make someone else bleed. Either way worked.
Lucian was still fast asleep next to me, we had stayed awake late talking about anything and everything, so I let him sleep while I crept as quietly as I could to the bathroom to empty my bladder and have a shower.
I stepped under the warm spray and let the water work its magic, waking me up and refreshing me. The screen door slid open behind me, and I felt Lucian press his hardness against my back. His arms came around me and his mouth came over my shoulder to lay kisses against my cheek.
"Good morning, beautiful."
"Mmmm, good morning," I murmured, raising my arm over my head to cradle his against me, "I was going to let you sleep in for a bit longer."
"I do not want to sleep love."
His hard length was pressing against my back, reaching behind me with my free hand, I grasped it and squeezed, feeling it pulsate in my grip. He grunted, thrusting his hips towards mine as if he could get any closer. One of his hands snaked between my thighs, putting one of my feet on to the shower seat, I opened myself up for him. My own grunt left my lips as two of his thick

fingers entered my pussy, pushing in and out and using my own wetness to draw circles over my clit. His mouth caught mine, leaning over my shoulder and drawing my head back towards him, his tongue mimicked his fingers, circling my mouth and playing with my tongue.

I couldn't keep my hips still, they moved of their own accord trying to make him move quicker but wanting it to last longer at the same time. My senses were assaulted from all angles, my mouth, my pussy, and when his other hand reached up to pluck at my nipple, I couldn't make it last any longer, I came all over his hand, my juices mingling with the shower still hammering away at us. His mouth left a trail of heat down my neck as he kissed his way down and back up again, while he pushed my upper body forward. I braced both hands against the wall, my palms trying to find purchase on the slick wet tiles, and hold myself up for his entry. I tilted my hips towards him, "Lucian." I panted. Looking over my shoulder to watch him, he held his hard cock in one hand and lined it up with my entrance, his other hand gripping tightly to my shoulder. He was enraptured with the sight of himself entering me; I watched him as he watched our joining, his eyes burning with lust and need until I couldn't keep my own eyes open. My head fell forward, unable to keep the weight of it as the pleasure intensified with the stretch of my pussy.

His cock thrust shallowly inside me, not filling me up the way I wanted him to.

"Lucian please, give me all of it."

"Like this love?"

His hand pulled me bodily towards him, his length spearing me until he hit the end, the stretch of him was a burn that got hotter and hotter as he thrust inside me, hitting that sweet spot every time he bottomed out.

"Remember who this pussy belongs to," he thrust harder, his voice barely discernible as he growled out each word, "no-one else can have this sweet cunt, it's mine."

"It's yours...it's yours." My hands had nothing to hold on to as he pulled me back on him every time he pushed inside me, "please baby, I need to cum." I sobbed out.

He reached around me to thumb my clit, rubbing it hard and fast; that pressure built and exploded out of me in waves, making me scream out, his own yells joining mine as he emptied himself inside me; I could feel the heat of him as he spilled deep within me, filling me up and creating tiny shockwaves that made me shiver.

He slipped out of me and pulled me to a standing position, running his hands along my body and feeling the quivering of my muscles. He gently lifted my leg from the seat and placed it on the floor.

"Do you remember your promise to me?"

"Huh?" my brain wasn't fully working yet, so his question stumped me.

"Our first date, I asked you to promise me something, do you remember?"

"Ummmm, vaguely."

"You promised that no matter what, you would never hate me."

I turned around in his arms and looked at him confused for a second. Of course I remember him saying that, but I was at a loss as to why he was reminding me of that now?

"I remember, you asked me to vow it, and I did," I confirmed to him, "how could I ever hate you Lucian, you gave us a place to stay and be safe…" I quickly corrected myself, forgetting that he didn't know that part yet, "safe because we aren't from a particularly nice area you know, and you have treated my family like your family and…"

His kiss cut off my verbal diarrhoea thankfully, before I said something stupid.

"You do not have to thank me for that, love," he said, "I am here to keep you safe by any means necessary, and I just want the best for you all, and for the baby."

His hands began soaping me up and I was starting to think that washing me was one of his new favourite things to do. It was one of my favourite things too, feeling his calloused palms touch me everywhere ignited that spark inside me, but I had no time for that again, I had to leave soon.

His hands washed every inch of me, and when finished, he turned the shower off and reached for the large towel on the shelf outside the cubicle; I smiled to myself as he wrapped the fluffy hotel towel around me and tucked it around my breasts. I had noticed that about him, he was always doing little things for me, small things that show his caring side, like wrapping me up after the shower and patting me dry, as if taking care of me was the most natural thing in the world. Holding my hand, making sure i'm eating and always asking if I'm hungry or thirsty, holding doors open for me - which you would think that it was a normal thing to do but so many men were not raised to be gentlemen these days, but Lucian was old-fashioned, and I had never met a man as polite and traditional as him...I liked it.

I lotioned my body before dressing in a new pair of blue jeans and a light-weight red jumper that hung off of one shoulder, and all the while I dressed, I thought that my child would grow up to have manners and respect like Lucian...his or her daddy. I tested the word out loud, deciding that I was starting to love the idea of my child having someone so dependable to nurture them; they would have a proper family unit, with a mum and a dad, auntie and uncle. And a grandma if Sarah wanted to be. I wasn't including Jackie in that list, she wasn't worthy of that title at all.

I slipped into some black TOMs. They were the most comfortable things I had ever worn on my feet, I hadn't owned a pair before but I was addicted.

The soft soled shoes didn't make a sound as I walked to my bag that I had left in the - my - walk-in wardrobe, and checked that everything was in there; my phone, my purse, some gum....and the knife that I had taken from dinner yesterday. I debated on where I should keep it, in my bag, tucked into my jeans somewhere? But in the end I left it in the zipped compartment of the bag, just knowing that it was there made me feel a bit safer, it was a mantra that I had grown up with. *It was better to have it and not need it, than need it and not have it.* It was probably the only thing that Jackie had taught me that I was grateful for, the one smart thing that she had passed down to me and it had not failed me yet.

Slinging my handbag across my shoulder, I walked out to find Luc fully dressed and buttoning up his shirt, the sleeves were rolled up to below his elbows and his forearms were on display. I had never found forearms hot on a guy until I met Lucian, they were covered in dark hair, except the underside was lighter, and the veins on his arms stood out prominently. I watched as his fingers finished their job, and he turned to me with a strained smile on his face.

"Come here," he held his hand out to me, "I will be there outside waiting for you, remember."

I walked towards his outstretched hand and grasped it firmly in mine, "you don't have to sit there for hours and wait, Brian can come back, I can text you…"

"No." he interrupted.

I frowned at his abruptness, "I'll be ok Lucian."

His frown relaxed, and a real smile this time took over his face. "I know you will be fine. I just worry about you."

We stood facing each other, my hand cradled in his against his chest where he held it against his heart. I caressed his face, feeling his beard scratch at the soft skin of my palm, "I will be in the school the whole time, just *you* promise that you'll stay in the car."

I had been assured that Jacob didn't know where the coven was, and so Lucian should be safe sitting outside it in his limo doing his work, but still I wanted to be sure that he wouldn't wander off and be found. I was more worried about what Agnes could do to Lucian at this point, considering she had been adamant that I stay there and not with him, but I would take no chances with his safety. "Promise that you'll stay in the car."

"Are you worried about me love?"

"Yes, don't laugh at me." I smacked his rock hard chest with my free hand which he caught with his own and held it next to the other against his heart.

"I can take care of myself, trust me, but if you need me for anything…"

"I'll call you." I assured him.

His mouth crashed down on mine, stealing my breath and leaving me gasping as his tongue conquered my eager mouth. His hands still held mine captive against him, and I was trapped by his onslaught and his grip as his mouth ravaged mine. But I stood there and let him take what he needed from me to ease his worry, because I didn't want to be in that school all day worried about him worrying about me. The kiss ended as abruptly as it started, but he didn't release me from his hold; his forehead rested against mine, his shoulders hunched forward so he could reach me, his warm breath stroked across my face and I breathed him in.

He had become so important in such a short amount of time, and now when I thought about the future, he was always embedded in those images, like he'd been there forever.

"We should get going."

I nodded my agreement, because I still hadn't been able to get that foreboding out of my gut, that going to Agnes today was a mistake. I knew if I opened my mouth I would make excuses to stay and Luc wouldn't stop me. In fact, he would probably love that. But she had information for me, important information she said, and I wanted...no, needed to know what she had. And if it was a waste of my time, well then Luc was just outside and we could make our getaway quick, and I never had to grace their doorstep again.

I doubted they would try anything with me anyway, they had seen what I did to the wall, I was the most powerful witch there, stronger even than Agnes, their high priestess, they wouldn't try anything.

Plus, I patted my bag, I had my trusty little stabby-stab, sharp enough to make a blood witch bleed, and I would bleed all over the fucking place if they pissed me off.

Lissa and Nathan were waiting outside their own doors as we walked out, still in their pyjamas - lucky gits.

"You're off?"

"Yea, I won't be long," I told Nate, "I'll be back by dinner, hopefully earlier."

He stepped up and wrapped his arms around me, squeezing me and lifting me until my toes barely touched the ground. "Just be careful ok." He whispered.

I pulled back and pulled his head to me, placing a kiss on his forehead, I smiled at him. Turning to my best friend, I hugged her. "You're staying in the hotel today?"

"Yea babe, I have a spa day booked downstairs," she stated smugly, "facial and a mani-pedi here I come."
"I'm not doing that." Spluttered Nate.
"I never said you had to do that, besides, I only booked it for me," she scoffed, "I knew you wouldn't like it."
"Thank god," he sighed, "because I have a date with Netflix and there's this new series that everyone is raving about and I've been wanting to watch it for aaaages."
I nodded at him, because once he got started on a new series, he would binge it until it was finished, so he would be entertained for hours - or days.
I took Lucian's hand again and led him to the lift, waving at the other two behind me, and we stupidly laughed and waved at each other until the doors to the elevator slid shut.

  The limo was as comfortable and well-stocked as I remembered it being. The stuff we had used days ago had been replenished, and it smelled like it had been cleaned. I sat as close to Lucian as I could, every part of my side rested against his, his body heat feeding into me until I was almost asleep from the warmth and the constant rocking motion of the limo as it weaved through the London traffic.
"Are you ok?"
"Mmmhhmmmm."
"What things do you need to do at the school."
My eyes shot open and stared unseeing at the empty seat across from me, what did I need to do at the school that I could tell Lucian about? "I have revision to do," I cleared my throat, but kept my eyes straight ahead, I didn't want him to see the lie in my eyes, "I have a...test thingy coming up soon, and I have to do some studying for it."
I felt him look at me rather than saw it. His stare continued as I locked my gaze with the window and watched the city pass me by in blurs of colour.
"Is there any...studying you can do at the hotel?" He questioned.
"Well, there are books and...stuff....that I need at the school, and the texts aren't online so…"
He didn't say anything more, but he rested his hand on my leg, holding it tightly against him and I closed my eyes and prayed

that one day, I could tell him about being a witch, and that hopefully he would still accept me, broomstick and all.

The limo jerked to a stop and the ignition cut out; the trip felt much quicker than the one I had taken to the hotel, but I looked out of the window and the familiar facade of the coven's house stood like a fortress amongst the other residences of the street. Its veneer covered the corruption that lurked inside the great manor.

I steeled myself for the questions and censure that I would receive upon entering, patted my bag again that was draped across my chest to soothe my worry and turned to Lucian beside me. "I'll see you soon."

I turned to climb out of the vehicle, the door opened by the trusty driver already, but Luc's hand tightened on my leg, halting my exit. "Don't go."

"I have to, they're waiting for me. I'm already here."

His eyes carried a look that I couldn't decipher, and he didn't say anything else; so I pecked him on the lips and climbed out, giving Brian a little wave and a 'thankyou' as I walked up the steps to the front door.

"AAAHHH YOU'RE HERE!" Rosie's screeching declaration pierced my ears as she threw her arms around me. "You came. I'm soooo glad you came."

Well, at least someone here was glad to see me. "Thanks Rosie, it's good to see you too."

"Are you staying long?" She threaded her arm through mine and pulled me through the entrance.

"I'm only staying long enough to get some info, then I'm leaving."

"Oh....ok." Her crestfallen look stayed in place as we walked upstairs, past the pictures that lined the walls. A discoloured area of wallpaper denoted a space where a photo used to be, but had been removed; the pattern faded to show that the image had hung there for long enough to leave it's mark.

Rosie paused outside Agnes' office, her hand raised and poised to knock. "I think you're a really nice person, Zoe." She whispered to me before knocking twice sharply and walking away rapidly. Okay, strange and a bit random.

I couldn't ponder her weird comment for long, because Agnes called out to enter, straightening my shoulders, I walked into her office. She wasn't alone though. Cunty-Jade was with her leaning against the wall behind Agnes' desk, her trademark smirk present on her overly made up face. Someone needed to teach this woman about contouring and that less-is-more. Amber was there too, stoic and dressed in her usual smock, but this time, it was grey with blue swirls; it looked like an arm-chair had been cut up and turned into her dress.

And lastly, the doctor. The woman who had tried taking blood from me, I couldn't even remember her name, Marsh, March something?

"Good Zoe, you are here," started Agnes, "we can begin."

I still stood just in front of the doorway, the door still open to the hallway behind me. Agnes waved her hand, a mutter under her breath and the door closed behind me with a soft click. Another wave of her hand had the chair in front of the desk swivel towards me, a hint to take a seat; I didn't really want to get comfortable here, I didn't want to stay long at all, besides I was completely aware that Lucian was anxiously waiting for me outside and I didn't want to make him wait too long. "What's with the get-together?"

"Ah yes, you remember Jade and Amber? Your short term mentors." I snorted under my breath, mentors? More like *de-mentors*. Then I snickered to myself at the Harry Potter pun, because I could totally see them sucking the happiness out of everything. "And you remember Dr Marchand. She helped you when you first arrived here."

I think her idea of 'helping' is greatly exaggerated; she took my blood pressure, listened to my baby's heartbeat and then tried to take blood…from a blood witch. Yea, not impressed.

"And they are here because?" I asked, "I thought you said you had important stuff to tell me."

"I thought they should be here for this as they all have your best interests at heart, dear."

I raised my eyebrows in disbelief, surely she didn't expect me to believe that, especially considering both Cunty-Jade and Amber made my short time here miserable.

Crossing my arms over my chest, I squared my shoulders and waited to hear what she had to say face to face, that couldn't be said to me over a damn phone. The high priestess pulled a brown manila folder out of her drawer and placed it gently at the edge of her desk. I looked at the plain folder, no text was written on it, just a blank, boring brown; but that ominous feeling from earlier settled heavier in my gut, and I knew I didn't want to see whatever was inside it.

"Take it Zoe. It is important that you see what is inside."

"Why don't you just tell me."

"You would not believe me, you need to see with your own eyes."

I stood there resolutely with my arms crossed, my fists clenched underneath my armpits refusing to touch the information that she offered.

She sighed at my mulishness, and leaning back in her chair, crossed her trouser clad legs, the epitome of elegance. "Inside that folder you will find all of the information that we have on one Lucian Garrick."

I inhaled sharply, my eyes widening at her audacity. "Are you fucking kidding me! This is the plan you came up with to get me to move back in here isn't it?" Ugh, I was so done. I turned around to leave, adamant that I would not let these bitches taint what I had just found, "you do not get to do this." I shouted over my shoulder.

"Lucian Garrick, born Lucian James Morris on 26th July...1530." I shook my head, this woman would make up absolute crap.

"I'm out." I pulled on the door handle, but it didn't budge. "Open this damned door now Agnes."

She walked around her desk, the manila folder in her hand now, "here is proof if you do not believe me."

"Oh I don't believe you. You didn't want me to leave in the first place, and you won't even be honest with me as to why you wanted to keep me locked in this...this cess pit."

"You are the last of your kind Zoe, if your line dies, your magic dies with you. Do you not care about that?"

"Obviously you care more about that than I do, I was perfectly happy with my boring job and my boring life and then all of this shit happened. You just happen to be right in the fucking middle of it, and not one of you has tried to help me but you want to *contain* me," I spat at her, "you want me to just go along with everything you say and be a good little blood witch that learns only the bare minimum so I don't threaten your little set up here." I took a breath and looked around the room at the women who were staring at me with open hostility. "I'm done with you all."

"Oh for fucks sake, you spoiled little child." Scoffed Jade. She snatched the file from Agnes and slapped it on my chest, the contents spilling out over the carpeted floor. "Always whining about your poor sorry life, well forgive us for not getting the violins out for you, but *some of us* give a shit that the last of your kind is shacking up with a goddess damned Lycan." She snarled out the last word as the remaining papers fluttered to the floor, facing upwards for the whole room to see. Pictures of Lucian scattered around my feet, all of them taken at different periods of time. I mean, there was a small painting of him wearing some old fashioned suit from Victorian times, his hair long and hanging around his shoulders; he was clean shaven - I had never seen him like that before, he had always had his beard - but it was definitely him. The artist had rendered his likeness perfectly.

I sank to my knees and collected them in my fists, looking at each one and memorising it. A picture of him in a suit like it was the 50's with his arm around some busty blonde. Another picture of him that looked like it was taken in the 20's, a black and white full length photo, with a different woman this time, dressed in her flapper dress.

"Where did you get these?"

"We actually keep track of all of the lycans as best we can," said Agnes. She had gone to sit back in her chair now that she had just fucked up my whole life - again. "We lost track of him for a while, he's not the most sociable of lycans. Most of them live in packs, he never has though."

"Why are you showing me this?" I sat back on my bum, tired of sifting through pictures of my new boyfriend from past eras, some with different women on his arm. There must have been two dozen images of him. Paintings, charcoal drawings, sepia photos fraying at the edges, polaroids. And the most recent one that looked like my Lucian. Bearded and suited up, I held it to my face, looking at the picture of him getting into his limo right outside the hotel we had been staying at.

"That one was taken just over a week ago. The first time anyone had seen him in years."

"This doesn't prove he's a lycan," I was grasping at straws here, but they were pictures of him in costumes, "you could have made all of this up, you're all witches after all."

"We thought you may say that." Said Amber, speaking up for the first time. Her trusty laptop was tucked under her arm, she pulled it out and placed it on the edge of the desk, opening the lid to afford me the perfect view of a paused video. Pressing play the video started with two lycans fighting. The video was wobbly and from an aerial view; but you could clearly see the savage display of the lycans. Actually, it was a big massive black beast trying to rip the head off of the one below him. The fight didn't last long, the victor already apparent from the size and viciousness of the one who clearly ripped the head off of the other without much effort

I had seen them up close, and I could imagine the size and strength it had to be to be capable of such an act. The transformation was probably longer than the fight. The beast went from four huge paws to kneeling on the dusty ground, his naked body glistening from the exertion. His shaved head lifted to reveal the familiar face of the man I was growing to lo...to care for. *Cared* for. My heart was in my throat as I finished watching him shift and dress in the clothes that I had seen before. "When was this?" I muttered.

"It was the day you went for lunch, Rosie took you. She dropped you off and circled back," I looked up sharply at Agnes' voice, "she had felt something was wrong that day, she was only trying to help you."

"She followed him, and she knew what he was and didn't say anything to me. I gushed about my date to her, and all the while she knew!"

"Do not be angry with her. She was doing what she was told."

I stood there, my eyes fastened on the still image of a clothed Lucian, staring down at the carnage he had created. Who was that other lycan? Was he one of the ones from the flat before? Anger like I had never felt simmered beneath my body. My skin felt tight, the way sunburn does when it's healing.

"Does he know who I am?"

"He is a lycan dear, of course he knows what you are."

"Also, he's like, the oldest lycan with the exception of dear old grandad." gloated Jade. "he can smell you a mile away." she cackled as she typed away on her phone.

I needed to sit down. I needed to leave, find somewhere to recoup and gather my thoughts.

"Yea, you should also know that your boyfriend here is only with you because he couldn't have Caitlyn. You're second….no, you're like the *only* resort"

"That is enough." Scolded Agnes.

But the damage was done. "What? What does she mean?" I looked at Agnes, who was glaring daggers at Jade.

She looked at me with pity, "rumour has it that Lucian was in love with Caitlyn - your ancestor. But Robert was a Lord, and they loved each other, or so the story goes. He was devastated when she was killed, he was also Robert's first…child." She stated, "the first one he turned on that new moon he was transformed."

I was a stand-in.

I was a replacement for his lost love.

"Sweetheart, I think you should sit down," she moved towards me, "I can call the hotel and have them pack your things…"

"What?"

"You should be here amongst your own kind."

"My own kind?" I whispered, staring blankly at the wall in front of me. There were none of 'my kind'. I looked down at the photo still clenched in my hand; screwing up the thick paper, I chucked it at Jade's feet. That anger festered inside me, feelings of betrayal, sadness and loss swirled around that simmering rot of rage and I swirled around intent on getting the fuck away from these people who had created this mess. I had been happy in my bubble, with my family, a baby on the way and…Lucian. That writhing, whirling storm erupted at the thought of his lies and I punched the heavy wooden door, splitting the skin on one of my knuckles. I watched the blood as it trickled down my fist, a physical embodiment of my pain; I heard the gasps and the scuffs of shoes as they noticed my hand. Glancing over my shoulder at them, I glared at each one of them, "I am not your fucking trick pony." I pictured the office door opening for me, and before the first drop of my lifeforce had dropped to the floor, the heavy wood crashed open, slamming against the outside wall and splintering apart on impact. I was not impressed with the force of my destruction, to hellbent on reaching that deceitful rat that waited outside for me.

As I made my way through the hall and down the stairs, his words replayed in my head *promise you will not hate me, promise you will not hate me, promise you will not hate me.* "Fucking lies." I raged.

The front door did not withstand my wrath, it blew off of its hinges and slid down the stairs, stopping at Lucian's feet. His polished black loafers didn't move an inch. He winced at the fire in my eyes, his face pale with worry. He should be fucking worried.

"You're one of *them*!" I screamed, "you're one of those fucking dogs that tried to kill me. Admit it."

"I am *nothing* like them love."

"Don't call me that. I'm not your 'love', I'm not your 'sweetheart', it's all fucking lies."

"It was never a lie. Nothing I have said to you was a lie." He stood there on the pavement like he had been waiting for me to exit the coven, "I knew they would fill your head with crap about me. I wish I had told you sooner."

"Then why didn't you?"

"Why did you not tell me you were a witch?"

"It's not the same!" I shouted, "as if I could just tell some guy I just met that I have magical blood, but you knew anyway," the windows of the limo rattled in their frames, cracks webbing across the glass, "you used me. You knew what I was all along and you used me to replace your dead woman."

His face slackened and he walked towards me, his arms stretched towards me, "Listen Zoe, you have to believe me…"
"Why should I believe you?" I was losing steam, my anger withering away and being replaced with grief. With the exception of my family, because they kinda had to love me at this point, I had never been chosen. I had never been someone's number one, someone's choice. My birth mum didn't want me. My foster mum didn't want me. Sean had nailed and bailed, and now Lucian; I was not his first choice, just like Jade had said. I was the last blood witch, he didn't have much of a choice if he wanted to be close again to the woman he had loved centuries ago. "I'm getting my stuff and we're leaving."
"Good, yes, we can talk, I promise that I never meant to deceive you."
"I think you misunderstand," he thought I meant that he and I were leaving together, "my family and I are leaving the hotel. I don't want you to follow us, or look for us."
"No, Zoe, wait…" He started towards me, a pleading look in his eyes, but I didn't want to hear his bullshit, I wasn't in the mood for it. I was done with today already and it was barely lunchtime. "Just give me five minutes to explain. Please?"
"Do not come any closer Lucian, I mean it." Tears streamed down my face as I watched him come closer; for just a split second, I considered allowing him to get closer and to wrap his arms around me like he did this morning.
But then I remembered the pictures.
I remembered that he was hundreds of years old and had probably killed my people. Just like Jacob had. Just like all of the other lycans I had read about; he was one of them. An animal who turned into a monster and feasted on the blood of women just like me.
"I said, don't come any closer." I felt the air around me condense and shoot out at his approaching form. The draft shoved him back into the door of his vehicle and held him there against the metal and glass; the wind continued to push him back, the groan of the metal bending under the weight of this man. The glass bent inwards and shattered into thousands of pieces, a symbol of my current emotional state.

His beautiful golden eyes locked with mine and I couldn't help but stare as he kept being forced back, the limo now being shoved into the middle of the road with each blast of air. "Zoe." His hand managed to break free and tried to push himself off of the bending metal, claws erupting to dig into the frame and help him haul himself away from the invisible storm I was creating. "WAIT." He called out to me as I turned towards the street, and without giving him a second glance, I ran down the sidewalk and out onto the next street that ran perpendicular to the one I was escaping down.

      I ran until my lungs burned and my feet ached, I ran until the physical pain overwhelmed the emotional one. I kept going in the direction of the hotel, hoping that I could find a black cab along my route to drive me the rest of the way. This was London, there were black cabs everywhere so I slowed to a trot and continued walking; each slap of my shoe on the concrete stung the balls of my feet, but at least my knuckle had stopped bleeding. I looked down at my fist, pleased to see that it had scabbed over already, it would probably be healed by tonight. For once, I was ashamed of how I had acted. I could have really hurt someone today. Yea ok, maybe they had deserved it by making me feel like shit, and rubbing my face in the fact that I had shacked up with one of them *unknowingly,* but a lot of the girls in that house were innocent and I shuddered to think about what could have happened if I had not ran when I did.

Was Lucian free now and looking for me? Or would he go straight back to the hotel to wait for me?

I rummaged through my bag still slung across my shoulder and pulled out my phone, comforted by knowing that Lissa and Nathan were safe at the hotel and had not seen my meltdown. Focusing completely on the device in my hand, pulling up Lissa's number to let her know what happened and to start packing, I wasn't paying attention to my surroundings. I should have known better, Sarah had taught me better than to not be aware of where I was going; she had told me the stories of women coming into the hospital after being out on their own. The attacks, the assaults. She always made sure we were prepared from the day we started walking to school without an adult.

But I was preoccupied. The day had turned to shit before my eyes and I had been blindsided by the truth. The truth that I was a gullible, desperate moron begging for attention. I had fallen for his crap hook, line and sinker. We were moving to a remote village in Europe somewhere, where we could grow our own food, and have some cows for milk. And we wouldn't need anybody else. Just us and the baby, when he or she got here.
It would be perfect.

I was considering all of the beach locations that we could visit in our new life as expats, when a shadow fell across me. I couldn't look up in time before an arm came around me pressing a sickly-sweet smelling cloth over my face.

I kicked back at who was behind me, aiming for anything; I tried to use my elbows but his other arm banded tight around me, locking my arms together at my sides. This fucker was strong and I was breathing in that smell. My head felt dizzy and my movements became sluggish; I couldn't get enough strength behind my hits, my legs gave out beneath me and I collapsed in the strangers arms.

"That's it, darlin', just go to sleep." His voice surrounded me and it was the last thing I heard before I succumbed to darkness.

CHAPTER 14

Zoe

  I woke up groggy, my head pounding like the time Lissa and I had necked Jagerbombs all night, and then spent the morning puking our guts up. But I couldn't remember drinking anything, actually, I couldn't remember much at all. I strained to think what I had been doing to feel so shitty; I remembered waking up with Luc and getting ready to go and meet the Hecate witches.
That was it so far.
I strained to think what had happened afterwards, but everything was a blank up until I had reached the coven. Did they do something to me?
My eyes were crusted closed, I could feel the gritty sandpaper-like grain sticking my eyes together; I tried to wipe them but I couldn't move my arms.
I laid there - for I don't even know how long - with my eyes closed trying to take stock of my body, and how I was feeling.
I was freezing; the floor was hard beneath me doing nothing to stop my shivering. Trying to sit up, I curled my body forward slowly, keeping my eyes closed as the movement was making me feel nauseous. "Ugh."
A blast of light behind my eyes had me cringing and ducking my head down to try and get away from the blinding pain in my head.
"Good, you're awake."
A female voice I didn't recognise echoed across the room, making me turn my head swiftly in her direction, but the light was bright for my sensitive eyes; squinting up at her, all I could make out was a blurry figure walking towards me. Shaking my head to try and lose the foggy feeling bought flashes of images to

my mind. Pictures of Lucian flashed in my head, his face contorted with…pain? I groaned at the pounding headache that pulsed behind my eyelids.

"Where am I?" I managed to croak out around the dryness of my mouth, my tongue wanted to stick to the roof of my mouth; I tried licking my cracked lips to create some moisture, but it was as dry as the fucking Sahara. "Could I have some water?"

"You can have whatever you want," she replied. I sighed with relief, imagining quenching this thirst, "as soon as Jacob says you can."

My eyes flew open and landed on the skinny woman standing just a few feet from me; the pounding in my head being pushed to the back of my mind as her word slowly sank in. "What…what did you say?"

"Where do you think you are, little girl. This ain't the Ritz no more."

I looked around me, the room was floor to ceiling white wood panelling and the floor was a solid stone. "What is this place? Where's Lucian?"

Her laughter reverberated around the room, her head thrown back and her hands on her non-existent hips; her box-coloured red hair lay limp around her shoulders, and her roots were growing in a dark muddy brown, it looked like it hadn't been washed in weeks.

"Lucian? That fucking dog won't find you here."

And at that, calling him a dog, it all came rushing back; the photos, the video of him shifting. My face must have shown my shock but she misunderstood it. "Yea sugar, he ain't gonna come for ya." She cackled.

My heart pounded in my chest as I took in everything at once, Jacob had me and I had no clue where I was. My hands were tied behind my back, my wrists held together with…was that fucking silk? I tried leaning far enough around to look over my shoulder and try and wriggle out of the bonds, but they didn't budge an inch.

"No use trying to get outta those, that's spider silk," she chucked a hard boiled sweet into her mouth, and tucking it into one of her cheeks said, "strongest and stretchiest material ever made; good for holding girls like yourself." She chuckled.

"Girls like myself?"

"Yep, you blood witches. Can't cut yourself on it, it's too soft, it's round your ankles too in case you hadn't noticed yet." She raised her eyebrows at me and looked to where my legs were stretched out in front of me; the pale silk was wound around and in between my ankles, tying my legs firmly together. I tried rubbing my feet in an up-down motion to loosen the fabric, but it was stuck tight to my trousers.

"Sticky that shit is, always get it stuck under my nails." She buffed her scraggly nails against her threadbare yellow shirt, then looked underneath them. "See, look." She turned them round to show me the dirty underside of her nails, black grime and gods knows what else caked under the nail beds. I tried my best to hold my gag reflex at bay.

"Oh...yea...I can see that." I breathed deeply through my nose and out through my mouth, the sight of her stained fingers almost making me wretch. They were prepared for me, they made it so I couldn't cut myself - on anything. There was nothing surrounding me, just four walls and a ceiling, and not a window in sight. I needed to get the fuck out of here and find my bag, as pissed as I was at Lucian right now, I was sure he was the ony one who could - or would - help me, and I needed my phone for that. So that meant I needed this weird woman on my side, so I pasted the fake smile on my face that I used for customers at the bookies and tried to strike up a conversation with her. She looked...pretty normal; maybe Jacob was keeping her locked up here too, and he clearly wasn't taking very good care of her.

"Hey, so, I'm Zoe, and not to be a massive inconvenience or anything, but could you maybe loosen the ties a bit, they're really tight and I can't even feel my toes." She stared at me blankly and I worried that she wasn't all there in the head, which may actually work in my favour. "And I'm bursting for the toilet," I let out a fake laugh, "being pregnant really plays havoc on your bladder, know what I mean."

Her angry snarl was enough warning to shut the fuck up right now. I stared at her mottled face and clenched teeth, *she* was angry for some reason? I was the one kidnapped and tied up on a damn floor.

"You think you're so fucking special!" She snarled.

"I really don't," I shook my head in denial, "nothing special about me, nope, just normal and boring."

"You, with your baby, rubbing it in my face because you know I can't carry a child. EVER!"

Woah. "I'm sorry, I didn't know…"

"LIAR." She screamed, before running at me with her raggedy claws extended; I tried shuffling back on my bum but I couldn't get far with my hands and legs tied.

"Now just hold on a minute…."

There was a burning pain as she grabbed my hair, my scalp feeling like it was about to be ripped off, I screamed in pain and anger, this woman had serious problems, but if I could get her to just scratch me - I shuddered thinking about all of the germs under her nails coming into contact with my skin - a tiny drop of my blood would do the trick and I can get the fuck out of this shit hole before Jacob can even get here.

"Ah ah ah, Lou, stop harassing our guest."

I shuddered at the low growl from behind my crazy attacker. It was too late, he was here. She immediately rushed to do his bidding, releasing my hair from her clutches and stepping back from my reach; she rushed over to where Jacob stood in front of the door that I hadn't noticed, it blended in with the white panelled walls, but now that I knew it was there, I could see where the hinges were and a handle - white to blend in.

He looked exactly as he had the last time I had seen him at my house; handsome and cruel. Lou glided over towards him, and like a dog in heat, rubbed herself all over him, literally. She was rubbing her face all over his arm, and gyrating against his leg. I wouldn't be surprised if she started humping his leg too.

"Ello kitten."

I swallowed the lump in my throat and sat up as straight as I could whilst being tied up. My legs in front of me and my hands tied behind my back, I grabbed a hold of every bit of courage I could, and stared straight at my kidnapper, the man who had essentially turned my whole life upside down. It was him and his pets who had come to my house causing us to flee and leave everything behind, and I was so sick of him.

"Look at you trying to be all brave and shit," he walked around me, skirting the room but his eyes fixed on my position laid out on the floor, "you did good Lou, you can leave now."

"But Jake, you said…" his icy glare turned to his comrade, "I said you can leave now."

Her hair hung limply over her face as she hung her head and turned away towards the still open door. "You said I could have the baby remember, just don't hurt the baby."

My whole body jolted at her words and I felt the blood drain my face. "My baby? You said she could have *my* baby?" I snapped, "what the fuck is wrong with you, you psycho."

"I'm doing you a favour pet, you will be too busy to take care of a baby," he laughed, "now Lou, get out before I make you." She scuttled out of the room with her shoulders raised above her ears, and if she had had a tail right then, it would have been tucked between her legs. "Apologies kitten, you weren't supposed to hear that, but I suppose it's best you hear it all now, and then we can move on to the good stuff."

"Why don't you undo these bindings, hand me my bag and we can get on to the good stuff."

"Now why would I do that? I rather like you on the floor at my feet," he leaned against the wall, his arms crossed, "at my mercy. You should make note of this, you will be doing it a lot."

"I won't do anything for you. You made a mistake Jacob, you thought that restraining me would keep you safe. I will blow you the fuck up!"

His amusement was written all over his face as he chuckled, "no, you won't." He stood up straight and walked towards me, "you will not touch me and you will do everything I tell you to do."

A snort laugh escaped me, because clearly all this time hunting me down had not taught him one thing about me, I was stubborn as fuck, and if he told me to do something, I would do the opposite just to piss him off, especially when he had plans to give my baby to that crazy whore.

He bent down on his haunches, too far away for me to try and kick him in the face, but near enough that I could see the endless

darkness through his eyes, there was not even a hint of his pupil, his irises were so black; It's what I imagine a wormhole to look like; empty, nothing.
"How do you think I found you?"
"I don't know Cujo, you probably had psycho lady sniff me out."
His maniacal grin caused a wave of unease to pass through me. "I don't really need to work that hard if I'm honest, not when I have friends in the most magical of places."
I sat frozen staring at him, grasping his meaning but desperately trying to come up with something else, anything else. The witches hated lycans, they wouldn't help him...would they?
"You're lying."
He made himself more comfortable on the floor, crossing his legs and resting his elbows on them as he leaned forwards. "You want it to be a lie, but the truth is kitten, you're a liability and certain people want you out of the way." He looked over his shoulder towards the wall where the door was, and as it opened a familiar figure walked through.

    I had a feeling. I knew she hated me, but surely the enemy of my enemy and all that crap was a real thing. But obviously not.
"Fucking Jade," I sniffed, "there's a reason we call you Cunty Jade behind your back."
Her contoured face turned an ugly shade of red under all that crap she painted on with a trowel. "Does Agnes know you're a dirty traitor?"
Her polished stiletto heels paused before she even made it halfway in the room, and she stared at my trussed up body, probably making sure I was tied up and couldn't get to her. When she was clearly satisfied that she was safe from me, she smiled and, sliding her manicured hands into the pockets of her black cigarette trousers, she let out a tinkling laugh. "Agnes knows whatever I tell her, I am her successor after all."
"What the hell did I ever do to you that you thought it was ok to give me to our enemy!"
"Like you have not been fucking the enemy."
"Ah yes," mused Jacob, "you've been banging the favoured son."
I glared at the arshole sitting across from me.

"You did nothing Zoe, that is the point," Replied CJ, "You were born with all of this power, and all you do is cry about what you lost, and how you want a normal life, it is disgusting." She spat. "You could have had everything. Immortality, power, wealth. But instead you shackle yourself to those Nulls and spend all of your waking hours talking about the bastard child you carry."

"Fuck you bitch."

"Blood witches of old used to choose the fathers of their next child with meticulous precision knowing that their daughters would carry the best of both lines. They chose Lords and Dukes and rich merchants...but you spread your legs for some nobody, and now your child will *be* a nobody." She looked down at me from her lofty position. "They would cast spells during their first trimester - the most important time - to make sure that their babies would be strong, you...you sit and binge Netflix. You are the worst excuse for a blood witch, and I would rather see your whole line die out than be this worthless, useless example of what used to be the greatest witch line."

"Are you stupid? I asked you, all of you to teach me, and no-one would. Not one of you wanted to help me and you have the nerve to stand there and tell me I'm not a good blood witch because I don't know what I'm doing? Well whose fucking fault is that huh."

She gazed at me with her icy eyes, hatred blazing down at me, and I just knew that couldn't be the only reason she went to all of this trouble to get me here, she wanted me to believe that she wanted me dead because I wasn't a good witch...after like, a week? she wasn't telling the whole truth. "You're lying."

"Excuse me?"

"That's not why you gave me up. You're lying."

Jacob's deep laughter rang out through the room. "Oh, she is on to you."

Shock covered her face. "What does it matter, I want you gone and Jacob wants you. Win win." She stroked her hand through his hair, and his eyes closed as if he was enjoying her caresses. "She wants the babies." Jacob's reply was like being engulfed with ice water, its frost encasing me; I couldn't move, I couldn't even breathe.

"For fuck sake Jacob."

"What does it matter if she knows? She won't be leaving here for a long fucking time."

"You are right, she can know, at least she will know what happens to her children," Jacob stood then, he towered over Jade as they stood side by side.

"Your daughters will be raised by the Hecate line going forward, their power will ensure I am the high priestess forever. I will be immortal, like you, and it's because your babies will be raised in deference to the great goddess, and I will restore our power, making sure that the Hecate line is, and always will be, the most powerful of witches. Your daughters will willingly sacrifice their power and their lives in honour of their mother - me."

I yelled my frustration at her. "You evil whore, you're a disgrace to all witches." I tried to stand, rolling onto my side and trying to get my knees beneath me, but I collapsed onto my front unable to get up. I screamed my hatred at her and her plans, the thought of any of my future children suffering under Jade's cult-like future terrified me.

"Hush kitten, it's not so bad." Jacob helped right me, seating me on my bum once again, but I thrashed in his arms trying to head butt him, or bite him, or anything that I could reach with my body parts that I could still move. "Now now, don't be difficult. You haven't heard the best part yet." He moved to retake his place beside that bitch.

"I do not think she likes this plan darling." Smirked Jade.

"Any son you conceive will be kept safe."

"Are you trying to make me feel better? Because it's a fucking shit way of going about it."

"Don't be so ungrateful kitten."

"You want me to be happy that you will only murder my daughters, but my sons will be...what? Your slaves?"

"They will be my sons and they will be the strongest lycans ever born, stronger even than Robert himself," he bragged, "I will take care of them, rest easy knowing that at least your sons will be loved."

"You seem to be forgetting a major flaw in your schemes." I explained.

"Oh?" He cocked his head to the side like a regular golden retriever.

"Yea, I refuse to be a part of this bullshit. I told you before, you can't make me give you my babies to murder."

I told him, he could tie me up, but I had teeth and I knew how to use them. They may not be 'Lycan' sharp, but all I needed was a bead of blood, a little nip, and I was out of this shithole. Bye-bye Jacob, bye-bye traitor.

I bit down hard on my bottom lip as I glared up at them; I felt the sharp sting as my teeth pierced the sensitive skin of my lip, and tasted the sweetness of my blood as it welled up. I smiled at them, narrowing my eyes as I pictured both of them bursting into flames. It was only right that they burn in hell for what they've done.

I watched, and waited for their screams of agony, for the smell of burnt dog hair.

But nothing happened.

They shared looks of triumph as they gazed down at me, "well done, I was unsure if it would work. But you have certainly outdone yourself."

Jade's chest puffed with pride, "thank you, it was quite easy actually."

Nothing was happening. I could feel the blood magic, a tingling around my lips as the blood continued to well and slowly trickle inside my mouth, but I couldn't make it do anything.

I had spent so long wishing that I wasn't this person, that I was normal; now I couldn't do magic, I felt...panic. "What did you do to me?" I shrieked.

"Did you think I would bring you here and not have a way of controlling you? Did you think I had spent all of these years tracking your kind and not know how to keep you in line?" Jade's tinkling laugh joined Jacob's.

I was restrained. I was trapped. And, I was...human. Fear like I had never known bubbled in the pit of my stomach. Dread filled my heart knowing that I couldn't protect myself or my baby, and these people would keep me here, magicless and helpless. They took delight at seeing the fear painted on my face, because Jade was bragging about how great she was, how talented a witch she was, that she had bested a blood witch.

I couldn't breathe and it felt like the room was closing in on me, I gasped for breath as they watched me struggle with no concern. Humour twinkled in their eyes as they had watched me try to use my powers and realise that I was unable to do anything. The realisation that I was stuck here with them, and that I may never see my family again…see Lucian again was devastating, and a sob tore from my throat.

"Oh for Goddess' sake, stop complaining. You're so dramatic," laughed Jade, "I did it while you were sleeping; just a little binding spell to keep you from doing anything drastic. It's an old spell, it used to bind young witches' magic until they learned to control it."

"How long does it last?" Questioned Jacob, his eyes still locked on me.

"It only lasts a few hours," relief filled me at hearing her words; my magic wasn't gone forever, it was just temporary, "but I will be back soon to re-do the spell."

"It doesn't matter, in a few hours she will be in her *new home*." He stressed the last words, and I figured my new home was *not* going to be a little cottage with a white picket fence and a 60 inch TV.

A tiny spark of hope lit up inside me, I had a few hours between being moved out of this room, and getting my powers back. I had to think and work smart and hopefully I'm provided with a window of opportunity and I can get the hell out of here.

The Traitor turned to me then, "you know Agnes has some of your ancestors Grimoires locked away in her room."

My ears perked up, and from my uncomfortable position on the stone-cold floor, I considered all the ways I could ruin Agnes when I got out of here. She had deliberately kept them from me, and kept me ignorant of the ways of my ancestors, knowing full well that she had all the relevant information to hand. She could have prevented some of this, but she was as much to blame as they were. I gave Jade my best death glare which didn't do much except make her grin even wider.

My shoulders throbbed from the position they were held in, and my bum was starting to go numb from sitting in the same position too long. I contemplated Agnes' position in all of this; does she really not know what Jade is doing right under her nose? In league with the monsters that she professed to hate. I tried to shift around to relieve some of the ache, but my arms strained against the silk bonds and pulled my shoulders back further, causing a pulsating heat to resonate down to my wrists. Psycho one and two were whispering between themselves while I tried to get comfy and come up with some ideas about escaping. It would be easier if the crazy lady - Lou, Jacob had called her - would come back and take over, she would have been easier to manipulate. I knew what she wanted, what she was clearly desperate for, and although I felt kind of bad for her, I knew I had something she wanted. I could work with that.

  Their muttering ended, and I hoped that meant they would be fucking off sooner rather than later. They looked cozy, cozier than people who only started working together should be. They shared small touches and secret smiles. No way could Jacob actually have *feelings* for The Traitor? They shared a look and a smile between them, "It's time for me to go now," she stated this louder, clearly wanting me to hear that she was going back to the coven, "Agnes will be wondering where I got to, can't have her asking any questions." Jade turned to leave, her heels click-clacking on the stone floor as she strutted towards the exit as if she was on a fucking catwalk, and not like she was planning on murdering my forced-upon-me future children. Children that I didn't even know could happen, because lycan's were infertile right? So many plot-holes and questions, how the hell did these people think this shit would happen and that they would get away with it!

She blew Jacob a kiss as she got to the door, then winked at me. "Have fun." The door closed quietly behind her, not even a *snick* of the latch catching.

Now it was just us again, an immobilised witch and a lycan with a superiority complex. The only noise in the room was the sound of my heart pounding in my ears. Now that his accomplice was gone, his relaxed stance had straightened, making him seem taller. Or was that just because I was still sitting on the damn floor?

He stood nearer to the door that Jade had just left from, his hands tucked into the pockets of his black slacks. I only just realised that they had been wearing matching outfits.

"Did you and Bitchface coordinate your wardrobes? Because if you did, it's lame." He looked down at his clothes, an annoyed look taking over his face.

"You are not really in a position to be insulting me."

I snorted, "you keep telling yourself that this is a done deal; but you should know that as long as I'm breathing, I will never stop trying to get away."

"And you keep telling yourself that you have a chance, it's amusing to watch you keep fighting me," his black loafers stepped silently towards me until he was only feet away, "I knew you would not be amenable to my - our - idea, so I had to come up with a contingency plan; a way of making sure you would be compliant." He took his hands from his pockets, crossing his arms over his lean chest and shouted at the top of his lungs for a Banner?

A scuffling noise outside the door had my stomach making twists and turns wondering what kind of shit he had thought up to try and keep me in line. All I could think was that Lucian had followed me here and now Jacob had him here too, and I knew I wouldn't sacrifice my baby, or future babies, to keep Luc safe. Any parent would do the same, and Luc would understand, he had professed to love the baby I was carrying already, so then he would be willing to accept any fate to make sure that my baby made it out of this safely.

A big ugly dude in a stained white vest and cargo trousers dragged a moving, writhing mass through the doorway and threw it at Jacob's feet. "Here ya go boss."

I struggled to comprehend what, or who, it was I was staring at, my brain would not let me believe what I was seeing and I tried to kick myself with my bound feet to wake me up from this nightmare. A sob fell from my lips as I stared at the bruised face of my little brother. "Nate?" His name fell from my lips like a plea, begging him to open his eyes and let me know he was ok.

"WHAT DID YOU DO YOU FUCKING MONSTER." I wriggled as hard as I could, wanting to touch him and feel for a pulse, but I couldn't move, I stared intently hoping to see the rise and fall of his chest but the tears were blurring my vision and I couldn't fucking see anything.

"Why? He's just a kid."

"He's just a human kid that you love; I told you I would get you to do what I wanted."

A moan of pain was dragged from Nathan's lips as he struggled to his hands and knees, his head raised slowly to look around him. "Zoe?" He moaned out.

"I'm here sweetie." I cried. Tears poured from my eyes and my head hit my raised knees in relief; he was alive, that was all that mattered.

"What happened Zo? Where are we?" He mumbled around his split lips; someone had been using him as a punching bag, both of his eyes were starting to swell closed, the beginnings of bruises a shadow underneath his eyes; blood crusted his nose and his lips were split in at least two places.

My beautiful boy. He had never suffered like this before, he had never even fallen over and cut his knee, he was always so careful; someone had harmed him badly, and my heart screamed for revenge at the cunt who would strike a kid, my kid, like that.

"I thought you were at the hotel with Lissa? Where is she? Did they get her too?"

He looked at me, fear prevalent across his face, he tried to crawl towards me but Jacob grabbed him by the scruff of his shirt and dragged him back. Nathan's cry of pain as his collar pulled against his throat had me shouting at Jacob to release him, I spewed threat after threat at the filthy bastard who was holding my brother to him like a dog on a leash.

"I'm sorry Zo, I'm so sorry, I didn't mean to leave," he sobbed while his head was pulled back against our tormentor's chest, "you text me, you said you needed me..."

"What? No!" I looked at Jacob's smiling face, "you fucking planned this, you lured him out you fucking psycho."

"You text me, you needed me, I had to come," he wept, his body shaking with great heaves as he tried to get his breath back, his

arms hung limply by his sides as he struggled with telling me what happened, "I was just...just watching...and you text....and I had to meet you...and I couldn't...couldn't lose you..." His words were punctuated with racking sobs, my heart shattered knowing that they had used Nathan and his big heart against him, knowing he would try and save me, the only family he had.
"And now kitten, you have a very tough choice to make."
"Please," I begged, "let him go, I will agree to anything you want, just please don't hurt him. He's innocent Jacob." I pleaded as much as I could while laying on the floor trussed up like a fucking turkey, I hoped my acquiescence would be enough to get Nate out of here and to somewhere safe. I would have all of the babies Jacob wanted me to if Nathan was just left out of this.
"Well, you see, I can't really trust that you will follow through with your promise, so you need to make a choice," he pulled Nathan closer to him, his hand still gripping Nate's collar and his other hand now clamped around my brother's shoulder, "you can leave here right now, the door is open, I will cut your bonds and you can go back to loverboy."
I held my breath not daring to say anything or even risk moving when he was giving us a way out, "and Nathan?"
"Nathan stays here with me, we will be new best friends. So make your choice. Little brother?" He shook Nate, just enough that his head bobbled back and forth, "or Lucian?"
A whimper from my brother pulled my attention to him, "I won't leave you Nay Nay, I promise."
I used to call him Nay Nay when he first arrived at Jackie's house, a scrawny little five year old, he loved the nickname, begging me to call him it every night because he had said no-one had ever given him a nickname before. A glimpse of that scared little boy flashed across my teenage brother's face, the fear and uncertainty that he would be left alone, that I would take Jacob's offer and leave him to his fate.
"I won't leave him, are you crazy," I snapped, "we stay together."
"I was hoping you would say that." It was all the warning I got, that and the glint of malice in his eyes as his fangs elongated and he sank them into the crook of Nathan's neck.

Screams were ringing in my ears, and I couldn't tell if they were mine or Nathans. His blood coursed down his shoulder and over his chest as Jacob held Nathan to him and kept his fangs embedded in his body. Nate's arm stretched towards me as his cries tapered off until they were merely whimpers of pain falling from his lips.

But I couldn't do anything. I watched in agony as Nate's lifeless body dropped to the floor, his face turned towards me and his eyes closed, his dark lashes prominent against his pallid face. The screams were still echoing around the room, and I realised it was me; I dropped my face to the floor and squeezed my eyes closed as I screamed out my pain and agony.

  I wanted to wake up from this nightmare, I wanted to be back in my shabby but comfortable living room with Nate sprawled out on the floor with his headphones on while Lissa and I laughed at the antics on Love Island. I had never wanted to hear Jackie's hacking cough as she walked through the front door more than right now, because that meant that this was all in my imagination and I hadn't failed in keeping my brother safe.

I had brought him with me so that I could protect him, so that Jacob wouldn't go looking for him, and in doing so, I had painted a bright red target on his back.

"Don't cry kitten, he'll be fine."

I couldn't look at him, I kept my eyes clenched so that I didn't have to see his filthy smug face. "Stop fucking calling me that."

My screams had died along with my brother's humanity, and now my throat felt like I had swallowed razor blades. I watched Nate lying prone on the floor for the slightest twitch waiting for something, anything to happen. Because if he was still alive and he survived the bite, then he would be one of *them.*

I had read enough about lycans at the coven to know that Jacob's bite was a death sentence.

"You know I saved you from a lifetime of pain. He's immortal now, like you; don't be so ungrateful for the gift I willingly gave him."

"A gift," I spat, "how the fuck is turning into a mindless beast a fucking gift?"

He glided towards me on silent feet, stealthy and menacing in his anger. He grabbed the material of my shirt between my breasts and dragged me upright until my nose was brushing his. My arms were aching after being tied up behind my back for so long, and now I wasn't lying on them I tried to wriggle them around to ease some of the throbbing in my shoulders and wrists.

"I didn't have to do it this way," his hot breath covered my face, my brother's blood still coating his chin and drying around his mouth, specks of red flew at me as he carried on, "I could have done it the way I did it last time, but it was a bit of a hassle mind you. Your mother was always a pain in my arse."

My eyes widened at his confession, he had known my birth mother. "What are you saying?"

He dropped me unceremoniously on the floor, I landed flat on my back with my arms taking the whole of my weight, I felt a sudden sharp pain in my wrist but I grit my teeth against the onslaught and locked eyes with him.

"She shouldn't have ran from me Zoe, and then she wouldn't tell me where you were; she was useless to me by the end."

I sucked in a breath, gasping at the knowledge that Jacob had been the reason my mother had left me; she kept me safe from him. He was pacing up and down, running his hands through his thick hair so it was standing on end; he was starting to get a crazed look in his eyes, they were shifting back and forth between human and lycan. He was losing control of himself. I glimpsed Nathan still lying in the same spot he had been dropped, but I could see his chest rising and falling in shallow pants, and sweat beaded his top lip like he had a fever. It was happening.

 He kept going on and on, muttering about damned witches getting in his way, "she took you from me kitten, you won't get away from me again." His obsidian gaze trailed over my face like he was committing it to memory. "They promised me a blood witch of my very own, and now here you are," his eyes dropped to my stomach, "but we have a problem, don't we."

I lay there on my back, my arms squashed beneath me, daring not to breathe or make a sound in case I set off the crazy beast inside. He had just admitted to killing my mum so that he could have me - when I was a baby.

"Do you know that some species in the wild will kill the offspring of a female, so that the death of the young will trigger her heat cycle again, and the male will attempt to breed his own child on the female?" His back was to me now, his gaze lost to some inner musings, I didn't know what he was getting at, but at that moment, Nate let out an inhuman cry. His back arched off the floor and his unseeing eyes were pointing towards the ceiling, his ankle let out a deafening crack as it bent backwards on itself; his hoarse shout of agony and terror resounded through the room.

"Nate!" I shouted out, if his attention was on me it might take his mind off of what was about to happen to him. "Nate, look at me." His stare remained fixed on nothing as tears streamed down his face while his body started contorting in unnatural ways; the sounds of bones cracking and scraping filled the air along with his sounds of suffering. An intense hatred the likes I had never felt before filled my very soul as I caught Jacob enraptured with Nate's first transformation.

Almost shaking himself free of his reverie, Jacob turned towards me, his smile beaming.

"Do you see? Do you see what we would have together," he declared, "you can have your brother forever, and we can have as many sons as you want." He clapped his hands together in delight, and I flinched at the next sound of anguish that howled from Nathan's lips.

"Can you let me go so that I can go to him?" I whispered, "he needs me…please."

      The smile fell from his lips as he watched me with an almost deadly calm. "Yes, he needs you doesn't he." He walked towards me and I breathed a sigh of relief that I would finally be let loose from these fucking ties, and with that bit of freedom, I could try and figure a way out for both of us. We could go to the country somewhere, a place that Nate could run around and have space to run in his newly acquired form, and he would need to hunt too probably, all of these new scenarios were running through my mind, plots and plans were taking shape as Jacob reached me. "Young Nathan does not need some filthy human boy interfering with his development, he will need all of your love and attention for a while...at least until I beget my own son on you."

"What do you...UGGH." My whole body shifted backwards at the force of his booted foot in my stomach, I brought my knees up to try and protect my baby while I retched and heaved at the sudden pain and breathlessness. He moved towards me, determination in every step. "Wait, Jac..." His heavy foot came down on my side, rolling me over onto my bound arms leaving my whole body exposed. I wriggled around to try and give him my back, but I was helpless to his assault. "Please don't do this. I beg you. I already told you that I'd do what you wanted." I cried out.

"This is for the best kitten. The child doesn't belong in our world."

"But...but what if it's a girl? I thought you wanted more blood witches?" I begged. It was my attempt at buying more time for us.

"It's a boy child, and he's useless to me."

His face showed no remorse as his heavy foot raised off the floor, My whole body was shaking in fear and pain; this was normally the time in movies when the hero bursts through the door and saves everyone, killing the bad guy. But there was no-one coming for us. I watched as if in slow-motion as he brought his foot flat down on my stomach. He stomped on the delicate curve where my baby - my son - was growing. And he relished in the pain he inflicted on me.

  White-hot agony tore through my midsection, an ever increasing tide of pain swept through my whole body as his foot continued his stamping tirade; I couldn't scream, the torment too intense. It continued on as Nathan's screams joined my tortured groans everytime his foot landed.

There was no way any child could survive this, and tears of devastation fell as grunts of pain left my lips. I kept my eyes on Nathan as Jacob's beating continued, unable to move except take every kick he gave me, they weren't just centered on my stomach now; they fell on my sides, my legs. My ribs were taking a lot of the impact, the sharp pains that came along with the stomping of his feet made me heave, bile erupting with my moans of pain, splattering on the cement floor.

A rush of warmth between my legs confirmed what I already knew.

My baby was dead.

I lay on the cold floor, my arms crushed beneath me, blood saturating my jeans and dampening my thighs. The life my child had deserved so cruelly ripped away. Nathan's agonised screams had lowered to growls of pain as each crack of his body filled the room; and I screamed to the Goddess with all of my pain, suffering and anger. I screamed until my throat went hoarse and the fire in my stomach spread through my veins. Lava coursed through my blood, the pain of the fire inside me taking over every other hurt until I felt like I was burning from the inside out.

I screamed for Haima to hear me and take away this anguish. Knowing I was this all-powerful being that could not take care of my loved ones caused a ripple of self-loathing; I should have been able to protect them.

I screamed until I felt a swell of that heat inside me merge into one agonising mass.

Before I could even register that Jacob had stopped his beating and stepped back, I concentrated all of my rage and grief at the lycan, and sent it hurtling towards him. The tidal wave of magic exploded across the room, engulfing Jacob, and to my horror, Nathan too.

"NOOOOO." I watched helplessly as his half-shifted form was thrown against the wall, the wooden slats cracking with the impact and bits of wooden debris falling around him as he crashed to the floor unmoving. I didn't know where Jacob had been thrown, but with the amount of power that I had thrown out, he must have been obliterated in the blast - I could only hope.

My whole body wracked with pain, I tried to shuffle and slither my way over to my fallen brother, but I didn't get very far before gunshots sounded from above me. Exhaustion swept over me, I let my head rest against the floor for a minute, listening to the bangs happening above as I watched for signs of life from Nathan. His transformation had stopped when I had accidentally blasted him, and he remained in a half-formed state, his jaw protruding like a muzzle, but the rest of his face still resembled my baby brother. "I'm so sorry. I'm so sorry." I sobbed my apology over and over. Sorry that I didn't save him, and sorry that I had got him into this in the first place.

My body refused to cooperate now; everything below my chest hurt, cramps in my abdomen pulsated and clenched over and over. The wetness between my legs was a stark reminder of what I had lost…of what Jacob had taken from me.

The icy feel of the floor on my cheek was enough to keep me from slipping into unconsciousness, and so I lay there staring at Nate and waiting for whatever was upstairs attacking the place to find me. I didn't hold out hope that it was someone here to help, because so far, no-one had helped us unless it personally benefited them.

A sharp stabbing pain in my stomach had me curling inwards and crying out, another reminder that I was alone here; my baby was dead and my brother…I thought that he was probably dead too. He hadn't moved in so long, not even a twitch.

My pain subsided into dull throbs with the occasional sharp pain, but I noticed that if I laid still and didn't move, the pain wasn't as bad; except for the pain in my heart, I doubted that would go for a long time - if ever. I just wanted to close my eyes and be anywhere but here, somewhere my family was still whole and healthy.

I'm not sure how long I laid there on my side, curled into a ball with my cheek pressed to the floor, but the chill had ceased; I wasn't cold anymore. Heat surrounded me, and part of me wanted to keep my eyes open and watch for what would happen next, but the other part of me wanted to just close my eyes, give into the beckoning warmth and sleep.

I wanted to dream and imagine I was back at the hotel, just waking up with Lucian beside me. I could imagine that this heat I was feeling was his arms wrapped around me, I would forget even going to the witches and stay in bed with him. They say ignorance is bliss, and I wanted to be ignorant for a while longer.

I closed my eyes against the chaos surrounding me, and drifted off into a painless slumber.

"ZOE!"

Pain.

Everything hurt.

"ZOE?"

Was I dead? But then why was there so much pain? Isn't heaven supposed to be painless? Unless I wasn't in heaven? That's why it was so warm here, burning even. What on earth did I do to deserve Hell? I mean, there was that time I had lied to Jackie about bunking school for a whole week, but I had been a kid, surely that wouldn't mean I would be made Satan's Bitch for all eternity?

"ZOE? WHERE ARE YOU?"

Someone was calling for me, that's what had woken me. Trying to lift my head caused shooting pains throughout my whole body, so I resigned myself to staying still and hoped that whoever it was would find me down here. "I'm here." I whispered weakly. My words came out with a shuddering cough just as bits of plaster fell from the ceiling and landed around me. Smoke seeped from under the door, black and grey tendrils starting to fill the room.

Fire. Something was on fire above me, and the smoke was slowly taking over.

At least I would die from smoke inhalation before the fire got me. Being burnt alive didn't sound fun at all!

The door to my prison crashed open, smashing against the white panelled wall that was slowly turning black from the smoke; a hulking figure stood framed by the doorway, the black mass writhing around him. For a split second, I thought it was Jacob coming back to finish the job, but then I remembered that I had blown that fucker up.

He ran towards me, dropping to his knees beside me. "Mo ghràidh, dè rinn iad dhut."

I had no idea what he was saying, but just hearing his voice, knowing that he had come for me, made my heart crack, gratitude filling in some of the broken pieces.

He reached over me and sliced through the silken bonds, blood flushed through my wrists, and I felt prickles and stings as I started to get feeling back in my hands. They had been tied up too long, and I dreaded now to think of what my feet would feel like when they were released too.

"Lucian…"

"Sshhh, do not speak my love, I'm getting you out of here." His gentle hands ran over me from the top of my head to my feet, where he sliced those ties too. When his hands stopped at my stomach, seeing the carnage that *he* had done to me, he hung his head.

He bent down to whisper kisses across my face, an area that was relatively untouched from Jacob's beating, so his lips didn't hurt me. But when his hands slid beneath me to lift me towards him I cried out, the sudden movement jarring all of my injuries. I had managed to forget the pain while I had been laying so still, but changing my position brought all of that fiery agony to the forefront.

"Stop, stop, it hurts."

"I'm sorry darling, we need to leave, this whole place is coming down."

"Please no…" I cried, "just leave me here."

Shock covered his handsome face, and tears created rivulets through the soot on his skin. He was crying for me?

"Is tu mo bheatha. I will never leave you again," he curved his hands around me tighter, "brace yourself, I have to lift you."

Pain ripped through me as he brought me up with him, resting me against his chest. I cried out because it felt like I was being stomped on all over again.My useless hands tried gripping onto him, trying to find something to hold but they flopped uselessly beside me. I had no energy, and the pins and needles were stabbing my hands and feet, like tiny daggers were impaling me.

"I have you, I'm sorry." His hands held me tenderly and I could feel his thumbs brushing against me, but it was too much, and I could feel myself slipping away again. "No, Zoe, stay awake. Stay with me damn it."

I could feel the swaying as he moved, trying to move as quick as he could while trying to keep me as still as possible. But something was in the back of my mind, something I had forgotten to say. The rocking motion was almost soothing me back into unconsciousness; I was safe now.

But that niggling feeling was still there.

Cracks along the wall entered my vision as we got closer to the door, and I remembered.

"Nathan."

"What?"

"We can't leave him," I croaked out. With every bit of strength I had left, I lifted my hand to where my brother had fallen, "he's there. Jacob…" I couldn't finish, I couldn't acknowledge what had been done to him. I left my head to rest on Lucian's chest, while my tears soaked his shirt.

Lucian's harsh intake of breath informed me of when he noticed Nate and what had happened to him.

"They turned him."

I nodded my head against him."Don't leave him here, we can't."

His golden eyes caught mine, and I saw the stunned look in his eyes. "What the hell is he doing here?"

"Put me down, I can walk."

"You cannot walk Zoe, look what they did to you."

"You need to carry Nathan, and this house is fucking burning; I can walk!"

"ROSIE!" His gruff voice shouted loudly, carrying up the set of stairs just outside the door that I hadn't noticed was there. A basement. That's why there are no windows.

Footsteps pounded down the wooden steps, delicate booted feet gave way to cargo pants and Rosie's face carrying a massive gun. She was covered in ash and blood, but there were no visible cuts on her; she came to a sudden halt inside the room and gasped when she took in my condition. I must have looked worse than I felt.

"Zoe…I…"

"We do not have time," Lucian started towards her, "I need you to take her, can you manage?"

"I'm stronger than I look." she snapped back.

"Good, take her, I need to get Nathan."

"Nathan? But he was…"

"I know! Just take her to the van as quickly as you can."
She swung her gun behind her back, the strap criss-crossed over her chest, and stepped towards us. As Lucian lowered me into her arms, everything moved and that ever-present fire ravaged my body, the pain increasing as her hands wrapped around me, touching on every single bruise and wound that had been inflicted on me. Her whispered *sorry, sorry, sorry* repeated in my ears as she took the stairs quickly.

Heat enveloped me as she jogged down the hallway, past leaping flames and broken furniture. The smoke was thick and cloying and the coughing aggravated the agony in my stomach. It was like lightning was shooting through my abdomen, causing echoes of agony to rip through every bone, every muscle; black filtered through my vision, and sparks of light pierced my brain.

And through it all she carried me until clean air filtrated my system. I took great gasping breaths of a crisp, cool breeze. Rosie laid me on the grass outside the property, I could feel each blade of grass rubbing against my sore skin. Looking down at myself for the first time, I could see black discolorations, bruising under the skin that were beginning to form, and blood staining the crotch and legs of my trousers.

Rosie just sat there as if she had seen a ghost.

"I'm sorry."

What was she sorry for? What happened to me? She was there this morning when I was at the house. "Did...did you know?"

"No, I promise, I didn't know she would...could...do this," haunted eyes fixed on my trousers, "I didn't know." She repeated in a whisper.

I turned my head from her and closed my eyes; I couldn't even look at her knowing it was *her* kind that had tricked me, manipulated me. This was as much their fault as Jacob's.

Her choking sobs did nothing to me, I didn't feel anything; because no-one heard my tears and pleading when my baby was being murdered, no-one cared then, why the fuck should I care now?

Dots still danced in my vision, and Rosie's sobs turned to thunder in my ears as everything, the pain, the death, the chaos, swept over me in a wave of exhaustion so strong I couldn't stay awake any longer. I drifted off to the roar of the flames and the crying of a traitorous witch.

CHAPTER 15

I didn't wake up this time like I normally do; an easy, slow coming-to with the light shining on my face through the thin, cheap curtains that Jackie kept in the flat. No. It was rapid, as if someone had pressed the 'on' button and there my brain was, ready and active. That didn't mean my body was ready to go.
My eyelids shot open, and it was as if the glaring of the light from the wall of windows opened a door for every other ache and pain to invade my senses. I tested my body, firstly flexing my fingers and toes, and when that seemed ok - a bit stiff - I slowly brought my legs up, raising my knees until they pointed towards the ceiling.
Um, nope. Not the ceiling. A canopy. Black gauze surrounded the huge bed that I lay in, smothered with huge blankets and a mountain of pillows. That was why I was so warm and cosy amongst the aches and pains.
I hurt, but it felt like when you press down on a days-old bruise - tender. The amount of pain I was in last night, there's no way I feel this good now. I should be suffering far worse. I gingerly pressed against my belly, feeling nothing and that made me feel terrible; I should feel sore there too, it should ache after what I had lost. But there was no feeling at all.
Pulling myself up carefully to rest back against the pile of pillows, I looked around and took note of where I was. It definitely wasn't the Shangri-La.
The room was massive, and painted a dove grey; chairs of crushed velvet sat in a semi-circle around a fireplace that was flickering with its dying embers. A large painting above the fire depicted the silhouette of a man astride a black stallion, flying towards a sunset of reds and golds. It was stunning.

There was nothing personal though; nothing in the room could tell me where I was and whose house this was. I thought that maybe I should be panicking a little bit more, worried about where I was, but what would be the point? Everything had been taken from me, what else was there to lose?
I relaxed back against the soft mound, someone would find me soon enough.

I must have summoned someone with my thoughts. *Could I even do that?* A light knock on the door preceded my host's entrance, and Rosie walked in carrying a tray with a steaming mug and something that smelled so good my belly let out a tremendous gurgle of happiness. I couldn't remember the last time I had eaten, and my body was making its hunger known.
"You're awake," she placed the tray on the bedside table next to me, "I brought you some tea, and there's some freshly baked bread and tomato soup here." She stepped back from the bed, wringing her hands in front of her, she looked like she hadn't slept in days.
"Where am I? How long have I been asleep?"
"Oh, well...we are at Lucian's Scottish home, you slept the whole way here..."
"And how long have I been asleep?" I repeated.
"Um..." She looked towards the door, discomfort evident on her face, like she wanted to be far away right now, "three days."
"How the fuck did I stay sleeping for three fucking days?"
"Please don't be mad, I gave you a sleeping drought, it helped you heal while you dreamed, I'm sorry...please don't be mad."
A deep sigh left me and she cringed against what she thought would be my anger, but to be honest, I wasn't angry at her; she's a victim as much as me. I saw the way the Hecate witches used her, used her kindness. I truly believe that she didn't know what Jade was planning, and last night....no, three nights ago, I didn't tell her that. I wasn't in my right mind when she brought me out of that house, I didn't see her as a traitor. But she probably thought I hated her now.

"I'm not mad at you Rosie..." before I could even finish my sentence she had thrown herself on her knees at the edge of the bed, grasping my hand.

"Oh, thank you, thank you. I'm so sorry about what happened. Goddess forgive me. I didn't know what Jade would do, if I had known I would have stopped you, stopped her," the words spilled out of her mouth as she held tightly to me, "I'll never forgive myself for what you suffered."

I grabbed her hand with my free one, "no, you don't take this!" I vehemently instructed, "this is not your fault, it's theirs. Do you understand?" She looked at me with bloodshot eyes, "do you understand Rosie?" I said it softer this time, but just as firm, and she nodded her head. Maybe she didn't believe it all right now, but I would make her believe it, she was not to feel guilt for anything that had happened.

We both heard the heavy footsteps before seeing Lucian enter the room, "I heard your voice, I knew you were awake."

I soaked in the sight of him. If Rosie looked like she hadn't slept in days, well...Lucian looked like he hadn't slept in *weeks.* His hair was growing out, and it was now about half an inch long growing in all directions; it looked like he had been trying to run his hands through the short length and I wasn't used to seeing him look so unkempt. His beard was a long scraggly mess, sticking out all over the place, and his eyes were red-rimmed; his clothes were rumpled, as if he had been wearing them for a while. "You look terrible."

His laughter filled the room, "thank you love." He walked towards the bed, and at this point, Rosie took that as her cue to leave, quietly shutting the door behind her. Lucian took her spot beside me, leaving one leg on the floor as he faced me, "you should eat something."

"I will, I just...need you to tell me...what..."

"What happened?"

I nodded, clenching the blankets in my fists. I needed to know what he had done with my brother's...with Nathan.

"After you ran off, I was kept at the coven, your magic lingering well after you had left."

My face showed surprise, because I hadn't thought he would go back that far, neither did I think my spell would last much longer after I had made a run for it. I let him continue, because as much as I wanted to know where Nate's body was, I also wanted to put it off for a bit longer. You know, that whole 'ignorance is bliss' thing.
"Once the spell had dissipated, I followed your scent until I lost it, but there was the smell of lycan, and I knew they had you then."
Looking down at my hands tangled in the blankets, I remembered when that guy had come up behind me; the fear I had felt as he covered my face.
"I ran back to the house to get my car, and that's when I found Rosie outside; she had heard another witch on the phone talking about you…about having you."
"Jade, I saw her there, she cast a spell so that I couldn't use my magic, but then…"
He waited patiently for me to finish, but I couldn't say the words. How could I tell him that I had killed my little brother? That my power had sent him hurtling through the room into a damn wall.
"I knew where Jacob lived, but it was heavily guarded, so we set fires around the perimeter; small controlled explosions, but it got out of hand and…"
"and that's why there was a fire." I interrupted.
He nodded, "we didn't anticipate him having a propane tank buried on the property, and it exploded, it caught the house."
His hands reached out and cupped my face, his thumbs stroking along my cheeks as he raised my head to look at him, "I'm sorry I did not get there in time. The baby…" I covered his mouth with my hand, stopping what he would say next. I couldn't talk about the baby yet, not now; it was too soon. I needed to focus on grieving for one loss at a time. Because if I thought about having to mourn both my baby *and* my brother, I would suffocate under the weight of the pain.
"Where is Nate?" I choked out his name, my hand falling to my side to grasp at the blanket again, clenching it in my fist.
"I put him downstairs for now."
"Can I…can I see him?"

"That's not a good idea right now, the transition is still too new, he…"

I shot up, grabbing his shirt in both hands, my heart pounding in my chest. "He's alive?"

He looked confused for a second, before his puzzlement cleared. "You thought he was dead."

Burying my head in his chest, hot tears spilled out, and I couldn't stop the sobbing heaves as I cried with relief and gratitude. He held me there, until I was a snivelling mess, and I didn't even care that my snot and tears got all over him.

"He was too far into the transition, nothing would stop it love. But it's best not to go down there for a while," I looked at him questioningly, "he's stable for now, still in his lycan form, but the smell of a blood witch may send him into a frenzy," strong hands wiped my face of tears. "Soon, ok?"

He was the expert on lycans I suppose. I paused, remembering how I had gotten caught in the first place "I ran from you." I whispered.

"It's my fault, I should have told you; I kept putting it off hoping that by the time you had gotten to know me, it wouldn't matter what I was."

"Yea, you should have told me, but I wasn't honest with you either."

"How were you to know? How would you have known that you could talk to me about being a witch?" Raising each hand to his mouth, he kissed the back of each hand. "No more lies my love, I promise."

He took a breath, still bent over my hands, his eyes reflected the pain I felt in my chest. "What happened in there, before I got to you?"

Ripping my hands away, I scooted back against the pillows, just asking that question brought up all of the reminders, and flashes of past events that I didn't want to re-live.

"I need to know what happened darling, Jacob needs to pay for what he did…"

"Jacob's dead, I did it myself."

Guarded eyes looked at me, filled with wariness. "Your blast didn't kill Nathan, it would not have taken out Jacob."

The realisation that he could be right, that my attacker may still be out there had me clutching my throat, desperate for air. I couldn't breathe, and the less air I took in, the more I panicked. It couldn't be true, he had to be gone; the pressure in my chest was like a balloon inside of me, filling up and getting bigger and bigger, not going down and unable to go anywhere. And what happened to balloons when they were filled too much? They burst!

"Zoe, love. You need to breathe, I need you to take a breath." Lucian's words did nothing to pierce that balloon in my chest, in fact, it felt like he was making it worse. My hands flailed around, desperate to find something to hold on to but also desperate to keep moving and try to get rid of this dread that was taking up residence inside me.

Around my gasping breaths, I heard muffled shouts from the hallway, and as clear as day, a shouted "WHERE IS SHE?" Lucian was trying to calm me down, but that voice…I needed it. The door flew open, and standing there, her great chest heaving, still wearing her blue scrubs over her considerable weight and her bright red Crocs, her hair shorter than Lucians but her eyes blazing; stood the only mum I had ever known.

She rushed over to me, shoving Luc out of the way. Picking me up like an infant and cradling me on her lap, I felt like a child again. She slowly rubbed circles on my back, telling me it was ok, she was here now, and everything would be alright. It was exactly what I needed to calm my racing heart and pop that pressure filled mass inside me; slowly, I started taking in small gasps of air, until I was able to take in more and more. "Sarah?" "I'm here sweet'eart." Her big arms - strong from carrying patients - cradled me, rocking me from side-to-side until I was lulled into a dreamlike state; here but not, awake but…not. I just laid on her, my arms and legs tucked in to make myself as small as possible so that I could fit on her lap while she rocked me and comforted me.

Her voice seemed like it came from miles away, "you can leave now boy, she don't need you 'ere fussing over 'er. Give her some space."

Lucian, she was talking to Lucian and just called him 'boy', if I had the energy to laugh right now, I would, but all I could muster was a twitch of my lips that I hope he didn't see; I don't want him to think that I was laughing at him.
"Boy? Lady, I have centuries on you"
His reply had a snort coming out of Sarah's full lips. "Until you can prove to me that you're a man, then your age means nothin'. Now, out."
Sarah was a big woman, always has been, and she can be quite abrupt, but if you really knew her, then you would know that she's actually just a massive teddy bear, and her gruff orders were just from years of dealing with drunk and disorderly patients. She didn't take shit, and obviously not even hundreds-of-years-old lycans could scare her.
She made me eat the food that Rosie had brought me, and although I had been sleeping for three days, I was exhausted..
"Go back to sleep sweet'eart, I'm not goin' anywhere." As Sarah got comfortable beside me on the bed, her feet crossed at the ankles and humming under her breath, I fell back to sleep.

It was dark when I next woke up, and I was alone. Dotted around the room, wall sconces let off dull light, and everything was in shadows; I didn't know where Sarah had gotten too, but I hoped Rosie was taking good care of her.
Guilt gnawed at me as I lay there wrapped in a thick duvet, my head pillowed by fluffy cushions. Lucian had said that Nathan was downstairs. What was downstairs? More rooms like this one, or a basement like Jacob had kept me in? What was his life going to be like now that he was one of them? Lucian wasn't mad like the other ones and I didn't know why he was different...but that was a good thing, he could teach Nate what he knew, and I would get my little brother back - just a little bit hairier.
There was a squeak as the door to my room was slowly pushed open, and Lucian tip-toed in. "Why are you being so quiet?"
"I do not want to wake your nursemaid," he whispered, "she's in the next room with Lissa, asleep."
Lissa's here too?"
"I sent for her yesterday, she had been safe at the hotel for the time being, but she kept calling me...every hour on the hour until

I relented and sent a car for her." He crawled onto the bed, laying down gently beside me, his head resting on the same pillow as mine. He was so close, I could see the gold flecks in his eyes, feel his warm breath on my cheek, and I relished in his closeness.
"Thank you. For bringing Sarah and Liss here," I shifted so I was on my side facing him, "and thank you for getting me out of there. I didn't say it earlier." His long fingers threaded through mine until our palms were clasped together, his hand engulfing my smaller one.
"You never have to thank me for keeping you safe mo ghràidh." The first thing I was going to do in the morning was google what that meant.
"I had to wait for Sarah to go to sleep before I could come and see you; she guarded the door like a rottweiler." I chuckled quietly, that sounded like Sarah. "It's true, everytime I came near your door she would glare at me with her evil eye. I swear, I thought my balls were going to shrivel up and crawl back inside me."
Laughter burst out of me at the thought of this man, who could turn into a gigantic beast, scared of a little nurse.
"Sshhh, she might hear you and wake up, then she will make me leave; I'm not ready to leave you just yet."
His words were sobering; I wasn't ready for him to leave yet either...maybe not ever.
"I have something for you." He sat up and switched on the bedside lamp so I could see better, not that he needed the light, but I appreciated the gesture; even with the wall lights on, it was still quite dark.
He pulled out a long thin case from the drawer by the bed, and carefully placed it in both of my hands. The woodwork was exquisite, filigree carved into the edges of the oak box.
"When the massacre happened hundreds of years ago, I was a new lycan, and I hated what Robert had turned me into," I listened intently, enraptured by the story he was weaving about his past, "after a few weeks of being...this, I went looking for the coven - your ancestors."
I looked up sharply, this was my history too?

"I found only death. The pack had obliterated everything and everyone in their path; Robert was nowhere to be found, off with his tail between his legs, guilt for creating these…monsters…and me."

He stared sightlessly at the dim light, as if he was seeing something entirely different, memories of a past life.

"Their blood saturated the ground I walked on, the stench of decay infiltrated my senses, and I vowed then and there that I would never be like them. I would never use your kind, or harm them. When I first felt your magic, I was relieved that there were more of you left; I was filled with a purpose that I had given myself centuries ago…to protect you, to care for you."

He blinked, coming back to himself, "and then I saw you for the first time, and I knew that just protecting you would not be enough for me…I wanted it all," he nodded to the box I still held, "open it."

Lifting the lid of the case revealed a bed of black satin, and an elaborate knife with an onyx handle, rubies encrusted into the hilt. Lifting it out of the box, I saw my reflection in the steel, and it glittered in my hand as I turned it this way and that, watching the light reflect off of the metal and gems.

"I sharpened it earlier, for you."

"You gave me a knife."

"It's an athame, it was Caitlyn's, your direct ancestor."

I spared him a glance before returning to gaze at the beauty in my hand. The feel of the smooth stones against my palm was calming, and I released a pent up breath, feeling myself relax against Lucian as I continued my assessment.

"I found it when I went back to the forest to look for survivors; I found it in Caitlyn's house…"

"And you took it, why?"

"I found no sign of the child, Robert's daughter, or Caitlyn, so I took it and what books I could find, and left. I hoped that they had survived, and I was keeping their most important possessions safe, but I later heard of Cait's death, and so I just kept them locked away."

"It feels like…mine." I whispered.

"That is because it is yours. It would have been passed down to each daughter as they came of age, a ceremonial dagger to aide in spell-casting and rituals. It has been in your family for centuries. Some even say it was the first blood witch's dagger that she passed onto her first daughter, and so the practice started of first-born girls inheriting the athame."

"Jacob said it was a boy."

His big body froze next to me, "he couldn't know that, it was too early to tell."

"He was adamant…and I…believed him."

He carefully took the blade from my hand, and laid it gently back in its silky lining, putting the lid on and placing it back in the drawer before laying on his back and pulling me gently on top of him. I rested there, listening to his heartbeat and feeling his body heat seep into me while he continued to tell me about the past.

"For years afterwards, I would hunt down the lycans who had joined in the massacre. Some of them got sick of being in Jacob's pack and taking orders, so they would go off on their own. They were easier to pick off one-by-one, and the pack didn't miss them as they had already run off." I felt him sigh where I lay on him, "some of them hated what they had become, and tracked me down themselves, begging me to release them from their curse. They wanted forgiveness too, but I…couldn't give that to them, that was between them and their God."

I lifted my head off of his chest so that I could look at him.

"What I am trying to say is, I have never been like them, and I never will be."

"You'll tell me more? About the blood witches?"

"I can do better than that my love, with the books I kept and that knife, I can help you have some semblance of control over your magic; we can practise, so that this doesn't happen again."

I breathed a sigh of relief, because as much as Lucian said he would protect me, I couldn't be at his side 24/7, I needed to be able to protect myself too, and besides, what kind of witch would I be if I didn't know how to use my magic. This was what I had wanted since I found out what I was, to learn how to use it.

"Good, because so far, all I've done is blow shit up, and as fun as it is, I need to know how to do more. I want to know everything."

Lucian laid there, his arms wrapped all the way around me keeping me locked to him.

I thought about my family who were all safe in this house, alive. I thought about Nathan and everything I could do to help him through this new phase of his life, because there would be no school in the foreseeable.

And lastly, I thought about my baby, and if Jacob had been lying, then my daughter would have inherited that same dagger that Lucian just gave to me; a piece of my history that I could have passed down to her.

But I didn't cry.

I had cried almost all day, and I had no more tears left.

No, I didn't cry. I wouldn't cry anymore.

But I was the last of my kind, daughter to a murdered witch, mother to a murdered child.

And I would have my revenge.

The end...for now.

KEEP IN TOUCH

Find me on Facebook and Instagram for more information about Zoe's revenge and what she has planned for those who have wronged her in Book 2. (Coming soon)
@kellycoulterauthor

Remember, your reviews are precious, so please consider heading over to Amazon and posting an honest review.

Thank you.

Kelly

ABOUT THE AUTHOR

Kelly Coulter

Born and raised in North London, Kelly found a love of reading at a young age, demolishing books at a rapid rate. She would often get in trouble at school for reading when she should be studying, hiding her romance novels within science texts to try and keep them hidden from teachers.

A lover of all things romance and horror, Kelly decided to combine aspects of the two to create her first book: Blood Witch. Despite being a lover of everything 'Zombie', there are no walking dead within these pages.

Kelly currently resides in Oxfordshire with her awesome husband and crazy, beautiful sons.

Printed in Great Britain
by Amazon